snapdragons

OTHER BOOKS AND AUDIOBOOKS
BY SARAH M. EDEN

CHRONOLOGICAL ORDER OF ALL RELATED
SARAH M. EDEN GEORGIAN- & REGENCY-ERA BOOKS

Snap-dragons

*A determined bride
and a runaway groom—
arranged marriages
don't always go as planned.*

SARAH M. EDEN

Covenant

Covenant Communications, Inc.

Cover image © Richard Jenkins Photography https://rjenkins.co.uk/

Cover design by Hannah Bischoff, copyright © 2024 by Covenant Communications, Inc.

Published by Covenant Communications, Inc.
American Fork, Utah

Library of Congress Cataloging-in-Publication Data

Name: Sarah M. Eden
Title: Snapdragons / Sarah M. Eden
Description: American Fork, UT : Covenant Communications, Inc. [2024]
Identifiers: Library of Congress Control Number 2024934677 | 978-1-52442-564-7
LC record available at https://lccn.loc.gov/2024934677

Printed in the United States of America
First Printing: November 2024

30 29 28 27 26 25 24   10 9 8 7 6 5 4 3 2 1

Chapter One

Cambridge University, 1774

INDEPENDENCE WAS PROVING TO BE highly overrated.

Niles Greenberry had come to Cambridge specifically because his very large and very involved family had always attended Oxford. He had a brother and quite a few cousins at that university even now. Other than Niles, there were no Greenberrys at Cambridge.

And he was a little lonely.

Not lonely enough to rush home to the crush of siblings, parents, aunts, uncles, grandparents, and cousins, who filled their corner of Cornwall. And not enough that he was willing to switch universities. But just enough that he had decided to do something he very seldom did: talk. To people. People he didn't know.

Over the course of his first term at Cambridge and throughout this first half of his second, Niles had been inarguably intrigued by a group known to all as the Gents. Theirs was a tight-knit circle, all in their first year at university, who had almost immediately become the stuff of legend. Nearly every student at Cambridge wished to be part of their very exclusive and lively brotherhood.

It was with that aspiration in mind that Niles tentatively approached Stanley Cummings, who was generally assumed to be the head Gent and who was sitting on a low wall in a courtyard. Niles had been hoping for a chance to approach Stanley. He'd been thinking of him by his Christian name in an attempt to feel less intimidated.

The Gent was by himself, which didn't happen often. It was Niles's best opportunity to begin what he wished would eventually become a camaraderie. First, though, he had to actually speak to the man.

Courage.

Niles wasn't a coward, truly. But putting himself forward was a highly uncomfortable prospect. He preferred listening over orating, going along over blazing a trail. Niles enjoyed a lark and an adventure as much as the next person, but he didn't generally instigate those adventures. Among his family, he'd been the reliable companion when a brother or cousin had undertaken a bit of mischief. Surely the Gents could use an accomplice.

Before Niles managed a single word, Stanley looked up and saw him hovering nearby. "How are you, Greenberry?" he asked quite casually, almost as if they'd spoken dozens of times rather than not at all.

"You—You know who I am?" Not the bold beginning he'd meant to make.

Stanley smiled. "Niles Greenberry. You hail from Cornwall. You come to Cambridge from Harrow. You're studying classics, but I suspect you don't enjoy it."

"Yes, but what did I eat for my midday meal today?"

That earned him a laugh, something the Gents were famous for. Laughter and larks and unwavering loyalty.

Stanley lifted the book he was reading. "My father has me studying classics as well. It's not to my liking, but that doesn't seem to matter."

How familiar that was. "My family doesn't allow me many choices in life. I had to browbeat them to be permitted to attend Cambridge when they far prefer Oxford."

"Browbeat?" Stanley looked a little doubtful. And well he might be. Niles was not one to put himself forward, an obvious trait to anyone paying the least attention, and he suspected Stanley paid attention to a great many things.

"'Browbeat' sounds better than 'beg and plead like a child.'"

Again, another chuckle. This was going better than Niles had feared it would. Stanley and one of the other Gents, Lord Jonquil, had returned from Nottinghamshire only a few days before. One of Stanley's sisters had died, though Niles didn't know the circumstances. Both gentlemen had returned heavier of countenance. Niles hoped Stanley appreciated having a reason to laugh, even lightly and briefly. He hoped it eased his pain a little.

"I—I thought maybe—" Niles wasn't eloquent, but he didn't usually stumble *this* much over his words. It was less a matter of not having mastery of the words he wanted and more of being so unsure of the outcome of the request he meant to make. "Should you ever need another person for—When you are undertaking a cricket match, if you're ever in need of another on your team, then I would—"

Stanley didn't laugh then, which was a relief. And he did seem to be listening. "I've not ever seen you play cricket."

"I'm good at it." Niles wasn't boasting but was stating the unvarnished truth. "I know I'm not the tallest of men, and I'm not built like an out-and-outer, but I've yet to find a sport I'm not good at."

"Truly?" That intrigued Stanley.

Niles could hardly blame Stanley for not immediately believing him. The quiet, small, overlooked people were never assumed to be good at anything beyond books and deep thinking and knowing the precise distance from a fireplace to achieve optimal snugness.

"I know you and the Gents have a good team as it is, especially with Fortier on your team. That surprised everyone, truth be told."

"People can be extremely surprising; it is one of my favorite things about them."

This was his moment; Niles knew that instinctively. He would never forgive himself if he didn't seize it. "I think I could be surprising in good ways. If the Gents are ever looking for someone to round out numbers or do some of the less glamorous work on an adventure."

Stanley eyed him with a studying gaze. "Are you petitioning for membership?"

No doubt plenty of others had done precisely that and had been humiliatingly disappointed. Niles refused to be discouraged so quickly. "Only offering my services as an aide-de-camp."

"That's the thing, though, Niles Greenberry: in our brotherhood, there are no subordinates, no underlings."

Well, that was his luck running out, then. He wasn't good for much else.

At that moment, Lord Jonquil happened to step into the courtyard. He was one of the most jovial people Niles had ever encountered, yet he looked completely downcast. That had been a jarring change in him since returning from Nottinghamshire.

"Lord Jonquil has taken your family's tragedy very much to heart," Niles said.

"My sisters are like sisters to him," Stanley explained. "Losing Charlotte and nearly losing Julia has torn him to shreds."

Niles hadn't realized these gentlemen had endured a near-double tragedy. It was little wonder they were both so weighed down by it.

"My family is loud and domineering and often more than I can endure," Niles said, "but I would be devastated if anything happened to any of them."

He looked back to Stanley once more. "I am sincerely sorry you both have had to endure such a loss."

"Not everyone here has been so compassionate." Stanley appeared to be watching Lord Jonquil, but when Niles looked as well, he spotted the actual focus of Stanley's gaze.

Timothy Baker had proven himself a source of misery to any number of his Cambridge schoolmates. It was believed he had caused difficulty for local families and shopkeepers as well. Why were some people like that? Taking delight in causing people pain? And why did his group of lackeys enjoy taking part? All three were walking alongside their leader in disagreeableness.

"You're not strutting around so much anymore," Baker said to Lord Jonquil, walking alongside him, though he most certainly hadn't been invited to do so. "It's about time you were brought down a peg or two."

Lord Jonquil didn't say anything but continued his slow walk across the courtyard, his expression pulled in what could be described only as broken-heartedness.

Baker's group kept pace with him.

"Everyone has decided you're pathetic," one of the group said.

Stanley set his book down on the wall, standing as he closely watched what was happening. Niles kept an eye on it as well.

Lord Jonquil still didn't answer. He didn't look annoyed or aggravated. He looked sad, grief-stricken.

Then Baker tossed in one more barbed comment. "She wasn't even *your* sister."

"She was *mine*." Stanley stormed toward them.

"Half sister," Baker corrected with a smirk.

In an instant, a brawling bout of fisticuffs broke out. Baker's group had two on one over Stanley and Lord Jonquil.

Niles rushed into the fray.

"You'll get pummeled," Stanley warned, ducking away from a coming fist.

"I won't," Niles said.

With ability born of years of secret effort, Niles landed two punches in quick succession, leveling one of Stanley's attackers. Niles spun about and felled one of those going after Lord Jonquil. He turned and punched the last of Baker's band in one fluid movement, then shoved him backward onto the ground.

He then rounded on Baker himself. What he saw was shock, and not merely on the face of Cambridge's most dedicated and obnoxious tormentor. Stanley and Lord Jonquil looked just as surprised.

Niles motioned toward Baker with his chin. "This one deserves a facer."

"Agreed," Stanley said with a shrug. "But I'd settle for letting him and his little band toddle off looking . . . pathetic."

And they did. Niles didn't for a moment think they'd stop being utter nuisances, but maybe Lord Jonquil had gained a temporary reprieve.

"Lud, man," Stanley said to him. "I hadn't heard you were a pugilist."

Niles stretched out the knuckles in his hand, working out the sting that a bare-knuckle brawl always caused. "I decided at Harrow that I needed to be able to defend myself."

"Don't tell me Harrow had people like Baker," Lord Jonquil said.

"*Everywhere* has people like Baker."

Stanley snatched up his abandoned book. "I've learned a lot about you in the past months, but I didn't realize you play cricket." He motioned with his head for Niles to walk alongside them. "I don't think anyone knew until today that you brawl like a bruiser. But it doesn't surprise me that you jump to the defense of people's sisters. That is precisely the sort of person I was sure you were."

"You've taken that much notice of me?" No one ever did.

"I have. *We* have. The Gents have wondered if you'd eventually consider joining us."

Niles nodded, unable to find the words he'd formulated in his mind when he'd imagined making a petition for membership.

"I was certain you would when you were ready," Stanley said. "But I meant what I said: no underlings, no subordinates. When you join this group, you become one of us, wholly and completely and on equal footing."

Niles swallowed. "I'd like that."

"Which leaves only one question," Stanley said.

"What question?" Niles asked.

In unison, Stanley and Lord Jonquil asked, "Do you speak French?"

"*Oui, je parle français.*"

They exchanged smiles of acknowledgment.

"Well then, Niles Greenberry"—Stanley shook his hand—"welcome to the Gents."

Lord Jonquil shook his other hand. "I hope you're ready for an adventure."

Niles grinned at them both. "Always."

Cornwall, Autumn 1787 (thirteen years later)

Niles had known since he was a child that a marriage would eventually be arranged for him. The Greenberrys believed in curated courtships the way other families embraced religion or politics. It was woven into the fabric of who they were. But Niles wanted nothing to do with any of it.

Grandfather had already made matches for Niles's older brother, two younger sisters, and every cousin of marriageable age. He had avoided this reckoning for as long as he had, thanks to the tireless efforts and persuasive abilities of the best friend he'd ever known. It was more than just a shame that they'd lost Stanley so young; it was an unmitigated tragedy.

"Mrs. Seymour is known to be quite the most fashionable lady in Dublin society." Mother stood beside the tailor, whose shop they were at in Plymouth Dock. Niles was to have a new wardrobe, as Grandfather didn't wish the Seymours to have a poor first impression of the Greenberrys.

"Does *Miss* Seymour have an opinion on such things?" Niles asked, looking over the lengths of silk and satin the tailor was considering. Putting a fashionable foot forward wasn't a terrible thing now and then, but Niles generally preferred being comfortable to being modish.

"I am not at all acquainted with her feelings on the matter."

He had received some variation of that answer whenever he'd inquired about the lady who had been chosen to be his wife. Her family was important and influential and in favor of the match, and that was all Niles seemed destined to know about Miss Penelope Seymour.

Mother added two waistcoats to the order, and the tailor scratched her instructions into a small book before rushing into a back room to fetch buttons for Mother to peruse.

"If we undertook this during the next Season in London, Digby would be more than happy to assist," Niles said. "I'd be so fashionable, it would be painful."

His mother smiled a little sadly and a lot consolingly. "Your grandparents would never hear of the delay. You've already been granted more time than your siblings or cousins. And we've managed to delay things for three months now." She set her hand on his arm, giving it a light squeeze. "You cannot possibly avoid this forever."

"But I don't wish to be married. And the only circumstances under which I could imagine that changing are those in which the person I am marrying very much wishes to be married *to me* and I to her. Specifically. Because we *chose* each other."

"That simply doesn't happen, dear." She watched him with a little too much pity, something he'd cringed at again and again the past months. Mother was a wonderful woman and the best mother he could imagine, but she did sometimes treat him a little too much like a child despite his being thirty years old. "Marriages aren't a matter of romantic connections in our family, or on our rung of Society."

"Two of the Gents married by choice rather than by arrangement," Niles said.

"I worried that would cause you discouragement." She shook her head. "Your grandparents won't be swayed. But take heart. The matches they have brokered for your siblings and your cousins have proven very happy."

While that was true, it was not terribly comforting. Outside of his immediate family and the Gents, Niles hadn't found many people who gave him a second thought, let alone came to like the person he was. Part of that, he fully acknowledged, was his own reticence. The rest was owing to how immediately forgettable he was. It wasn't an observation he made out of self-directed pity; it was simply the truth.

He didn't mind that most people thought that of him. But to be required to build a life with someone who found him entirely forgettable was a miserable prospect.

But Mother was correct: his grandparents would not change their minds on the matter. Niles had always known that.

Mother continued consulting with the tailor. Niles took the opportunity, as he'd done countless times over the past four months, to reconcile himself to his fate.

His grandparents truly had chosen well for the others. Grandfather was particularly careful to address material considerations and needs. Grandmother made certain the social benefits were sufficient. And Niles felt certain they gave at least a little consideration to the personalities and preferences of their individual grandchildren. There was some comfort in that.

Father arrived at the shop, having finished his business for the day. They would all be returning home the next day, and preparations would begin for the Seymours' arrival. Niles dreaded it. Legitimately and fully dreaded it. But what could he do?

They finalized their order with the tailor, then climbed inside the carriage to ride back to the inn, where they would pass the night.

"Is there anything you can tell me of Miss Seymour?" he asked his parents. "Anything to help me form some idea of who she is?"

"I suspect you know most, if not all, of what we do," Father said. "She is twenty-five and Irish. Her family is well thought of."

His father's suspicions hit the mark. That was, in reality, very nearly the sum total of what Niles knew. So impersonal, so unencouraging.

"The Seymours are known for their horses," Father added.

That *was* new information. Niles liked to ride, and he knew a great deal about horses. Here was a small hint of hope.

"The only sticking point your grandfather has encountered involves the property Miss Seymour inherited from a great-uncle. They have insisted it remain hers rather than become yours, as is customary upon marriage." Father shrugged a little. "And they are further insisting that the trustees appointed upon her inheritance remain the trustees overseeing it."

"Did Grandfather agree to those terms?" Niles, of course, would be the one signing the marriage agreements, he having long since reached his majority. But Grandfather always negotiated the contracts.

"Regardless of who is technically the owner of the estate," Father said, "you would have a place to live and raise a family. It would be an odd arrangement, though not unheard of. Still, having a home is a valuable thing."

A home, but not one he owned. To almost anyone else, that wouldn't be the problem it was for Niles. He'd known for some time that were he to achieve one of his most personally important goals, he had to eventually own land. *He* himself. Not his wife.

Land ownership was a qualification for seeking election to the House of Commons. He'd wanted the chance to sit in Parliament and make a difference in the world ever since Stanley had left to fight in the war with the colonies. He'd wanted a voice in those decisions that had the potential to irrevocably change lives. But he didn't own land, so he didn't qualify.

Pursuing that goal had motivated him for years, leading him to save as much of his income as he could and to listen closely as Henri and Aldric, two of the Gents, discussed which areas of the country had property at lower prices and which areas cost more but were worth the added expense because their locations offered important advantages. He'd made plans and done calculations. And he'd known in the back of his mind that there was at least a possibility that when his family chose a match for him, the lady in question would bring land to the marriage.

He'd told himself that the possibility of having claim on an estate and finally being in a position to move forward with the one future he'd found himself excited to pursue would make the prospect of an arranged marriage palatable.

"Miss Seymour's family won't budge on the matter of her retaining ownership of the estate?" Niles hadn't heard of this aspect before, and his brain was struggling to sort through it.

"Not even a little."

Mother offered another of her pseudo-pitying glances. "The house and land would still be yours in all ways except that one. Not all young gentlemen without estates of their own are so fortunate."

He didn't feel fortunate.

"And," she added, "the next time it is your turn to host a gathering of your friends, you needn't hold it at *our* home."

"Did you mind so much?" Niles asked.

"Not at all."

Father added his agreement to Mother's declaration. "And I hope all of them will come to Cornwall for the wedding in a few weeks."

A few weeks.

Miss Seymour would be in Cornwall in only another month. There'd be no escaping at that point, no chance for claiming what he wanted and avoiding the fate that had been chosen for him.

He needed more time.

Chapter Two

Cornwall, one month later

"WHAT DO YOU MEAN HE'S not here?"

Penelope Seymour didn't need to ask the question out loud because her brother, Liam, did so first. They'd made the journey from Ireland to Cornwall so she could meet her betrothed and so he and Liam could sign the marriage agreement.

She had anticipated awkwardness between her and Mr. Niles Greenberry, had *planned* on it. She had bolstered herself to endure discomfort and hesitation. She had spent some time rehearsing in front of her obliging mirror a few responses to questions she thought her soon-to-be husband might ask, including why it was that her mother hadn't bothered to make the journey. She'd even practiced keeping her expression neutral so she'd keep hidden all indications of pain and rejection.

She'd not made plans for the possibility that her betrothed would be absent entirely.

Mr. Greenberry's father, who had been introduced to her as Mr. David Greenberry, not to be confused with the multiple other Messrs. Greenberry in the area, offered a quick explanation. "Niles made an unexpected journey to the home of a friend almost a month ago with every intention of returning before your arrival. We expected him back days ago."

"Inclement weather, perhaps?" Liam asked.

Mrs. Greenberry offered a small shrug. "That is a possibility."

But, Penelope would wager, based on the hesitancy she saw, the lady didn't actually think *weather* had delayed her son's return.

"He will, no doubt, rush into the house while we are all at supper, embarrassed at his tardiness and explaining the . . . carriage difficulties he had or something of that nature." The missing groom's father didn't seem to fully believe the explanation he was suggesting either.

Penelope was admittedly nervous about marrying a stranger, but she'd not ever considered the possibility of running away. Had Mr. Niles Greenberry done precisely that? Surely not.

"Is the Royal Mail so dawdly here that a letter of explanation couldn't have reached you since the time he was meant to have left his friend's home?" Penelope asked, searching about for some kind of clarity.

Her future in-laws exchanged uncomfortable glances. 'Twas answer enough, really. The missing Mr. Greenberry would have sent a letter, either from the home of his friend or from a roadside inn, if his travels had gone awry, and that letter would have arrived by now.

He'd piked off.

This was not going at all the way Penelope had anticipated. She had a groom who was nowhere to be found. Now what was she to do?

"We are to dine tonight at Ipsworth with my parents," Mr. Greenberry said. "Please rest from your travels until then."

There was a hint of desperation in the invitation and a look of worry lurking in the gentleman's eyes. Did he think Penelope meant to run off as well? She was made of sterner stuff than that.

They were shown to the adjacent guest chambers, where they were to spend their time in Cornwall before the wedding.

Mere moments after being left there by the housekeeper, Liam joined Penelope.

He eyed her with palpable misgiving. "Now what do we do?"

"Dress for supper, I suppose."

"Do be serious, Penelope." He dropped into a chair near the fireplace. The poor man looked defeated already. "We've come all this way after so many months of correspondence, and Mr. Niles Greenberry couldn't even be bothered to be here."

"I'd not assume his absence is a matter of indifference."

Liam shrugged and nodded in unison. "A gentleman will most certainly have an opinion on the matter of his impending marriage."

What, then, was her betrothed's opinion?

"Mr. *Robert* Greenberry didn't give you any indication that his grandson was opposed to the match?" she asked, referring to the family patriarch, whose house they were eating at that evening.

The grandfather of her intended had undertaken all the discussions and negotiations. That had seemed odd at first. She'd worried that Mr. Niles Greenberry was weak or simple or lazy or . . . A great many concerning possibilities had occurred to her. But after a few letters, the inner workings of the Greenberry family had grown clearer.

Each generation appeared to defer to the one before. It almost felt like a little kingdom nestled away in Cornwall. The eldest Mr. Greenberry was the king. Even a monarch's own grandchildren deferred to him without that being an inarguable indication of moral or intellectual weakness. Of course, it could be both. A prince could be deferential *and* feeble, obedient *and* spoiled.

"If the eldest Mr. Greenberry had given any indication that his grandson had the least objection," Liam said, "then *I* would have had hesitation myself."

Where, then, was the grandson?

"The *middle* Mr. Greenberry didn't seem to truly believe his son was simply late."

Liam's brow creased in that way it always did when pondering something he found overwhelming. "Suppose the absent Mr. Greenberry doesn't return?"

Penelope wasn't nearly as ready to admit defeat as Liam seemed to be. "We've only been here for an hour. I don't know that I'm ready to bring in mourners to weep and wail for my dashed hopes."

He chuckled a little, and she breathed more easily. Laughter had always helped her face life's difficulties.

"Have you set your heart so much on this gentleman you have never met?" His lips pulled downward, drawing his eyes in the same direction. "I suppose . . . I could try"—he drew the word out long, emphasizing it in an inarguably doubtful way—"to find someone else."

Someone else she had never met. She would, of course, far prefer to marry someone who actually liked her, who cared about her. In her most imaginative moments, she had even let herself dream of marrying someone she loved who loved her as well. But that was not her lot in life. She had to hold out for those important aspects of a match that she could reasonably fight for. "How probable is it that this hypothetical 'someone else' would agree to our terms regarding Fairfield?"

Liam rubbed at his temple. "It is unusual enough for a lady to inherit an estate. Our great-uncle created a very odd situation leaving it to you."

An odd situation, yes, but he'd also given Penelope greater hope for her future than most ladies had. That hope had ebbed, though, when she'd realized that a lady's property, by default, became her husband's upon marriage unless the marriage agreement specified otherwise.

"If the Mr. Greenberry we are waiting for doesn't return or does only to refuse the match"—heavens, she hoped neither scenario played out—"we could find someone else."

Liam looked miserable and exhausted. "I know I just said I could try. But I already have, Penelope. I tried with everyone I could think of in Dublin. I tried with any number of English families I had any kind of connection to from my days at Shrewsbury and the one Season I spent in London." He stood and crossed to the windows, tension rippling off him. "I've been trying for years. But you have no dowry, and Fairfield, which under normal circumstances *would* be a dowry, is not to serve in that capacity. Our family hasn't any enviable connections or lofty standing." He looked back at her, misery in his expression. "I have been attempting for years to secure a match on the terms you wish for. Years, Penelope."

It was decidedly discouraging, but she didn't mean to entirely abandon this possibility too quickly. "Mr. Greenberry will return soon enough."

"What if he doesn't?" Liam pressed.

Penelope took a slow breath to steady herself. "Then, I'll be in a spot of difficulty, won't I?"

"*You* will be in a spot of difficulty?" Liam shook his head. "I'll be the laughingstock of Dublin."

"And I will be the jilted old maid."

"Neither of us will emerge from this fiasco unscathed." His posture slumped. "Is Fairfield worth all this?" Liam clearly had his doubts.

"Yes." Even if Fairfield were the only consideration, seeing this match through would be worth the current discomfort and uncertainty. But it wasn't the exclusive reason she needed the wedding to move forward as planned and without delay.

She'd begun making arrangements for living at Fairfield and for making it the profitable horse-breeding endeavor she knew it could be. But most merchants and virtually all banks and creditors were hesitant to work with an unmarried lady. She had a chance to purchase a stallion at a price she knew she'd not ever see again. The animal had good bloodlines and a regal bearing. It, along with the stallion and two brood mares that were already hers, would allow her to begin immediately building her lifelong dreams at Fairfield.

But the loan she needed was contingent on her being married. The stallion wouldn't be available forever. And after her repeated insistence that she was soon to be married, should she then fail to marry, the bank might never trust her again. That would undermine her for years.

"There must be someone else who would allow me to keep Fairfield."

"Niles Greenberry is not merely your *first* option. He is your *last*."

"I assure you, Miss Seymour, Niles was raised to be more mannerly than the current situation would indicate." The eldest Mrs. Greenberry—the *queen*, as Penelope thought of her in order to keep them all sorted out in her mind—sat with palpable dignity as supper was served with still no hint of the missing gentleman. "I am certain he will return horrified at having not been here and deeply apologetic for the inconvenience he has caused." There was a hint of "he had better" underlying her declaration.

The lady's son and daughter-in-law did not appear as convinced as she was. The nervousness and uncertainty that had been in their expressions earlier remained. If anything, it had increased.

The *king* of the family was proving the most unbothered by the situation. Penelope didn't for a moment believe he was truly indifferent. He, after all, had invested months of correspondence in bringing this match about. What appeared to be a lack of concern was actually confidence, which helped keep Penelope from fully panicking.

An awkward silence settled over the table, broken only by the clink of crystal and the ping of silverware against china. It seemed even the footmen were holding their breath.

Penelope wasn't *fully* panicking, but she was *partly* panicking.

She pushed around the pease porridge and ham on her plate, doing her best to appear to be eating, but in truth, she had no appetite. She didn't consider herself a pessimistic person, but she couldn't entirely convince herself that Mr. Niles Greenberry was soon to return, and every dream she had depended on his return. Every last one.

"Your family's reputation as preeminent horse breeders and trainers is quite impressive," Mr. David Greenberry—father of the missing Mr. Greenberry—said into the uncomfortable quiet.

"Thank you, we have worked hard to become so," Liam answered, though Penelope did far more to continue that tradition than he did. She'd learned long ago to let her father, while he'd been alive, and now Liam, take credit. Liam grew easily embarrassed when he thought his sister was outshining him in matters generally seen as belonging to the men in a family. Her pride in what she had accomplished didn't require him to suffer indignities.

It was, truth be told, for the best that in the matter of their horses, Liam take the credit anyhow. The Greenberrys struck her as a very traditional family. She couldn't imagine they would look with approval on a lady being directly and deeply involved in a business endeavor that fell outside the generally accepted bounds of accepted behavior. The situation was already precarious with Mr. Niles Greenberry so conspicuously absent. She couldn't afford to make a horrible impression on his family.

And in that was another reason she needed to marry. Having a gentleman attached to the equine efforts she intended to continue at Fairfield would give them a legitimacy that would be lacking if she alone were seen to be undertaking them. And it would preserve her reputation, allowing her to have a place in Society, to perhaps have friends.

"I hope when Niles returns," the younger Mrs. Greenberry said to Penelope, "that you will have the opportunity to ride with him. He is quite an adept horseman."

That was revealing. "Which means his delay isn't likely to be the result of a riding mishap."

"He will return soon enough," the monarch of the family declared over the rim of his cup. "The Greenberrys have been married in the chapel here for generations. He will be the next."

Penelope studied him. He took note of her scrutiny. For just a moment, his confidence remained undented. But that moment gave way to a dropping of his eyes to his plate.

This family had reason to believe the prodigal prince stayed away intentionally and, worse yet, didn't actually intend to return and do his duty.

Her partial panic grew.

"We had hoped your mother would be making the journey to Cornwall," the queenly Mrs. Greenberry said, clearly thinking it a casual conversational topic.

'Twas anything but.

"Our mother intends to make the journey closer to the wedding day." Liam's answer was accurate if incomplete.

Mother had bemoaned the inconvenience of traveling to Cornwall, something her only daughter's wedding apparently did not justify. And she had further complained that none of her particular friends would be there, a more important consideration than whether her own children would be. Penelope didn't think her mother was truly selfish . . . merely inconsiderate.

That was what she told herself, at least. Just as she told herself that Liam wouldn't be required to search out another match who would inevitably snatch away all her dreams for her future. The banks and the stallion and the preparations needed at Fairfield would not wait forever.

Mr. Niles Greenberry was, as her brother had stated, her last option. Her *only* option.

She needed to find out where he was.

Chapter Three

"I SHOULD KNOW BETTER THAN to concoct schemes with you." Niles sat slumped in a chair in Pledwick Manor's formal drawing room. "Every time we have done so in the past, it has ended in disaster."

Digby Layton, whose estate Niles had essentially been hiding at, scoffed in the overly dramatic way he had long ago perfected. "On the contrary, we've had some brilliant schemes. Don't forget that time we 'borrowed' Timothy Baker's chaise-cart. That didn't end in disaster."

"No. It ended with the cart on the roof of the library at Trinity Hall."

Digby's smile turned into an absolutely wicked grin. "Yes, it did."

"Stanley was so proud of that." Niles laughed lightly at the memory.

"Rightly so. The man was an inarguable genius in matters of mathematics and physics. Being able to not only calculate how to do that but to execute it flawlessly . . ." Digby shook his head, clearly still in awe of what they'd managed.

Niles's spirits fell a little. "I miss him."

"So do I." Digby's gaze unfocused, and his mouth turned down a bit. But his quiet contemplation didn't last more than a moment. "No matter that we aren't the planners he was, I think Stanley would approve of you doing all you can to avoid a path you fear will bring you misery. And not only for your own sake. He would remind you that Miss Seymour, no matter that she is agreeing to this arrangement, would not be rendered happier by having a husband who is miserable."

Niles rubbed at his forehead. "But to simply refuse to go home . . . that feels rather cowardly."

"Oh, it is."

"That's very helpful, thank you." Niles made the dry comment as he stood. "I think I would be more at ease if I'd heard from my family. I can't imagine they would simply shrug upon reading my letter and say, 'Well, that is that.' And Miss Seymour will have been in Cornwall for at least a week now. Some word should have arrived."

"Perhaps they did send word, but the letter went astray."

"Or," Niles countered as he began to pace, "they are so angry with me that they cannot put it into words and are simply waiting for me to return so they can murder me."

"Murder? The Greenberrys?" Digby clicked his tongue and shook his head. "You certainly have the numbers to kill swaths of people, but I don't know that your vast family has enough of a violent streak."

"They might not be violent, but they will be disappointed. That is worse."

"Worse than being murdered?" Digby's theatrical scoff returned and, as it always did, helped a little.

"Somehow, you've managed to avoid being roped into a match of your family's choosing."

"A person's family must care at least a little about him to bother making such arrangements. Since what family I do have doesn't care if I live or die, I suspect there will be very little familial interference in my life." Digby almost never spoke of his family. The Gents knew just enough from what Society whispered and the hints he let slip now and then to be fully aware that the Layton family was in the midst of a decades-long internal war, with Digby being too often used as cannon fodder.

"The Gents consider you family," Niles reminded him. "And we absolutely care if you live or die."

"Do you intend to arrange a marriage for me?" Digby eyed him sidelong. "Heavens no."

"And I don't intend to simply give up and let your family force this one on you." Digby's tendency toward the dramatic meant a lot of people underestimated him. But he was one of the cleverest people Niles had ever known.

"Miss Seymour is probably a perfectly lovely person, and I've just caused her no end of embarrassment," Niles said. "And for the record, I do not begrudge any lady her wish to retain possession of a property she has inherited."

Digby rose and crossed to him, setting a reassuring hand on his shoulder. "You're entitled to hold fast to your ambitions and hopes for the future as well. What you need and what she needs are in conflict. That would make a terribly shaky foundation on which to build a life together."

It was a logical argument, yet it didn't entirely assuage Niles's guilt. "A gentleman is not meant to break an engagement."

Digby's gaze narrowed ever so slightly. "You said the arrangement hadn't been finalized."

"Miss Seymour and her brother were traveling to Cornwall so the marriage contracts could be signed and so she and I could meet. Grandfather was at least considerate enough to allow that before requiring that the match go forward. He left open the possibility of us not proceeding if we discovered we despised each other."

"See there? You are simply taking the exit he allowed for."

"But I still feel badly."

Digby tugged at his lace cuffs. "That is because you, Niles Greenberry, have a conscience. I do not recommend it, as it causes such inconvenience."

Niles laughed. Digby had a knack for dredging up humor even in the most difficult of situations. "Perhaps I could try selling my conscience. If I received enough blunt for it, I could simply buy the land I want. Then Grandfather could marry me off to any lady he chose."

But he inwardly winced at that. Giving up his hopes for his life's work was a harrowing prospect, but marrying someone he didn't love would be a far more difficult pill to swallow.

"I stand by the first plan I suggested," Digby said. "Don your yellows, resurrect The Cornish Duke, and win the rest of the money you need."

"I don't fight anymore." Niles was firm about that.

"But, Niles, you were so blasted good."

He couldn't help a satisfied smile. "I know."

His fists, after all, were what had gained him entry into the Gents. And those fists had won him enough purses to be achingly close to having land of his own. But there were risks in pugilism that he could no longer justify.

The butler entered a few minutes later. "A visitor has arrived, Mr. Layton."

Digby offered Niles an explanation. "I wrote to the Gents to tell them you were in a bit of a bind. No doubt they've jumped at the opportunity to scheme with us a little."

No doubt.

"Begging your pardon, sir," the butler said, "but it is not one of your friends."

"Then, who?" Digby clearly had no better idea than Niles did.

"Mr. Liam Seymour and Miss Penelope Seymour."

Miss Seymour. Niles's entire body froze. He didn't move. Didn't blink. Didn't breathe.

Digby turned slowly to face him and mouthed, "Miss Seymour?"

That snapped Niles back into motion. He crossed directly to Digby and, in a low voice, said, "Her Christian name *is* Penelope."

"This scheme was a bad idea," Digby whispered.

"You just said it was brilliant."

"What do I know about brilliant ideas?" Digby threw his hands up. "I'm not the *strategic* Gent; I'm the *handsome* one."

"Where was this humility when we were concocting this no-longer-brilliant scheme?" Niles demanded in a harsh whisper.

"We were both a little cup-shot," Digby said.

"I was not drunk."

Digby shook his head. "Then, this is to be laid at your feet, because I was definitely bousy."

Niles knew perfectly well that Digby was resorting to ridiculousness in an attempt to defuse a tense moment. But the man's usual approach wasn't going to help just then.

"What do we do?" Niles asked. "She is *here*. Now."

"First things first, we get our story straight." Digby held his gaze. "What did you tell your parents in your letter?"

"I said I wasn't feeling well and needed to delay my return trip."

Digby's brow pulled low. "You told them you were unwell, and they didn't even send well-wishes? That doesn't sound like your parents."

It didn't, actually. But that was hardly the most pressing issue at the moment. "Miss Seymour is *here*, Digby. What do we do?"

"You can start by pretending to be dying," Digby suggested.

Niles sighed. "I didn't say I was dying, only a little unwell."

"Then, lie weakly on the chaise longue or something. Try to look pale."

"I cannot simply will myself to be pale."

Digby gave him a look of overblown reprimand. "Well, if you spent less time riding horses or playing cricket or beating people to a pulp—"

"I haven't beat anyone to a pulp in—" Niles shook his head. "We don't have time for meandering conversations. Miss Seymour is here, no doubt looking for me. What do we do?"

His friend, thank the heavens, grew serious at last. "Look as though you've been through something harrowing."

"Which I have," Niles quickly added.

Digby nodded. "And we'll navigate this as best we can." That was not terribly reassuring. To his butler, Digby said, "Show them in, please."

Though Niles had protested the request that he grow pale, he felt the color drain from his face. He was not a dishonest person, nor was he irresponsible, yet he'd exaggerated his feelings of unease to give the impression of being unwell, and he had, for all intents and purposes, run away from home rather than do what was expected of him.

Niles should have gone to Norwood Manor instead of Pledwick. Aldric *was* the strategic Gent; he would have formulated a plan that might have actually worked.

Digby smoothed his clothes and fussed a bit with his hair. Niles didn't bother with either. It was taking all his mental capacity to simply remain on his feet. He'd have no difficulty appearing to be worse for wear.

The butler returned and announced, "Mr. and Miss Seymour."

Niles spared only a glance for Mr. Seymour, all his attention falling on the man's sister.

She was tiny, no more than an inch above five feet tall, if that. There was a wispiness to her that made her seem almost otherworldly. And she was shockingly beautiful. *Shockingly.*

"Welcome to Pledwick Manor, Mr. and Miss Seymour." Digby's manners were, as always, flawless. "How kind of you to make so significant a journey out of concern for Mr. Greenberry."

"Concern?" Mr. Seymour sounded genuinely confused.

"Surely," Digby continued, "his family told you he had been delayed due to having fallen unwell."

"They did not," Miss Seymour said. "All they could tell us was that Mr. Niles Greenberry hadn't returned home and they'd not the first idea when he intended to do so." She had that unique mixture of an Irish and English accent so often heard among those in Ireland who were either educated in England or had English governesses.

"I did send a letter." Niles sounded like a child standing in front of his parents, having been scolded for some misbehavior or another.

Miss Seymour's gaze shifted from Digby to Niles. She studied him silently. He was so seldom the focus of anyone's pointed attention that he hadn't the first idea what to do. When one drew about as much attention as the furniture, one didn't need to worry about scrutiny.

"It seems you ought to send another letter, Niles," Digby said. "Your first one appears to have gone astray."

"That would explain why they didn't write back." Niles could feel Miss Seymour's gaze still on him, though he'd turned to Digby. Embarrassment kept him from looking back at her. Instead, he addressed her brother. "Was my family terribly worried?"

"I would say they were more confused than worried." He wasn't scrutinizing Niles the way Miss Seymour was. And he didn't really sound Irish at all. "They were very apologetic."

Niles had put his family in an untenable situation. "You didn't have to journey all this way."

"I think we did," Miss Seymour answered.

He made the mistake of looking at her again. *Shockingly beautiful* was an inadequate description. She was gorgeous. Breathtaking. Bewitching. And clearly disappointed in him.

Her brother spoke to Digby once more. "We are hopeful that you will not begrudge us your temporary hospitality, Mr. Layton."

"Of course," Digby offered with perfect and, no doubt feigned, equanimity. "You are welcome to remain at Pledwick Manor for as long as you wish."

For as long as you wish.

This scheme was, without question, turning into a disaster.

Chapter Four

Niles had sat through his share of awkward meals, but supper that night topped them all. Miss Seymour hardly said anything. Her brother said far too much.

Between the first remove and Digby's declaration that the gentlemen would forgo their after-supper port, Mr. Seymour spoke of his family estate and his education at Shrewsbury, which accounted for his lack of an Irish accent. He further spoke of Dublin, any number of people only he and his sister knew, their unpleasant voyage across the Irish Sea, their equally unpleasant journey from Cornwall to Yorkshire, and a great many stories about their family's interactions in Dublin society. Through it all, Digby did an excellent job of appearing unwaveringly interested. Miss Seymour didn't entirely hide her embarrassment at her brother's lack of awareness. Niles mostly wished the ground would open up and swallow him whole.

But no obliging holes appeared, and he found himself seated among the Seymour siblings and Digby in the drawing room, where the same dynamic repeated itself.

In the midst of one of her brother's long recountings of a social gathering in Dublin, Miss Seymour spoke in quieter tones to Niles, he being seated nearest her. "My brother didn't talk nearly this much in Cornwall. He doesn't, generally, unless he's trying to impress someone."

As Digby was the one to whom most of Mr. Seymour's comments were directed, it wasn't difficult to determine who it was the man wished to impress.

Miss Seymour turned a bit in her chair, enough to face him more directly. She had the brownest eyes, deep and rich and . . . filled with suspicion.

Still speaking quietly, she asked, "Have you *actually* been ill?" Her tone and expression told him she sincerely doubted it.

"I—There has—" He'd realized there was a great likelihood he would eventually have to confess to the exaggeration, but he'd not expected it to happen so soon or so directly.

"You needn't fear you'll offend me if your answer is no." A smile lurked in those umber eyes. A smile? That was certainly unexpected. "You'd not be the first gentleman to invent creative ways of avoiding me."

"I doubt that," he muttered. He couldn't keep his eyes off her; he suspected the men in Ireland couldn't either.

"Is—"

Before Miss Seymour could say anything more, the butler stepped into the drawing room. "More visitors, Mr. Layton," the butler said.

"Show them in," Digby said as he rose.

Niles stood as well. Doing so gave him a distraction from Miss Seymour and her questions. *And her beguiling eyes.*

The butler moved back to the doorway and, after a quick nod to whomever was in the entryway, announced to the room, "Lord Jonquil and Mr. and Mrs. Barrington."

Digby had predicted a Gent might arrive. In all honesty, two at once wasn't very surprising. The Gents often traveled in packs.

Lucas bounced into the room first. "Look who I found wandering the Yorkshire roads." He motioned to Kes and Violet.

What would Miss Seymour think of the extremely informal arrival? A quick glance revealed the same studying gaze he'd received from her earlier that day but this time directed at Lucas. She appeared to be very astute. He didn't imagine there was much she missed.

A subtle elbow from Kes to Lucas's side brought a little more decorum. All three of the new arrivals seemed to have quite suddenly taken note of the unexpected additions to the party.

Digby, dignified and gracefully proper, moved to where his newest guests stood. "Allow me to undertake some introductions. Mr. and Miss Seymour, this is Lord Jonquil"—he indicated Lucas—"and Mr. and Mrs. Barrington." He motioned to Kes and Violet in turn. "Friends," he addressed the three, "this is Mr. and Miss Seymour of County Wicklow in Ireland."

Bows and curtsies were exchanged along with words of pleasure at making one another's acquaintance. Niles received so many furtive glances that any discretion his friends might have been trying to employ was lost entirely.

Digby had said he'd written to the Gents, informing them of at least some of Niles's predicament. If he'd mentioned Miss Seymour by name, or had at least mentioned that the match chosen for Niles had been an Irishwoman, this introduction would feel very significant to them.

Kes, despite being known among them as Grumpy Uncle, could be counted on to be circumspect. Lucas, who had fully earned his moniker of the Jester, on the other hand . . .

Violet proved the most immediately helpful. She crossed directly to Miss Seymour. "What a pleasure it is to find another lady present. How long have you been at Pledwick Manor?"

The two ladies sat on the sofa and engaged in what Niles hoped was a perfectly unexceptional conversation. Digby asked Mr. Seymour to excuse him a moment, then he pulled the rest of them aside.

"We received your letter," Kes explained. "Since we're the closest, we thought we'd best make the journey."

Digby looked to Lucas. "You were in Nottinghamshire."

He nodded. "And still arrived ahead of Kes."

"By thirty seconds," Kes countered.

Digby held up a hand to stop the pretended argument. To Lucas, he said, "With you so recently a father again, I can't imagine Julia is overly pleased with your departure."

Word had arrived about six weeks earlier of the newest member of Lucas's growing family, a son who'd been named for Digby and Henri.

Lucas reached into his pocket and produced a folded bit of parchment, which he handed to Digby with an almost smug look.

Digby unfolded it. Niles and Kes flanked him and read silently over his shoulder.

> *My dear Gents,*
>
> *I am absolutely certain you are convinced that Lucas has made a horrific miscalculation and has abandoned his recently-delivered-of-a-son wife without giving sufficient thought to the decision. I insisted he make the journey. Niles is too dear to us to ignore his current difficulty. While I cannot make the journey with Lucas, I am not truly abandoned. Both of our boys have two grandfathers and a grandmother here who are spoiling them unabashedly.*
>
> *Niles, I do hope you can sort this out before it becomes a catastrophe.*
> *The rest of you: behave!*

Yours, etc.
Your Julia

"Well, that's us put in our place," Digby said with a smile.

Kes was back to the matter at hand almost immediately. "This Miss Seymour of Ireland is the same Miss Seymour of Ireland your family chose for you?"

Niles nodded.

"And you stayed here instead of returning to Cornwall in order to avoid the match?"

He nodded again.

"And she tracked you here like a hound at a foxhunt?" Lucas barely held back the laugh Niles could see in his eyes.

"Sniffed him out with deft precision," Digby said.

"Didn't know you were such a prized commodity." Kes offered the dry observation with as much indication of amusement as the others.

"And I'd wager you didn't know Miss Seymour was breathtaking," Lucas said.

Niles ran a hand through his hair. "And she's clever. She saw immediately through the scheme Digby and I concocted."

"She did?" Digby winced a little.

"Dare I ask what it was?" Kes rubbed at the bridge of his nose.

"We'll share the details later," Digby said. "For now, though, if the Seymours ask, you are welcome to tell them you made the journey because you'd heard Niles was sick."

"Oh criminy." Lucas chuckled.

"We didn't have Aldric here," Digby protested. "We had to improvise."

"I'd like to point out that we *still* don't have Aldric here." Niles released a tight breath. Aldric was the General among the Gents, and for good reason.

Aldric had only just been given the running of an estate and was finding his footing there. He was unlikely to make the journey to Yorkshire. For the time being, at least, this motley group was Niles's best hope.

Oh criminy, indeed.

Chapter Five

PENELOPE DISCOVERED THE NEXT MORNING that the others at Pledwick Manor didn't rise early. Thus, she arrived at the stables with no one else around other than the grooms and the horses, which suited her. She'd tossed and turned throughout the night, her mind spinning with all she knew and all she needed to sort out. She did her best thinking when enjoying equine company.

"Are you wishing to ride this morning, miss?" The groomsman who asked the question didn't entirely keep his doubt hidden. She understood and wasn't offended. Her boots were suited to a visit to the stables, and she was dressed warmly for the winter air, but she hadn't donned a riding habit and wasn't wearing her riding gloves.

"My home in Ireland is a horse estate, and I could not contain my curiosity any longer," she said. "I've come to see Mr. Layton's stables and to determine if my suspicions are correct: that he has very elegant preferences when it comes to his horses."

Pride shone in the groomsman's eyes. "Everyone who knows horses is impressed with Mr. Layton's stable."

Just as she'd hoped. "I will keep out of the way of the staff," she said, "but I would very much like to wander about, meeting the horses."

He nodded. "Of course, miss. Some of them belong to the visiting gentlemen."

Here was an opportunity for an insight. "Which is Mr. Greenberry's?"

"Morwenna," he said. "But Mr. Greenberry's out for his usual morning ride, so the mare's not here just now."

An early riser who rode every day. They had that very much in common. Did he realize that? Would it make a difference if he did?

Penelope stepped up to the nearest stall, where a chestnut gelding with a slightly arched neck and a shorter back quietly nibbled on hay. The animal was very pretty but also had a build that promised a smooth ride. The horse walked to the stall gate. Penelope allowed it a moment to smell her and decide she was welcome. Then she rubbed the gelding's forehead, softly running her hand toward his muzzle. She shifted her hand to pat his neck. He continued chewing the hay in his mouth, both undistracted and unconcerned.

Though she'd only just met "Autumn Ember," as the plaque beside the stall gate identified him, there was such familiarity in the interaction that her mind could ponder on her difficulties with a degree of calm.

She knew that Niles—she'd met too many Messrs. Greenberry in Cornwall to keep them all straight without resorting to Christian names at least in her own thoughts—*had* intentionally avoided being present when she'd arrived from Ireland. She further knew that he was lying about the reason he'd stayed away.

What she didn't know was what had changed his mind after so much effort to finalize this match. And she hadn't the first idea what to do next.

She moved to the next stall and made the acquaintance of a black mare with the lines of an Arabian and a striking white star and white sock. The mare was more standoffish but also decidedly more curious. Penelope thoroughly enjoyed interacting with horses whose minds she could practically see spinning. "Midnight," according to this horse's plaque, could almost certainly see *Penelope's* mind spinning. Niles hadn't met her yet when he'd changed his mind, so it couldn't have been an objection to her personally. It couldn't have been her Irish origins, though that'd give some Englishmen pause, because he'd already known that about her. It couldn't be his family's objections; they'd not had any.

Perhaps he'd never been in favor of the match but hadn't told his family, or had told them and had been ignored. Or maybe he'd stayed away because he was a spoiled princeling having a tantrum. Or maybe the Greenberrys were enacting some scheme to convince Liam to concede more in the marriage agreements.

The only thing they could be holding out for was Fairfield.

The Greenberrys she'd interacted with in Cornwall hadn't so much as mentioned the property, though, which suggested the arrangement didn't bother *them*.

If anyone had changed his mind, it was Niles. Which meant *his* mind was the one she needed to change back.

A little filly running around a small pen outside the stable captured Penelope's attention, and she wandered out into the early morning light to watch. The young horse had a very elegantly high step, a highly sought-after trait in horses ridden by those wishing to appear very impressive. If Mr. Layton didn't intend to keep the filly, he could ask a hefty sum for her.

Penelope's eyes wandered beyond the paddock and stables and out over Pledwick Manor's side acres. This area of England, with its starkly stunning moors, was quite different from her family estate in the Wicklow Mountains, which was different still from what she'd seen of Cornwall. But nowhere she'd ever been had managed to supplant Fairfield in her heart.

She had made the journey to Surrey several times since she'd inherited it from her father's uncle when she was still a child. From her first moments on the land that was hers, it had felt like home. It was peace and hope and the promise of freedom, of a life she could choose. No matter that there were more vast and impressive estates, she couldn't imagine loving a place more.

From the very beginning, Mother had insisted it was folly to think of Fairfield as anything other than bait to snare a husband. It would be taken from her, Mother had warned. She wouldn't have the running of it, Mother had insisted.

It wasn't until she was grown that Penelope had learned that all Mother's warnings would prove correct if Penelope didn't take pains to avoid it. And she'd further discovered that not marrying at all wasn't a truly viable option either. Merchants, men of business, creditors, potential purchasers of horses, Society, neighbors . . . seemingly *everyone* looked painfully askance at a single lady living alone and attempting to establish herself as a successful woman of business, even when she was particularly qualified in the area of business she was pursuing.

"Have we fresh hay in Morwenna's stall?" someone in the stables called out.

"Just tossed it in now," someone else replied.

Morwenna was Niles's mount. Niles, who had hidden here rather than return to Cornwall and follow through on their arrangement.

"You agreed to this," she whispered, looking out over the land, knowing he was out there somewhere. "I can't simply let you change your mind. I'd be destroyed."

But how did one go about persuading a gentleman of wealth and birth, one who'd already shown himself willing to use dishonesty and underhandedness, to honor an agreement that was not yet binding?

And do I actually want to marry someone like that?

She shook her head as she walked along the paddock fence. A lady who needed a husband willing to allow her the freedom and consideration she was asking for could hardly be picky. "Beggars," as John Heywood had written, "should be no choosers." And, "Women who kick against the rocks," as her mother had said, "are destined to be hurt and disappointed."

She'd taken some comfort in how uninvolved Niles had been with the marriage negotiations. It increased the chances that he would simply leave her alone in the years to come, and then what sort of gentleman he was wouldn't matter overly much.

How was this the best she hoped for? A husband whose best trait was that even with effort, he couldn't have been made to care *less* about her than he did? She had long ago decided that apathy was preferable to cruelty in a husband. But indifference was also a far cry from caring, even farther from love.

Be no chooser, she reminded herself. She had reached twenty-five years old without anyone showing a tender interest in her. Finding someone who loved her had long ago been shown too remote a possibility. She needed to focus on what was real and within reach. *I am going to sort you out, Niles Greenberry. I have to.*

Liam arrived at the stables just as her steps brought her back to that building. "I should have realized you would be looking over the horses."

"I can't help myself." She glanced back at the sweet filly. "I'm seldom happier than when I'm with horses."

"One would think you like horses better than people."

She shrugged. "Sometimes."

He looked instantly nervous. "You shouldn't jest about that among people who don't know you well. You'll give offense, Penelope, and I suspect our welcome here is a bit shaky as it is."

"Our host has given no indication that he would toss out two people on whom his dear friend and weeks-long houseguest had played so unkind a trick." Penelope was depending on that, in fact.

She had called upon every bit of persuasive reasoning she could think of to convince her brother to make this unplanned journey to Yorkshire. He had been ready to abandon the match entirely. He'd insisted during breakfast the morning after that awkward supper at Niles's grandparents' home that returning to Ireland and finding a "less complicated match" was their best option. Only by pointing out that returning with a still-unmarried sister after having been a bit smug about securing a connection to such a well-respected English family would be horribly embarrassing did she convince Liam to take this drastic step in the hope of bringing the whole thing about after all. She couldn't give up after less than twenty-four hours.

"While I have not seen all the horses, those I have seen are quite impressive," she said. "You should have an enjoyable ride this morning."

"Do you not intend to ride?" Liam eyed her. "You aren't dressed for it."

She sighed. "I wished to meet all the horses first. If my horses had been stabled here rather than having been sent to Fairfield, I would be out on the moors already."

That was another complication she needed to think through. She'd made the journey from Ireland assuming she would be taking up permanent residence at Fairfield after the wedding. Her horses had been sent there. Her books had been. Her little trinkets and personal treasures.

She was supposed to finally be going home.

Instead, she'd been rejected. Rather thoroughly, in fact.

She shook off the thought. She needed to keep her wits, not grow maudlin.

"Are you wishing to ride, sir?" The same groomsman who had spoken with her earlier addressed Liam.

"Yes," he said. "A mare with some spirit but not too much, if you have one. I'm not looking for a challenge this morning, but I'd also rather not be bored."

The groomsman nodded and returned to the interior of the stable.

"Had you a chance to speak with Mr. Greenberry last evening?" she asked Liam.

"He didn't speak," Liam said. "And no one seemed to expect him to."

Ought she to have given the possibility of his being a little simple more consideration? He'd said almost nothing to her. Certainly not enough to answer so significant a question. Her initial impression had been that he was embarrassed, perhaps feeling a little guilty.

"Perhaps he is a bit shy," she said, hoping to keep Liam from growing discouraged enough to abandon it all. "As we get to know Mr. Greenberry better, he'll grow more friendly. I'm certain of it."

"I am trying to be," Liam said. "These gentlemen hail from very exalted circles. We are very much out of our depth here."

"Mr. Greenberry agreed to this match once." She directed the reassurance more at herself than him. "That leaves open the possibility that he will do so again no matter his high connections."

"I really do hope so, Penelope." Liam's gaze flitted over the paddock but didn't linger on any one horse. "But I also need to be realistic."

She smiled at him. "You be realistic. I'll be optimistic. Between the two of us, we'll find the answers we're looking for."

Chapter Six

NILES HAD INTRODUCED THE GENTS to a very Cornish variety of ground billiards during that glorious, long-ago first term at Cambridge when he'd been brought into their circle. And it hadn't taken his newfound friends long to transform the game into something delightfully ludicrous. Lucas and Stanley had led the descent themselves.

Playing it again now with three of the Gents made the one they all still mourned feel a little closer.

It also gave Niles an excuse to pretend he hadn't made a mull of his life lately.

"Protect your brain boxes, Gents!" Lucas called out before striking the heavy wooden ball with his short-handled mallet and sending it careening through the air. The Gents' version of ground billiards enthusiastically violated the "ball should remain on the ground" rule that usually applied to the game.

Digby sauntered toward the spot where the ball came to a stop. Usually, when they played this game, there was a mad rush to reach the ball first, as points were awarded for getting the ball closer to the target, but they were playing a very casual version this time.

"Perhaps," Digby said, "we should tell Mr. Seymour that Niles took a ball to the head and that is why he didn't return for the signing of the marriage agreement." He hit the ball with his mallet, and it flew toward the king pin.

"He defected a fortnight ago," Kes said. "Unless this hypothetical blow he is meant to receive today was so significant that it mussed his mind retroactively, I don't think he can lean on that excuse."

Niles whacked the ball all the way to the king pin, then bowed in acknowledgment of the points he earned for hitting the mark. Upon standing fully upright again, he asked, "Why would we direct excuses to *Mr.* Seymour and not *Miss* Seymour?" It seemed to him, she was the one who deserved an explanation.

"Because he is in a position to potentially bring a breach of promise suit against you." Kes was the one who explained, but the looks on the other two Gents' faces indicated they were aware of that possibility as well. A possibility that had not occurred to Niles, and neither had Digby thought of it at the time they had concocted the harebrained approach they'd taken.

Niles pushed out a slow breath. "I would lose all I've saved."

"Very well might," Lucas acknowledged.

"And with it, the reason I took this risk to begin with." Why could nothing seem to work out the way he wished it would?

"You would be an excellent member of Parliament," Kes said. "Don't abandon your goal of gaining the land you need to be eligible."

Niles wasn't ready to give up, but he wasn't sure how to move ahead. "And I wouldn't mind having something of my own, even a very humble estate that I wasn't beholden to my family for." Realizing that didn't sound entirely the way he wanted, Niles amended, "I love them, I really do. And I wouldn't want to be cut off from them. I only . . . I just . . ."

"Families are complicated things," Lucas said, crossing to the ball lying in the grass next to the king pin. "You can love them and still need room to breathe." He hit the ball far in the opposite direction. They all hustled over to it to begin another round of Gents Ground Billiards.

"How much more money do you need to get breathing room?" Kes asked.

Though Niles hated to speak the total aloud, he didn't imagine it would do any good not to be forthright. "One hundred fifty pounds."

They all looked appropriately awed. It was not an impossible amount, but it was not insignificant either.

He'd done the calculations countless times. He was fortunate to have a relatively generous and guaranteed income from his family, though it was not quite sufficient to meet the income requirement for serving in the House of Commons. But if he had an estate that generated an income, he could qualify. Lud, there were a lot of "ifs."

Kes sent the ball flying once more. As they watched its path through the air, he asked, "Have you considered grave robbery? You could make a few extra coins that way."

Most who knew Kester Barrington would never guess that he had the sense of humor he did. Most who knew Niles wouldn't guess he was a dab hand at any kind of athletic endeavor. People were often surprising.

Lucas had trotted over to the ball, mallet swinging in anticipation. "Or you could polish up your dancing," he called back. "The theater is always hiring."

The ball cracked against his mallet and flew yet again. They were nearing the king pin. Niles started off, hoping to reach the ball first after the next hit, as that would allow him to knock it into the pin and win double points for the round. No one was truly keeping score, but he enjoyed knowing he had hit the mark.

As he walked toward a waiting spot, he spied Miss Seymour approaching. Anxiety clutched at his heart and throat. It was more than the hint of nervousness that he would expect when in company with a beautiful woman who had shown herself to be observant and intelligent and not easily distracted from her purpose. Miss Seymour had been unfairly treated and lied to. By him. He half expected her to soundly renounce him. He would deserve it, but he would also hate it.

She was within a few yards when the crack of a mallet against a ball echoed. Niles spun enough to search the sky for the hard and heavy orb. It was careening right toward them. The Gents were yelling out warnings. Miss Seymour wouldn't know to be looking for it.

Niles dropped his mallet and rushed back a few steps, watching the ball's trajectory. "Guard your head, Miss Seymour," he shouted just in case.

But he caught the ball before it could do any damage to the lady, who had endured quite enough already. The smack of it against his hand stung. He switched the ball to the other hand, then shook the pain from the one he'd used, all as he turned toward Miss Seymour.

"Our apologies, Miss Seymour." He looked for some indication that she was overset by the encounter. She didn't appear to be. "If we'd known you were so nearby, we wouldn't have hit the ball."

She motioned toward his hand. "Do you throw as expertly as you catch?"

"I—I do."

"So do I."

There was a riddle in that. "Yes, but does that . . . ?" He was so unaccustomed to being the one who did the talking that he sometimes tripped over the simplest of things. He wasn't shy or inarticulate; he was simply out of practice. "Does that mean you are equally *ad*ept or *in*ept?"

Penelope Seymour really ought to issue some kind of warning before she smiled so a fellow could formulate his thoughts while he was still able.

"Would you like to hazard a guess as to my athleticism or lack thereof?" She asked the question with enough mischief in her eyes to tell him she suspected the answer would surprise him.

He knew from his own experiences that people who were small—and Miss Seymour was *tiny*—were usually assumed to be lacking in physical prowess and athleticism. Ladies were met with that assumption more or less by default.

"Would you like to . . . ? Would you like to join us in this one?"

She glanced behind him. He could hear the Gents approaching.

"I hadn't intended to disrupt your game," she insisted. "I came in the hope of discovering the source of the odd cracking sounds I kept hearing."

From very nearly beside Niles, Digby said, "You are quite welcome to join us if you'd like. It's not a sophisticated game, but it's diverting."

She looked at Niles once more. "I am not overly familiar with ground billiards, but I'm a quick study."

He was surprised at how pleased he was that she wanted to join in and also at how nervous he was that she had directed her acceptance to him rather than Digby. "The game is relatively simple. It begins with the ball far afield from the king pin." He motioned to it. "Every hit that brings the ball closer earns the one who hit it a point. The person who hits the king pin with the ball earns two points."

"When we are playing competitively," Lucas added, "there is a great deal of running, as each person hopes to reach the ball first and earn a point for hitting it."

She nodded. "Unless the ball is at barely too far a distance to reach the goal and the one striking it will simply be offering the next player double points."

"Precisely." Niles held his mallet out to her.

"You need your mallet to play," she objected.

"If I get to the ball before you, you can simply trade back."

The corners of her mouth lifted, and his chest clenched at the sight. "Make certain you adequately emphasize the word *if* in that sentence."

The Gents quickly took up that line of teasing. Niles wouldn't hear the end of it anytime soon. He didn't mind. Jesting and good-hearted taunting were as much a part of the Gents' connection as support in times of trouble and cheering in times of triumph.

Miss Seymour eyed the ball and the king pin, gave the situation a moment's thought, then sent the ball sailing. To the pin. Right to it.

Shouts of "Huzzah!" and "Amazing!" rang out from them all. Her first time even attempting this game, and she'd made the perfect shot.

More than a little amazed, Niles said, "I really *should* have emphasized the word *if* more in that sentence."

She spun the mallet in her hand before holding it out to him. "Yes, you should have."

That set them all to laughing even more.

Miss Seymour was, at least in that moment, rather fun. The trouble was, Niles didn't know if that was a good thing or if it would only make the situation even worse than it already was.

Chapter Seven

A GENTLEMAN WHO HAD NOT only agreed to the admittedly unusual terms Penelope had asked for in their marriage agreement but who also hadn't disapproved or soured up when she had shown herself naturally adept at a sporting game? Until coming to England, Penelope hadn't known such a gentleman even existed.

Of course, that man was also an unrepentant liar. No gentleman who had been so horribly ill as to prevent a return trip home when doing so had been a requirement of honorable and proper behavior could possibly have engaged in so physically tasking a game as the one she'd joined in with the gusto he'd displayed. The Gents had already been at the game for some time before she'd arrived. And Niles had spent the half hour of her participation running almost ceaselessly without even growing short of breath. She would be surprised to learn he'd ever been ill a day in his life.

Her attempts to sort him out were leaving her only more confused.

Penelope hadn't been overly conversational during supper. She suspected no one had noticed. Liam might have if he hadn't been peppering Mr. Layton with questions. He seemed quite intent on making himself one of their host's friends. He had likely continued the effort after she and Mrs. Barrington had retired to the drawing room and the gentlemen had remained behind to have their port.

For her part, Penelope had something more pressing to attend to. "May I ask you a question, Mrs. Barrington?" She sat on the same settee as the lady. "It has the potential to be a bit of an uncomfortable and prying inquiry. But if I'm to have any hope of success while I'm here, I need to have it answered." Mrs. Barrington looked a bit surprised, and Penelope realized she'd made a familiar potential misstep. "I've often been accused of being very direct," she said by way of acknowledgment. "'Frustratingly forthright,' my mother often calls it."

"No need to justify your forthrightness. Personally, I find it refreshing. And the other ladies attached to this group of gentlemen—Lady Jonquil and Nicolette Fortier—aren't truly demure. Neither am I."

Penelope liked that. She would enjoy being in company with other ladies who were similar to herself. 'Twas yet more motivation to make sense of her current situation. "Is Mr. Greenberry simpleminded?" she asked.

Everything about Mrs. Barrington's expression said that had she been sipping tea, she would have spit it out.

"A bit too forthright?" Penelope asked.

"Unexpected more than anything," Mrs. Barrington said.

"What was it you *did* expect me to ask?"

"I don't know if I was set on a specific question, but I had honestly assumed you were going to ask something about *me*. People often have questions when we first meet. They hear the hint of trade in my voice and wonder what my background is. Or they notice the stiffness in my arm and wonder if it's an old injury. Or sometimes, they detect that I have some African ancestry and wonder at that."

Mrs. Barrington was certainly putting truth to her declaration of being very candid.

"I'm not familiar enough with the various English accents and dialects to have the first idea how to detect 'trade' in someone's voice. I'd noticed a stiffness to your arm and did assume you had an injury or rheumatism. I'd like to hear about your African ancestry."

Mrs. Barrington hadn't been cold to Penelope or standoffish, but there was an added warmth to her after this very small but very direct exchange. "Mine is a Portsmouth shipyard family, and the *ton* finds that . . . noteworthy."

"And not in a delighted way, I'm to assume?" Penelope thought she'd sorted what Mrs. Barrington was hinting at.

"Far from delighted." Mrs. Barrington gave her a significant look. "The stiffness in my arm arises from the fact that it is, in fact, a prosthesis, which I don't make obvious because that, too, would be considered *noteworthy*. And I'm sorry to say I don't know a great deal of the details of my ancestry other than our family pride in being related to a very well-known musician from Africa."

"Does the *ton* also find that connection 'noteworthy'?"

Mrs. Barrington nodded. "We don't often speak of it outside our family and close friends."

"But you are speaking of it to me now."

She gave a minute shrug. "I find, though we are not well acquainted, that I trust you. Your belief that Niles Greenberry is slow of intellect does make me question your judgment a little."

"No," Penelope was quick to counter. "I asked because I don't actually think he is, which I realize is confusing. His grandfather undertook the entirety of the marriage negotiations, which I decided either indicated a very fierce adherence to family hierarchy or a lack of faith in the younger Mr. Greenberry's ability to take on the task. And then, upon arriving here, I found that he very seldom talks and that no one seems to expect him to, but he doesn't actually strike me as being shy. While I don't truly think there is a slowness to him, I thought it best to know for certain before I decide how it is I ought to proceed."

Mrs. Barrington's open expression clouded with a hint of apprehension. "Does this mean you wish for *the marriage* to proceed?"

"Despite his defection and not knowing him well, yes. I am something of an unconventional person, and he agreed to some unconventional terms in the marriage contract, which gives me hope that he and I could be relatively well-suited. And even quiet as he is, I have the impression that he is a kind person, which I had hoped to find in a husband. Far too many ladies are married to brutes who mistreat them. Escaping that fate appeals to me very much indeed. Thus 'tis decidedly in my best interest to move forward if at all possible."

Mrs. Barrington did not look convinced. "There are any number of gentlemen who are kind. That is not so rare a quality that it requires pursuing a match with a gentleman who has, if you will excuse the bluntness of my language, shown himself willing to behave uncivilly in order to avoid the marriage you are seeking."

Blunt, yes. But also accurate.

"My situation is very odd. I haven't a dowry. My family's connections are limited to Ireland and, even then, are not among the most exalted spheres. What I do have to offer, in the end, would not be beneficial to my would-be husband. Every gentleman who has shown even the least interest abandoned any hint of that interest once he understood the situation. Until Mr. Greenberry. If he has, in actuality, permanently changed his mind, then I am out of options."

While Mrs. Barrington's expression had softened, it hadn't entirely cleared. "But Niles is not out of options. His family could make another match for him very quickly."

Penelope was well aware of that. "I would simply like a chance to discover if I might be a good option for him and he for me. I want to try. Gentlemen undertake courtships of hesitant ladies all the time. This wouldn't be entirely different."

Mrs. Barrington watched her more closely. "Are you considering *courting* Niles?"

Was she? She pressed her fingers to her lips, thinking. "I suppose I am." She rose and began to wander about as she pondered the idea. "I would like the chance to know him better. Though I have my suspicions that the other gentlemen would help him flee again if he asked them to."

"His happiness is important to all of us," Mrs. Barrington said. "The Gents will defend him to the hilt."

Penelope watched Mrs. Barrington closely, needing to know if she had lost this battle before it had even begun.

"What if," Mrs. Barrington asked, "you spend time here coming to know him and discover that while you find him perfectly pleasant, you don't feel any particular affection for him?"

Penelope had only ever allowed herself to hope for "perfectly pleasant." The idea of love and affection had been abandoned long ago.

"Or," Mrs. Barrington continued, "you do find yourself growing tenderly fond of him, but Niles doesn't return that regard? What would you do?"

Penelope held her hands up in a show of helplessness. "I don't know. I certainly don't want either of us to be unhappy. And though arranged marriages very seldom include affection as one of the considerations, to be cared about would be a wonderful thing. But it seems like far too much to hope for."

"The two of you getting to know each other better would not necessarily cause Niles any misery or harm." Mrs. Barrington's protective approach to Niles was both admirable and worrisome. Penelope, it seemed, needed to convince far more than her prodigal betrothed to look favorably on her. She needed to win over *all* his friends. "And should it become clear in the end that you two would not suit, the entire thing can be called off."

Though the last was spoken in tones of mere observation, Mrs. Barrington's gaze was anything but casual. Penelope understood the message. She had an ally in her efforts to make Niles's better acquaintance. But in the end, if her match with Niles wasn't seen as something more than a beneficial business-like arrangement, she would have an entire household of people sending her away *alone*.

"I would appreciate the chance to at least try," she said. "And though it would spell disaster for me, I give you my word that I won't force the matter if Mr. Greenberry does not wish to proceed in the end."

Mrs. Barrington nodded. "The gentlemen refer to themselves as the Gents, so you might as well also. And I suppose you had better call me Violet."

"Why *had I better*?" Penelope certainly hadn't expected this informality so soon after being interrogated and warned.

"Because you are going to need my help, and accomplices aren't meant to be overly formal."

"'Accomplices'? You mean to *actively* help me?"

Violet nodded.

"Then, you must have some faith that I will keep my word."

"I do," Violet said. "The fact that you are willing to try to sincerely determine if you could have some happiness together speaks well of you. And I am holding out hope that this attempted courtship will be the start of something lovely."

Tolerable had always seemed far more within her reach than *lovely*. What if it were actually possible? What if Niles was more than her *only* option and was actually also a wonderful option?

"No gentleman has ever found me intriguing enough to court," Penelope said, "so I don't have any experience with how it is undertaken. I have seen wooing from a distance. There were often flowers involved."

A little humor eased the suspicion in Violet's eyes. "And extremely emotional odes dedicated to beguiling eyes and luscious hair."

"Am I expected to write Niles poetry?" She didn't know whether to laugh or be horrified.

"And beg his hand for the supper dance at a ball," Violet added, her smile growing.

Warming to the exercise, Penelope said, "I could invite him to go for a drive in my impressive curricle."

"Only if it is *very* impressive."

In the midst of the laughter that followed, the gentlemen joined them.

"I would ask if you were laughing at us," Lord Jonquil said, "but I suspect I know the answer."

With an air of coyness, Violet said, "If the lot of you weren't so laugh*able*, we wouldn't be forced into it."

Mr. Barrington reached his wife's side. "How grateful I am that you endure us."

"*Endure* us?" Mr. Layton scoffed. "They, I haven't the least doubt, have been in here plotting against us."

Penelope widened her eyes in an expression of mock offense. "Plotting? We would never!"

Liam, whose gaze had been darting between Mr. Layton and Niles, moved swiftly to Penelope's side. "You aren't actually plotting anything are you?" he asked in a nervous whisper. "We do not claim standing high enough to make ourselves overly familiar like this."

"They all realize I'm simply joining in their jest." Penelope matched his volume. She looked quickly at Niles, standing a bit apart from the others, and saw in his face what appeared to be sincere amusement. "No need to worry."

Liam didn't look at all relieved. "They claim a rung on Society's ladder that we can't even see. Please don't embarrass us, Penelope."

"I think you are overreacting," she insisted.

Niles chose a seat a little apart from the others, yet there was nothing in his chosen location or his demeanor that indicated he was upset or uncomfortable. And none of his friends appeared to be surprised by his chosen location nor made any effort to change it. This was, apparently, a very common arrangement.

He seemed to feel most comfortable with a little bit of space. She could appreciate that.

"We have been doing a little plotting of our own," Lord Jonquil said. "What would you ladies think of an outing tomorrow?"

"That would depend very much on the outing," Violet answered.

"A hog farm," Mr. Barrington said dryly. "We will be mucking slop."

Mr. Layton shuddered. "Do not suggest such a thing, even in jest."

Across the way, Niles grinned. Something in the genuine delight in his expression pulled a smile to Penelope's face as well. Liam watched the group with a look of earnest uncertainty. Did he think he wasn't invited?

"Hamblestead has a lovely market cross," Mr. Layton said. "And the innkeeper at the Green Badger quite outdoes himself with the meals he serves. It would make for an enjoyable way to pass the day."

"And there are ruins of an old abbey nearby," Lord Jonquil said eagerly. "A fine place to explore." He turned to Niles. "Are you game for an adventure?"

"Always," Niles said without hesitation, one of only a half dozen words he'd spoken all night. But it was an additional insight. Niles Greenberry was very quiet, not entirely honest, surprisingly athletic, and "always" eager for an adventure.

"We could ask the innkeeper to pack a meal in a hamper," Mr. Layton suggested, "then enjoy a meal on the banks of the lake if the weather is cooperative."

"There is a lake?" Violet seemed particularly pleased by the idea. She was, apparently, fond of water.

"A lovely one," Mr. Layton said. "It is quite deep in some places, and the water looks nearly black, but in the shallower areas, it is a delightful shade of blue."

"That sounds gorgeous," Penelope said.

"We, in the area, think so."

"Then, I am certain we all will as well," Liam said. "How very good of you to arrange the outing."

Mr. Layton's expression remained perfectly friendly, but there was the tiniest, fleetingest look of exasperation in his eyes. "I find myself unexpectedly the host of a house party. Thinking of ways to keep my guests entertained is part of the associated responsibilities."

Liam was all apologies for the inconvenience when addressing Mr. Layton and silent expressions of concern when looking at Penelope. Though she did think her brother was overreacting, there was also reason to proceed with caution.

She was about to embark on a courtship, which she hadn't planned on and was not at all certain how to approach. She had promised Violet that if Niles didn't prove interested in the end, she would abandon her efforts. These were Niles's friends. If she failed to capture his affection, they would make certain she kept that promise.

Chapter Eight

NILES HAD ALWAYS LIKED HAMBLESTEAD. It was small enough to be idyllic, while also large enough for a new arrival to not draw a great deal of notice. He often preferred to be overlooked. Miss Seymour, however, didn't appear to overlook anything or anyone.

"Why do you suppose the Seymours haven't returned home?" Niles asked as he walked alongside the Gents during the group's excursion to the village. He spoke quietly, not wishing either of those he was discussing, or Violet, who had become fast friends with Miss Seymour, to overhear the question. The three of them were a few paces ahead of the Gents, having their own conversation.

"Because of my innate ability to make any and every guest at Pledwick Manor feel instantly both at home and in awe?" Digby suggested.

"And your willingness to generously lend people access to your remarkably capable staff?" Lucas asked, clearly not serious.

"Your willingness to lend me a member of your staff has certainly made *me* feel very welcome," Lucas said.

Digby gave him a withering look. "I ought to have left you to sort the matter on your own when you arrived without a valet. Inexcusable, Lucas."

"I'll find a new valet soon enough," Lucas said. "But in the meantime, I intend to take full advantage of your generosity."

"Which brings us back to my original point," Digby said. "If not for my superior ability as a host, Niles might not be in so uncomfortable a situation."

Niles wasn't distracted from the worry that had weighed on his mind for days. "Do you suppose they intend to try to force my hand on this match?"

His friends exchanged looks that told him they'd been wondering the same thing.

"We talked about it," Kes said. "All of us intend to stay here as long as the Seymours do. They'll not be able to browbeat you into acquiescing with all of us present to act as buffers."

That made Niles sound like a helpless infant when he really was simply unaccustomed to demanding autonomy. He was further inexperienced in being ungentlemanly. His current predicament arose from having recently done both and the need to continue doing them.

"Digby," Violet called back to the group from her place at a shop window. "We need your opinion on these shawls."

"Gents." Digby struck a very serious pose. "My expertise is being called upon. Do excuse me whilst I see to this utterly crucial matter."

Lucas leaned a little closer to Niles and Kes as Digby joined the others. "Watch *Mr. Seymour.*"

Niles did. The gentleman greeted Digby warmly, which wasn't surprising. Mr. Seymour had seemed intent on gaining Digby's good opinion. But then he nudged his sister a little closer to Digby. A subtle but unmistakable movement.

"I've wondered since supper last night," Lucas said, still watching the scene play out. "But I'm more and more convinced that the focus of the matrimonial efforts might be shifting, at least from Mr. Seymour's view of things."

"Do we need to be acting as a buffer for Digby, then?" Niles didn't know if that was more relieving or guilt-inducing.

Kes shook his head. "Digby acts empty-headed, but we all know perfectly well that he is entirely capable of looking after himself."

"He has been doing so since he was a child," Lucas added, looking genuinely sorrowful on their friend's behalf. Lucas had known Digby far longer than Niles had and knew aspects of his history that no one else was privy to.

Digby was deep in an animated conversation with the two ladies about the items in the window. Niles didn't feel equal to that topic, and Lucas and Kes wandered to the window of the next shop over to look at something there. Niles set himself against a wall, waiting.

Twice a year, a fair was held near Hamblestead, which brought in people from miles around. Digby had played host a few times when the Gents had attended. The autumnal fair would be held soon, if Niles was remembering correctly. And if he was further remembering correctly, it was here in Hamblestead that he'd bought a bit of incredibly delicious cheese. He ought to find that shop again and purchase a bit.

They were wandering the village while waiting for the hamper of picnic foods they'd requested from the Green Badger. The sky was overcast, but otherwise, the weather was beautiful. Niles had a bit of time. He made his way down one side of the market cross, where he thought he'd made the purchase before.

A villager tipped his hat to Niles as he passed. Niles nodded back.

He passed two men conversing outside a shop.

"Heard Martin might be arriving to fight for t' purse," one of them said to the other, who whistled in response, impressed.

Fight for the purse? Was there to be a pugilistic bout? Niles hadn't heard as much.

A woman with a little one in tow passed by. "I know you're jiggered, love, but we can't move slow. We've laundry to see to."

Niles reached the end of the road without finding a dairy or a shop that looked like it might carry cheese. He'd apparently remembered wrong. That was unfortunate.

"Mr. Greenberry?"

He spun about at the subtly Irish voice speaking his name, knowing even before he looked that Miss Seymour had spoken.

She smiled softly. "The food hampers are ready. I'd not wanted you to be left behind."

"The Gents rarely forget to bring along their Puppy."

Her confusion reminded him that she didn't have the necessary information to recognize the jest he was attempting.

"All the Gents have nicknames we use among ourselves. Mine is—" He'd never before been embarrassed by his moniker but was more reluctant to share it in that moment than he could have anticipated.

"Is it Puppy, by chance?" she guessed.

He nodded. "It's not ill meant."

"I'd not have assumed it was."

They walked beside each other back in the direction of the Green Badger.

"I had a nickname when I was a little girl, given to me by a neighboring family, and it *was* ill meant."

She didn't look hurt by the recollection, so he felt he could continue the thread without causing her pain. "May I ask what the nickname was?"

"They called me the Little Banshee."

He wasn't familiar with that term.

Miss Seymour smiled once more. "I can see that doesn't have the impact it would if told to an Irishman, so allow me to explain. A banshee is an Irish folk creature: female, unbearably loud, fearful, and an omen of horrific things, up to and including death. To be called a banshee is not a compliment."

"Were you particularly loud as a child?" he asked.

She laughed lightly. "That part of the name was merited, I'm afraid. But the rest was simply unkind."

"You were not a harbinger of death, then?"

"I've killed very few people." Her extremely serious declaration was quickly countered by the tug of merriment in her features.

"If the neighboring family wasn't included in your short list of victims, then I would say you missed an opportunity."

She laughed out loud at that. Niles was not the humorous Gent—that designation was Lucas's. There was something rather nice about inspiring a sincere laugh in that moment.

"In what little I've learned of you over the past months," she said, "nowhere did anyone mention that you were bloodthirsty."

"And no one told me *you* were a murderer," Niles countered.

Again, she laughed, and he didn't think it sounded insincere or forced. Did she legitimately find him funny? He certainly had a sense of humor, and he did sometimes make the Gents laugh but not many people beyond them. He didn't know quite what to think of Miss Seymour doing so, not only easily but also more than once in quick succession. It was . . . confusing.

They caught up with the rest of the party just outside the inn. Two hampers had been prepared, and Lucas and Kes now held them. Their coachmen carried wool blankets and cushions, as did a couple of stableboys. Digby guided the group around the inn and down the gravel walkway in back, which led all the way to the banks of the lake, where they would be spending that afternoon.

They clearly were not the only people to decide the day would be well spent in that setting. A small group had gathered a few yards away. What appeared to be a young family was equally as far in the other direction. A third group sat on blankets and cushions even farther along the banks.

In the end, they chose a spot just beyond the third group, on the other side of a small boat launch. The location afforded them a great deal of privacy while not being at an inconvenient distance from the inn. The coachmen and stableboys were invited—*encouraged*—to join in the leisurely meal, and they did so, but in their own grouping, a bit apart.

Through slight maneuvering, Mr. Seymour managed to see his sister seated beside Digby. Lucas tossed a knowing look at Niles and Kes. It seemed there was some truth to Lucas's theory that the focus of Mr. Seymour's matrimonial aim for his sister was shifting.

Did that mean hers was as well?

The moment the question flitted through his mind, Niles pushed it aside. If the Seymours' efforts were adjusting, that would help him in the end. And as Kes had pointed out, Digby was well able to look after himself. Their easy abandonment of him was reason for Niles to breathe more easily. Instead, he found himself with yet another thing to feel guilty about: Digby's growing inconvenience.

"I suspect one of you Gents might be known as the Sorcerer or some such thing," Miss Seymour said. "This is the most cooperative weather we've experienced since arriving in England."

"Alas," Lucas said dramatically, "we do not have a Sorcerer. The Jester." He motioned to himself. "And"—he motioned to Kes—"Grumpy Uncle."

That brought a surprised smile to Miss Seymour's face.

Lucas motioned to Digby. "The King."

That didn't seem to surprise her at all.

Lucas turned to Niles.

"I know this one." Miss Seymour said. "Puppy."

"Either he told you his moniker," Digby said, "or *you* ought to be known as the Sorcerer."

She pulled her eyes wide. "You'll never know which," she said in a foreboding voice.

Digby looked expectantly in Niles's direction.

"I won't risk the wrath of a possible sorceress by spilling her secrets," Niles said.

"Wise," Lucas said, overly solemn.

"Do they truly mean to call you the Sorceress?" Mr. Seymour asked his sister in a heavy whisper. He didn't seem to realize, or at least appreciate, that they were joking.

"Of course not, Liam," Miss Seymour answered.

Her brother looked at them all, clearly unsure how he ought to respond.

Violet smoothed over the uncomfortable moment by insisting they all begin eating. They distributed the food, and everyone settled in to enjoy the meal. Their conversation was general and friendly, and Niles was entirely content to let the people around him speak.

His attention wandered. The coachmen and stableboys were skipping rocks on the lake water. The family they'd passed on their way from the inn appeared to be enjoying their meal. The group nearest them was sitting on their cushions, watching as two of their servants stood at the end of the boat launch, placing items in a rowboat. The younger of the servants watched the water nervously, poor lad. Someone was out on the lake already, rowing slowly on the calm water.

Niles returned his gaze to the group around him and found Miss Seymour watching him, perplexed and inquisitive. Had she said something to him and he hadn't heard? Was she expecting him to make conversation? Was she simply letting her frustration with his engagement defection show?

But the expression left her face almost immediately, replaced by a light smile. Niles didn't know what to make of that either.

Sometimes she studied him. Sometimes she laughed. Sometimes she smiled. Sometimes she watched him with suspicion. Penelope Seymour was impossible to sort out.

Without warning, Lucas tore off his buckled shoes and, as he sprinted toward the boat launch, pulled off his coat and tossed it to the ground without slowing.

The nervous younger servant was nowhere to be seen, with the other motioning frantically toward the water.

Niles jumped to his feet and ran in that direction as well. Ahead of him, Lucas dove off the boat launch and into the water. Niles could hear frantic voices behind him, likely as worried about Lucas as the missing young man. But Niles knew Lucas could swim like a fish.

At the edge of the launch, Niles dropped onto his belly, ready to reach out when he was needed. Kes was beside him a moment later.

In the water, Lucas had an arm around the young man, pulling him to the surface a short distance from the boat launch.

"Get—him—out—first." Water sprayed from Lucas's mouth as he pushed each word out.

Niles and Kes each took hold of one of the young man's arms and helped him up onto the boat launch. He was no more than fifteen years old, and though he wasn't unconscious, he was clearly shaken to his very core. Miss Seymour was there on the boat launch and wrapped the young man in one of the wool blankets they'd been using for their picnic. It was grass stained but dry.

They pulled Lucas up out of the water as well. Miss Seymour immediately wrapped him in another blanket.

"What happened?" Miss Seymour asked the servant who'd not fallen in.

"He slipped. Slipped right into the water. He don't know how to swim."

Through chattering teeth, Lucas asked the sodden young man, "Why are you . . . tending to a boat . . . if you . . . can't swim?"

Shivering as well, the boy answered, his voice identifying his homeland as India, "Because . . . I am . . . expendable."

"No person . . . is ever expendable," Lucas said.

The group of picnickers the young man worked as a servant for were making their way slowly toward the boat launch, none looking motivated by compassion. The young man watched them warily and with a hint of worry.

"Don't you fret about them," Kes said.

"I will be . . . dismissed without . . . references." Poor young man sounded despondent in addition to being cold.

"Concentrate on warming up," Miss Seymour insisted.

Holding his own blanket tight around himself, Lucas moved to the young man's side. "We'll walk with you . . . back to the inn. If your employer objects . . . we'll deal with that as well."

"You are . . . very kind, sir."

Lucas motioned for him to begin walking. "What's your name?"

"I am . . . called Wilson."

An entire crowd had gathered around the boat launch, including all the others from Pledwick Manor.

Miss Seymour spoke quietly to Niles. "You managed to get rather wet as well. You ought to find a fireplace at the inn to sit near for a time."

He took a look at himself and found he *was* a bit soaked from the ordeal. "You were thinking fast on your feet, bringing the blankets like you did. Well done, Miss Seymour."

"Tell my brother that, if you get a chance. He'll be upset that I was running as fast as I was, which is generally not considered very ladylike."

"No matter what he says, coming to the aid of another person is heroic."

With a smile that proved unexpectedly tender, she said, "Then, you, Mr. Niles Greenberry, are a hero."

Chapter Nine

Mr. Layton had sent his coachman back to Pledwick Manor to fetch a change of clothes for both Lord Jonquil and young Wilson. Both water-logged men had spent the interim in rooms at the inn, sitting in front of fires, and once the coachman had returned, they had changed into dry clothing.

In the meantime, the rest of the party had gathered in the inn's private dining room, joined by the group Wilson worked for. Penelope didn't usually pass judgment on people upon first acquaintance, but she found herself entirely displeased with those who'd joined them.

"I will not pay for the room that boy has been in," one of the others said to the innkeeper when he came in to stoke the fire in the dining room. "He ought to have been sent to the stables."

Mr. Layton spoke up before the innkeeper had to. "You *aren't* paying for the room; *I* am."

"That boy already has ideas above himself," the same sour-faced gentleman said. "You are making a great deal of trouble for my household, making him think he warrants special treatment."

"Do you consider *not* being required to tend to a boat when one doesn't know how to swim to be 'special treatment'?" Niles asked, standing near the fire.

The room seemed to jump a little, not in surprise at what he'd said but in having, apparently, forgotten he was there.

"He is a stablehand," the most talkative member of the other group said. "Tending to boats during excursions falls under his responsibilities."

"If you make a habit of requiring your stablehands to risk falling into water," Penelope said, "you might do better to make Wilson a footman."

A lady in the group gave Penelope a wrinkled-nose look of distaste. "I assure you, we have two footmen already, and they are nearly perfectly matched."

Penelope turned a bit away. In a quiet voice, she asked Niles, "What does she mean, 'perfectly matched'?"

He seemed a little surprised that she'd turned to him, but he answered just the same, keeping his voice quiet as well. "There are some in English Society who consider it the height of sophistication to have footmen who are as close to indistinguishable from each other as they can be."

"And they are chosen solely because they'll 'match,' as she put it?"

Niles nodded.

'Twas a difficult thing for her to imagine. "That is something one does with furniture, not people."

"Unfortunately," he said, "for some people, servants and furniture warrant the same level of consideration."

Penelope shook her head. "I've known that to be true for some in Dublin society as well, I'm grieved to say." She eyed the lady who'd spoken. "Seems there are unfeeling people everywhere."

She'd apparently not spoken as quietly as she'd intended to.

The lady's nose scrunched up once more. "Seems there are *Irish* people everywhere."

Niles took a single step away from the fireplace, putting himself the tiniest bit closer to the sour-faced lady than Penelope. "I beg your pardon. You spoke too quietly for me to clearly hear your comment to Miss Seymour." Though Niles spoke softly, there was a sharpness underlying his words that wasn't lost on the recipient. "I would hate for anyone here to *not* know what you said to a lady who claims such a close and personal connection to the titled and influential people you see all around you."

The lady sputtered a little.

"What was it you said?" Niles's expression absolutely dared the lady to repeat her unkind words.

Penelope's sudden and unexpected nemesis made no further attempt. She returned to the rest of her group.

Penelope turned to Niles, so touched by his defense of her that she couldn't seem to find the words to express her gratitude.

"She ought not to have said what she did," was the extent of his explanation before he returned to his spot hovering near the fireplace.

You really are heroic, Niles Greenberry. And I suspect you have no idea that you are.

In the next moment, Lord Jonquil stepped into the room, dressed in dry clothing, his cravat quite expertly tied and his hair, though still looking a bit damp, fashionably coiffed. Young Wilson followed behind, looking uncertain and keeping close to Lord Jonquil.

Those not attached to Pledwick Manor eyed Wilson's return with obvious displeasure, though they did show Lord Jonquil more deference than they had at the lake, no doubt owing to their having learned that he was titled.

After a quick nod from Lord Jonquil, Wilson stepped up to his employer— the sour-faced gentleman—and, chin held high, said, "I no longer wish to be in your employ, sir."

That sent eyebrows upward all around the room.

"Think carefully, boy," the gentleman said. "You'll have no references, and you'll find yourself unable to secure a new position."

"I'll take that risk, sir."

The scrunched-nose lady eyed Wilson with her familiar expression. "How dare you speak to him so flippantly."

Niles moved to the door and opened it. "As Mr. Layton is paying for the privilege of his houseguests using this room and you are no longer connected to the concerns of this young man, I believe you can return to your picnic."

Penelope would wager no one in the room was forgetting Niles's presence now. He was proving a complicated person, more difficult to predict than she would have guessed. He was also proving inarguably remarkable.

Their temporary companions vacated the room, though not without a few lingering looks of mingled confusion and disapproval.

"Good to see you two looking a little less like drowned rats," Mr. Layton said to Lord Jonquil and Wilson. "Your cravat is exceptionally well tied, Lucas."

Lord Jonquil motioned to the young man, who dipped his head in acknowledgment.

Mr. Layton looked immediately impressed. "Well done, Wilson."

"He was wasted as a stablehand," Lord Jonquil said.

"You are in need of a valet," Mr. Barrington added.

"Precisely. And Wilson is now in need of a position. Seems fate is smiling on us."

"Grinning, I'd say." Mr. Layton looked directly at the young man. "My valet and I can offer you some training in being a gentleman's gentleman."

"I would be indebted to you, sir."

Throughout the exchange, Niles remained near the now-closed door, seemingly quite content to listen and not participate. He'd come to her defense despite his preference for remaining quietly apart. Realizing that, his defense of her touched her all the more.

Penelope walked toward him but was intercepted by Liam. "You have hardly spoken with Mr. Layton," he said in a tense whisper.

"I haven't precisely ignored him."

Liam threaded his arm through hers and pulled her away from the others to the far side of the room. "He is a gentleman of standing and wealth, without a wife."

She'd suspected Liam's thoughts had turned in that direction. "He is also a very close friend of the gentleman I am meant to be marrying. I sincerely doubt he is that disloyal to his friend."

"His friend has rather soundly rejected you," Liam countered. "There would be no disloyalty in his pursuit of Mr. Greenberry's . . ."

When the pause pulled out overly long, Penelope offered a conclusion to the observation. "Castoff?"

"That's not what I meant." But his attempt at denial made Penelope only more certain she'd hit close to his aim. "If there is a chance Mr. Layton would take an interest, we would be fools not to seize on it. His standing is remarkably high. And he hasn't rejected us out of hand."

"As unexpected houseguests," she reminded him. "That is far different than presenting himself as a potential suitor."

"I don't want you to end up all alone, Penelope. And we don't have a lot of options." A stubborn flavor of determination washed over him. "I have to at least try."

"Please don't."

But Liam wasn't swayed. He made his way to Mr. Layton's side. Her brother could sometimes be frustratingly oblivious to the impact of his behavior. She didn't doubt he truly believed Mr. Layton would welcome Liam's change in matrimonial goals for his sister, but his obtuse efforts would undermine Penelope's attempted courtship if she didn't begin making progress.

She returned to Niles's side once more.

"This is a more pleasant gathering now that it is our group alone," she said to Niles. "Our picnic partners did not prove very friendly."

"Not to you," he said. "Certainly not to Wilson."

"It was good of you to remove them so firmly. They'll not return and cause further grief."

In a quiet yet not weak voice, he said, "You seem surprised."

"*Pleased.*" She felt her smile turn a little smug. "But the lady with stanch opinions about the Irish, *she* was surprised."

He twisted his mouth a little, obviously hiding a smile of his own. "She never did repeat her comment, did she?"

Not trying nearly as hard to keep her delight tucked away, she said, "She did not."

"Imagine that."

Mr. Barrington called Niles over.

Penelope watched Niles leave, and her heart ached a little. She liked him. She hadn't known him long, but she had, in that single afternoon, come to know him a little better. He was heroic in his own quiet way. He had a good heart. He was kind.

And he thought her worth defending. Not everyone did. Her own family didn't always.

But Niles Greenberry did. Something in that realization made her want to cry.

Chapter Ten

PENELOPE WAS EMBARRASSINGLY NERVOUS.

There'd been no objection when she'd asked to join Niles and the Gents during their game of ground billiards. He'd not seemed annoyed that she'd spoken more with him than the others during their excursion to Hamblestead. He wouldn't be unkind, even if he was disinclined to accept her intended invitation.

Yet she was anxious as she approached the Pledwick Manor stables. Gentlemen asked ladies to accompany them on drives all the time. Were those hopeful gentlemen as nervous as she?

She'd seen Niles leave the house for his morning ride, and he was now standing outside the stables. This was her opportunity, if she kept her nerve. She was not ever this chickenhearted, but so much depended on the success of this courtship.

"Good morning, Mr. Greenberry," she said as she stopped at his side. Nervous she might be, but she wasn't a coward.

He was clearly surprised to see her but, to her relief, didn't seem displeased. "Good morning, Miss Seymour."

Courage. "May I join you on your ride this morning?" she asked.

He hesitated a little, and her nervousness increased.

"I can keep pace with you," she said in case that was a source of Niles's uncertainty. "I've had a chance to meet all of Mr. Layton's horses as well as a few of the Gents'. None of them gave me the impression of being too spirited for me."

"Even Morwenna?" Niles asked.

"Your mare appears to have ample fire. When I've watched her, she's also shown herself to be very intelligent. I would wager she regularly provides you with a challenge."

A subtle smile twinkled in his eyes. "I prefer to not be bored on horseback."

"So do I."

The more she learned of Niles Greenberry, the more convinced she became that they would make a not-miserable match if only she could convince him to consider it.

"Have you met the little filly?" She motioned to the tiny silver-gray horse standing at the far end of her small pen.

"I am the one who suggested Digby purchase her."

"Truly?" Penelope hadn't heard about Niles's involvement in the decision. "What was your reasoning?"

"She has a beautiful trot. With training, her already elegant high step would see her sold at a significant profit. Digby would have been foolish not to purchase her."

"That was precisely my assessment." They both had an eye for assessing horses and an understanding of the business considerations of raising and training them.

"She hasn't warmed to anyone yet." Niles watched the filly. "That will have to be overcome first."

Nervous horses weren't easy to train, and untrained horses were very difficult to sell. Did Mr. Layton have stablehands capable of easing the filly out of her skittishness?

One of the groomsmen crossed over to them.

"Will you saddle a mount for Miss Seymour?" Niles requested.

The young man nodded. "Which horse?"

Niles motioned to Penelope. "Whichever one she wishes."

The deference he so easily offered was somehow both unexpected and entirely in keeping with what she knew of him. "Saddle Midnight, please."

The groomsman made his way toward the stall where the Arabian mare was kept.

"Why Midnight?" Niles watched her with curiosity.

"I've watched her when I've visited the stables. She is spirited but also well-behaved and responsive. That will give me options. My ride this morning can be as sedate or challenging as I wish it to be."

"You are precisely correct."

"You know the animal well," she said, "though it's not your own."

He shrugged. "I helped Digby decide if he wanted to purchase Midnight a couple of years ago."

"Just like the filly." That was intriguing. "Do people often consult you on horse purchases?"

"All the Gents have done so at one time or another. I find horses endlessly interesting, and I have ridden dozens upon dozens. The Gents often ask for my thoughts, and I'm seldom wrong." He gave the explanation with dismissal in his posture and tone but not the sort that undermined what he was saying. It spoke more of modesty.

He had an interest in horses and enough of an understanding to be consulted about them regularly, though he wasn't already entirely convinced of his own infallible expertise, which far too many gentlemen had shown themselves to be when she'd mentioned her own experience with and understanding of horses. And while he was quieter than his friends, he had shown himself more than willing, and even comfortable, talking with her. He came to the rescue of servants and of insulted Irishwomen. He was kind.

None of this had been mentioned in the letters Liam had exchanged with Niles's grandfather. She wished it had been.

"The Seymours are quite well known in Ireland for our horses," she said. "I don't know if you were ever told that."

"My father did mention it." Niles didn't seem as excited as she was at having something so significant in common.

He was allowing her to join him on his ride though. That could be seen as a good omen, couldn't it? A stablehand led two horses out of the stables. Midnight was fitted with a side saddle. She really was a beautiful horse. Niles's roan mare was handsome as well.

"Does Mr. Layton have any white horses?" she asked Niles.

"Truly white, no," Niles answered. "The little gray filly will be a striking shade of white in a few years' time, but she won't still be here."

"I have a true-white mare. Pink skin, pink eyes. She's the most beautiful horse I've ever seen."

"A truly white horse is a rare thing," Niles said. "I think that makes them all the more awe-inspiring."

Oh, how could he not be excited to be discovering these connections between them? If she couldn't build upon these commonalities, she didn't know how to even begin winning his regard.

Penelope used a mounting block and the assistance of the stablehand to get into the saddle. Niles was quickly in his saddle as well, and they began at a leisurely pace as they left the stable yard.

"Why did you name your mare Morwenna?" Penelope asked.

"It is an old Cornish name," he said. "As mine is an old Cornish family, we have a tendency to find inspiration in that corner of the kingdom."

"My favorite pony when I was little had a very old Irish name: Cairbre. It was the name of two kings of Ireland, and I think the pony knew it."

"Rather pleased with himself, was he?" Niles spoke very personably and even seemed at ease. He didn't always.

"Extremely pleased with himself." She grinned at the memory. "He trotted about like a monarch."

"The most regal of kings do run about with saddles on their backs." Niles made the observation with such earnestness that had she not looked over at him and seen that now-familiar hint of a smile on his face, she wouldn't have realized he was jesting. How many people missed his delightful sense of humor because he offered it so subtly?

"I understand saddles are as much a royal accoutrement as a crown," Penelope said. "And so very refined."

"Indeed."

It felt good to have a slightly ridiculous conversation. There'd not been as much merriment in their family the last few years. Father's death had been a blow. Penelope's failure to make a match in Dublin society frustrated her socially ambitious mother. Liam had worked hard to find a husband who met Penelope's requirements, and that hadn't worked out well. Life had been far too heavy.

"Most ladies prefer a sedate morning ride." Penelope patted Midnight's neck. "But I am hoping this lass'll run."

"She will," Niles said. "I've seen it."

"Fast?"

He nodded.

"Faster than Morwenna?"

Penelope had encountered more than her share of men who grew irritated or offended when a woman even hinted at his horse or horsemanship being inferior. But Niles didn't seem the least threatened.

"I think these two mares are well matched for speed," he said. "But you're at a disadvantage."

"Why's that?" she asked.

"Because I know my horse very well, but you only just met yours."

She offered a coy shrug of one shoulder. "Which ought to even the odds for you."

His laugh was delightful. She'd heard it a few times since arriving at Pledwick Manor, most frequently during the game of ground billiards. He enjoyed active pursuits and friendly competition and had a teasing sense of humor. They were so alike, more than she'd ever imagined a chance-chosen match could be.

They rode through a passage in the hedgerow. Ahead of them, a gravel path stretched long and straight to yet another opening in another hedgerow, beyond which was a picturesque lake. The path continued past the shoreline, following a narrow strip of land that, clearly having been created specifically to do so, led to an island, on which appeared to be a columned gazebo.

The grounds of Pledwick Manor were not merely extensive; they were gorgeous. An objective observer would insist that Fairfield would never be its equal, but Penelope didn't need it to be. She loved her future home more than she could any other place in the world. It was more than an estate; it was every dream she had ever allowed herself to indulge in.

And Niles was key to claiming that.

"Shall we race to the next hedgerow?" She motioned to it up ahead.

"Will there be a forfeit for the winner?" Niles asked.

"I like flowers," she said.

Again, he laughed. "Before you become too attached to that particular prize, I should warn you that my favorite flowers are snapdragons, and they are not easy to find this time of year."

"Do I appear worried?"

"Not enough to boost my confidence." He shook his head. "It seems I ought to discover what *your* favorite flower is."

"I am inordinately fond of bluebells. I suspect they are equally difficult to find this time of year." She sighed as if she were enduring a tremendous disappointment. "Our forfeit, it seems, will be flowers that are not the winner's favorite."

Niles laughed a little. He then set his sights ahead of them again. "We'll go on your signal."

"At the ready," she instructed.

He bent forward a bit, focusing on their target. She did the same.

"And"—she drew out the word—"go!"

She nudged the horse with her legs, and the mare responded instantly. They sped down the path. The asymmetrical four-beat gait told her Midnight was at a true gallop. The feeling of flying during those moments when all four hooves were off the ground was as exhilarating as always. And the mare handled beautifully.

As far as Penelope could tell, she and Niles reached the far hedgerow at the exact same moment. On the other side, she allowed Midnight to slow and cool down. Niles was doing the same with Morwenna, and he was grinning as broadly as Penelope was.

"I think you enjoyed that, Niles Greenberry."

He turned back toward her. "I think you did as well, Penelope Seymour."

She took a lungful of rain-heavy air, feeling invigorated even in the quickly cooling breeze. "I always enjoy riding at a gallop, though my mother tells me I ought not do so away from home or in the company of others. 'Tisn't ladylike."

"Does she also share your brother's opinion about the unladylike nature of running?"

She hadn't expected him to remember that offhand comment but was deeply pleased to realize he had. "My brother's objections stem from worry that our family's standing is too precarious to endure overly close scrutiny. My mother's objections arise from her conviction that I am an endless embarrassment."

"Ought I to send her a letter informing her that you've managed to be here for days and haven't yet proven an embarrassment?" He was smiling but not in a way that negated his declaration; rather, it acknowledged the humor of his offering.

"I don't think my mother would believe you."

She couldn't always find reason for lightness when thinking of her mother's opinion of her, but she did in that moment. Niles likely didn't realize the kindness he had managed with his jesting response.

A drop of rain splashed on her nose, then her sleeve, followed quickly by several on her gloves. "It seems the heavens are of the opinion that we are too dry." She looked up to the thick clouds, and a raindrop crashed against her cheek.

Then the heavens split open. In an instant, they were in a deluge.

"The gazebo is closer than the stables," Niles said through the downpour.

She didn't need any urging. A roof over her head was far preferable to waiting for the rain to soak through her wool redingote.

They rode quickly over the narrow strip of land out to the lake island. The gazebo was larger than it had seemed from across the water, which was to their advantage, because the horses were able to be sheltered there as well.

"A shame," Penelope said. "I had hoped to ride longer."

"You can ride Midnight again when the weather is better." It wasn't exactly regret at not getting to ride longer *with her.*

She refused to be entirely discouraged. "Would you and Morwenna join us?" She offered a smile she knew was a little bit flirtatious.

He shrugged. That was all. A shrug.

Invitations to ride were apparently not an effective approach to this attempted courtship. She needed a different idea. He had enjoyed the game of ground billiards.

"Ground billiards was a great deal of fun." She let her enthusiasm show. "I think we made a good team during the game."

He looked genuinely confused. "Did you consider us a team?"

They hadn't been in the truest sense, but she'd hoped to emphasize that the afternoon had been enjoyable and that they'd both been good at the game and shown themselves well able to work together to share their mallet. "I suppose we weren't, were we?"

What other things did gentlemen propose when attempting to court a lady?

Another possibility occurred to her. Hopeful again, she said, "Perhaps Mr. Layton would allow us to borrow a pony cart." She opted for a smile that wasn't quite as flirtatious as she'd employed when asking if he would ride with her again, but she still felt confident he would see a small hint of it. Subtlety might prove a better approach. "We could go for a drive around the estate."

He tucked his hands into his pockets. His gaze remained firmly on the rain-pelted lake. Everything about him spoke of discomfort. "Violet would enjoy that, I'm certain."

"I suspect you know the estate better than she does." *Please accept. Please.*

"Digby knows it better than I do."

Decidedly *not* an acceptance. "I suppose he does." She managed not to sigh, but only just.

All around them, rain pelted the lake. The usual rings that flowed from rain hitting water were so frequent and so forceful that it created small, rippling waves. The trees along the shoreline rustled in the stiff breeze. It was beautiful and peaceful. And she was a little miserable.

She and Niles had discovered they shared an interest in horses, and he didn't seem to care. She'd coquettishly invited him to ride with her again, and he'd answered with indifference. A reminder of their enjoyable day of ground billiards hadn't seemed to please him. A suggestion that they take a cart around the estate had seen her passed off first to Violet and then to Mr. Layton.

The silence between her and Niles drew out long. Quiet didn't usually bother her, but she wanted to feel like she'd made *some* progress in winning him over. There had to be something she could say that he would respond to encouragingly.

"Mr. Layton has a picturesque estate," she said.

Niles nodded. "He is very fortunate."

"Your family's homes in Cornwall are lovely."

"They are also very fortunate."

Something about the longing she heard pushed her to ask a question that hadn't occurred to her before. "Do you have a home of your own?"

"I don't." His cheeks pinked a little, though that might have been from the chill in the air. "I will someday though." His gaze shifted out over the lake. "I will."

There was an almost desperate note ringing through his words of determination. Clearly, having a home to call his own was important to him. She understood that. Heavens, she understood.

He would have been told during the marriage negotiation that once they were married, they would have Fairfield. It would be his home as well as hers. He could ride horses whenever he wished, and she suspected he would enjoy being part of the equine venture she meant to tackle there. The Gents could come visit. His family could visit.

He would have a home. But it seemed he didn't want it.

Or he just really didn't want *her.*

Chapter Eleven

Niles considered himself a reasonable person. He didn't generally think ill of people unless they'd shown themselves to inarguably deserve it. And, thus, it frustrated him that despite not having concrete proof, he felt entirely certain Penelope Seymour was toying with him.

Asking to join him on his morning ride had been unexpected but also unexceptional. He knew of her family's connection to horses, and it stood to reason she would go riding in the mornings just as he did. And to ask to join him on a future morning ride would have been just as commonplace if not for the flirtatious smile that had accompanied the request.

He couldn't make heads or tails of it. Ladies regularly flirted with the other Gents but not with him. And Miss Seymour had not been the least flirtatious before that morning.

She'd also commented on their teamwork during ground billiards, no matter that they had been competitors, and she'd asked if he'd drive her around the estate. Those bits of conversation had involved smiles and slight flutters of her eyelashes as well, and absolutely none of it made any sense whatsoever. Unless she was laughing at him or attempting to manipulate him for some reason.

That rested heavy on his mind as he sat in the guest bedchamber he'd been using the past weeks. He'd changed out of his damp clothes but still looked a scraggly mess. Such was his distraction that he'd not even sent for his valet to help him put himself to rights, and it was in that state that Digby and Lucas found him.

"We heard you'd been out in the rain." Lucas looked him over, shaking his head and smiling. "You look it."

"I was riding Morwenna and was caught in a downpour."

"That is unfortunate for you," Digby said. "But a decidedly fortunate thing for Wilson."

Niles hadn't been expecting that declaration, neither could he make sense of it.

"What the King is attempting to convey," Lucas said, "is that we're hoping Wilson can address the current state of you as a means of practicing his valeting."

"We already spoke with your man," Digby said. "He thinks the young man would benefit from the practice, seeing as Lucas here looks inexcusably unkempt with unacceptable regularity."

Lucas pressed a hand dramatically to his heart. "Digby, you traitorous coward! How dare you malign me this way. The man said nothing of the sort."

From the time Niles had joined the Gents, and likely predating that blessed day, Lucas, Stanley, and Digby had routinely declared each other traitorous cowards in the exact theatrical tone of offended disappointment Lucas had just employed. It made Niles miss Stanley all the more. There was no one in the world like Stanley Cummings.

"I don't mind if Wilson gets some practice." Niles pushed a tuft of damp hair off his forehead. At least he would *look* like everything wasn't in shambles.

Digby gave a quick nod to Lucas, who stepped out of the room.

It was only Niles and Digby again, as it had been when Niles had first confessed that he was planning to do whatever he needed to avoid the match waiting for him in Cornwall. He'd not made so personal a confession to any of the Gents since Stanley.

"What's the matter?" Digby asked.

"Merely cold and a little wet." Niles tried to look convinced by his own explanation.

"I realize I look exquisite." Digby pressed his hand lightly to his indigo silk waistcoat with a confident and somewhat lavish bow. Just as quickly, his posture straightened and his expression transformed into one of annoyance. "But do I also look stupid?" he asked dryly.

"Never."

Digby gave a crisp nod. "Then, I will ask again: What's the matter?"

There was no point denying it any longer. "Miss Seymour is acting odd."

"Do you think she's ill?" Digby guessed.

"No. I think she's lying." Realizing he had just cast aspersions on a lady's integrity, Niles attempted to clarify. "Lying is, perhaps, too harsh a descriptor. She is—I haven't—If I were anyone else—Except—"

"This is the point where Stanley would have said, 'Take a breath.'" Digby watched Niles with concern and just a hint of amusement.

So, Niles paused and breathed in and out, giving his mind a chance to decide what he meant to say. "I am absolutely certain Miss Seymour was flirting at me."

"Flirting *with* you," Digby corrected.

Niles shook his head. "When have you ever known me to flirt?"

That seemed to give Digby pause.

"I have watched ladies flirt with the rest of you, and all of you do plenty of flirting as well. This was different."

Digby dropped into a nearby chair. "In what way?"

"It started suddenly and stopped just as abruptly. And in the moment before she started, there was a look in her eyes as if she remembered what she was supposed to be doing. And the expression that immediately replaced the coquettish looks was something I would interpret as contemplating her next strategy."

"What do you think her aim is?" Digby asked.

Niles shook his head. "I'm not entirely certain. All I know is it feels insincere, as if she wants me to think her feelings for me are more tender than they are."

"Thus, your declaration that you think she's lying."

"I do think it is insincere, which is disappointing. Is it so outlandish of me to hope that someone could *genuinely* feel tenderly toward me?" He'd been wishing for that for so long.

"Not outlandish at all," Digby insisted.

No woman had ever shown more than a passing interest in him, and he'd never had his head turned in any meaningful way. But the Gents had never belittled his wish to eventually fall entirely in love with a lady, no matter how increasingly improbable that had become over the years.

"Do you think I incorrectly evaluated Miss Seymour's flirting this morning?"

"It's possible," Digby said. "But given your situation, I would say you have ample reason to be at least a little wary."

Niles held his hands up in a show of frustration. "How will I know which it is?"

"You are attempting to sort out a woman." Digby shook his head. "You have little chance of *ever* knowing what *anything* is."

"That isn't very comforting," Niles said.

"Monarchs do not exist to offer comfort, Puppy."

Niles pushed out a tense breath. Why did everything have to be so frustratingly complicated?

Lucas returned with both Kes and Wilson in tow. Considering the young man was attempting to learn skills that would provide him with employment for possibly the rest of his life, he looked cool as a cucumber. Kes, on the other hand, seemed anxious.

"Have a seat, Niles," Digby instructed, rising from the chair he'd been sitting in and offering it.

Digby and Wilson gathered behind the chair after Niles sat.

"Mr. Greenberry's hair curls when it's wet," Digby said to Wilson, "but the curls pull out as it dries. Lord Jonquil's, on the other hand, retains a noticeable wave even dry." He continued on with his instructions.

Kes pulled the other chair in the room over and sat facing Niles. "I heard something from Violet last evening that I've been pondering, and I've decided you need to know what I heard." His earnest tone didn't bode well. "Miss Seymour has hopes of moving forward with the marriage her brother and your grandparents arranged."

Niles had more or less assumed that. Why else would she have tracked him to Yorkshire?

"I heard Violet ask her how the courting was going," Kes said. "And Miss Seymour said, 'It has not yet begun in earnest, but I have hope that it will prove effective.'"

"Prove effective?" Niles repeated the phrase, trying to sort out what Kes had overheard.

"Violet asked about *courting*." Lucas looked from Niles to Kes a few times. "Does Miss Seymour think Puppy is courting her?"

"I can't imagine why she would think that," Niles said.

"You haven't been making sheep eyes at her?" Lucas asked with an amused turn to his lips.

"Quite the opposite, actually."

Kes's gaze narrowed on him. "I can't believe you would glare at her."

"No, I mean *she* has been making sheep eyes at *me*."

Any other gentleman would have taken offense at the befuddled doubt that momentarily flitted over their faces. Niles understood it far too well to be even the tiniest bit upset.

"*She* is courting *you*, then." Kes gave a single nod.

Courting me. "That might explain the insincere flirting." He began turning his head to look at Digby.

The King leaned around Niles's shoulder from behind. "I realize you are up to your damp neck in romantic distress and are, because of your innate intelligence, literally turning to the most experienced person here, but could you attempt to hold your head still? Wilson is trying to perform a miracle."

"My deepest apologies," Niles said, looking forward once more.

"Let this be your first lesson in being a valet, Wilson," Digby said.

"That I ought to ask the gentleman to hold his head still?" Wilson asked.

"That gentlemen gossip every bit as much as the ladies do."

From the doorway came an unexpected observation. "If things have already devolved into gossip, then I suspect we have arrived too late."

Though Niles had been warned not to move his head, he spun on his chair, recognizing the voice of Lord Aldric Benick. Sure enough, the General had arrived. Henri Fortier—Archbishop—was with him. Other than Stanley, all the Gents were together again.

"If you two don't stop distracting Niles, I'll toss you out of my house," Digby warned.

Aldric eyed him as he and Henri stepped inside. "What has the King's crown crooked this time?"

"He is attempting to impart wisdom to young Wilson here." Lucas motioned to the young man in question.

"And he has discovered he has no wisdom to offer?" Aldric was in a rare mood; he didn't always join in their more ridiculous banter.

"Offer *your* wisdom to Niles," Digby said. "He needs it."

Henri sat on a nearby window seat. "Are we correct, then, in our assumption that your plan to remain here in order to avoid your match in Cornwall did not prove an ingenious scheme?" He spoke in French, likely not even realizing he'd done so. No doubt he and his new bride, Nicolette, exclusively spoke their native tongue at home. And Aldric had spoken French since birth, so their journey to Yorkshire had undoubtedly been conducted entirely in that language. How long had it been since Henri had even spoken English?

"The plan was not merely *un*ingenious"—Lucas spoke in English, which would help Henri make the transition—"it has actually left him more entangled in the matrimonial trap than he was before agreeing to the strategy."

Aldric, now standing near where Henri sat, studied Niles for the length of a breath. "More entangled *how*?"

Someone—either Digby or Wilson—pulled a comb through Niles's hair, tugging it but not painfully. "Miss Seymour sniffed me out."

"She's here?" Aldric didn't appear to know whether he found that impressive, worrisome, or hilarious.

To Henri's credit, *he* looked sympathetic. "Was she furious?"

"No," Niles said.

"Hurt?" Henri further guessed.

"No." Niles began to shrug but remembered the instruction to keep still and stopped. "She took it entirely in stride. And she and her brother are still here."

"Did *her brother* take it in stride?" Aldric asked doubtfully.

Lucas answered. "He might have been upset if not for Digby."

Aldric looked above and behind Niles to where the gentleman in question was standing. "What did you do?"

"I was simply my charming, delightful—"

"Unattached," Lucas added.

"Wealthy," Kes tossed in.

"—self," Digby finished. "That immediately made me Mr. Seymour's favorite person at Pledwick Manor." Then, quite obviously to Wilson, he said, "The ribbon should be tight, but the hair should be allowed to be softer."

"Did *Miss* Seymour also find herself similarly intrigued by the charming, delightful, unattached, wealthy host of this unexpected house party?" Aldric asked.

"The Irish lass is currently attempting to nab herself a Cornish Puppy," Lucas said.

"And that Cornish Puppy still doesn't want to be nabbed?" Henri asked.

Niles shook his head only to have Digby place his hands on either side of Niles's face to hold him still.

"My deepest apologies, Your Majesty."

"We require only a moment more of your cooperation," Digby said, using such a regal tone that Niles couldn't be certain if the *we* referred to both him and Wilson or if Digby was referring to himself in the royal plural.

Careful to keep very still, Niles said, "This Cornish Puppy hasn't changed what he wants for himself and his future. And being courted or wooed or whatever else this game is being called isn't changing that. It feels too . . ." How did he explain why Miss Seymour's efforts rankled the way they did?

"Coercive?" Aldric suggested.

That hit close to the mark, though it was not precisely what he was feeling. "I just don't know if she's sincere. I'm not saying she's a liar," he quickly added. "But I don't like the idea of being . . . manipulated."

"We'll not let that happen," Aldric said.

Niles made no argument that Miss Seymour was, in fact, interested in him and was courting him because she genuinely wanted to marry *him* and wasn't merely marrying the person who'd been chosen for her. All the other Gents had been swooned over and been the recipients of sincere adoration. All of them.

Except him.

"You said another year would see you with the £150 you lack?" Lucas asked.

"Assuming my family welcomes me home and saves me the expense of lodgings outside of the Season." No matter how upset they were with him, they couldn't cut him off financially; his income was stipulated in legally binding contracts. It hurt that he'd taken solace in that of late. His connection to his family had always been warm and secure. He'd risked all of that by rejecting his duty to his grandparents.

"I wish I had the money to lend you," Lucas said.

The others added their voices to the wish. Niles knew his friends well enough to have already guessed that every last one of them would have helped him financially if they could. Even though Lucas, Kes, and Digby had money enough to live quite comfortably, they all also had expenses attached to their estates. They didn't have much truly disposable income. Henri and Aldric barely had income, despite being sons of extremely wealthy families.

"Is there a possibility of finding an estate at a lower price?" Aldric asked.

"Not one that would provide me with the additional income I need to be eligible for a parliamentary seat." He didn't need to explain to any of them why that was so crucial. They knew his ambition, no matter that it was not often discussed among them.

"We'll see you safely through your current difficulties," Henri vowed.

Behind him, Digby said, "Your second lesson in being a gentleman's gentleman, Wilson, is that you'll sometimes overhear private conversations, but—"

"I know how to keep my mouth shut, sir," Wilson said. "And for Lord Jonquil, who saved my life, I'll keep every secret he needs me to."

Lucas looked entirely convinced of the young man's sincerity, which was reassurance enough for Niles. As Wilson gathered the tools of his sought-after trade, Digby stepped around and joined the Gents.

"Thank you," Niles said to them. "I've managed to get myself into quite a bind. I don't know how I'd survive this without all of you."

"Do you remember," Aldric said, "Stanley saying to us that everyone has a dream, but only the truly fortunate ones get to live theirs?"

Niles remembered that well.

"We're going to do more than see you survive this," Aldric continued. "We're going to see to it that you are one of those fortunate ones."

"One-hundred-fifty-pounds fortunate?" Niles asked doubtfully.

With a look of overdone pondering, Digby asked, "How do you feel about seedy gambling dens?"

That set the Gents laughing.

"And how do you feel about a courting counterstrategy?" Aldric asked. *His* look of pondering appeared entirely sincere.

"Counterstrategy?" Niles eyed the others, wondering if they had already sorted out what Aldric was hinting at.

"Miss Seymour is attempting to snatch up a Puppy," Aldric said. "And there's every chance Violet is already part of the schemes." He glanced at Kes, who nodded. "Which means Nicolette will not remain uninvolved for long."

"I would say her participation is a foregone conclusion," Henri confirmed.

Aldric met Niles's eye.

"Thus, the need for counterstrategy," Niles acknowledged the realization as he had it.

"Do you want us to tell Miss Seymour that Niles is a horrible person?" Lucas asked. "Maybe suggest that he has no table manners or that he has a tendency to toss insults at the vicar during sermons?"

"That won't be necessary." Aldric stood tall and confident. "Just stay close to our Puppy and be our usual obnoxious selves. That should prevent this courting scheme of hers from becoming a true entanglement."

"What if Miss Seymour proves more determined than that?" Digby asked.

"Or the ladies prove better strategists than our General?" Lucas added.

"Take care with the blasphemy." Henri stifled a laugh. The others didn't bother with the stifling.

Though they hadn't any true answers to his current difficulties, Niles felt better. He was in over his head, yes, but he wasn't alone.

Chapter Twelve

PENELOPE HAD BORNE TOO CLOSE a resemblance to a drowned rat upon returning to the house. Gracie, her lady's maid, had put her to rights as much as possible with Penelope's bones frozen and her nose red from the chill. She thought that reason enough to remain in her room for the afternoon, tucked under a blanket, watching the rain fall, and pondering how her attempt at wooing hadn't seemed to stoke the slightest interest in Niles.

Ought she to change tactics, or was persistence the more appropriate approach? She didn't wish to make a nuisance of herself, but without her effort, Niles wouldn't come to know her at all, and then there would be no chance of convincing him to choose her. And she wanted him to.

But he *doesn't want* me. That had been the conclusion she'd come to after the shrugging and confusion and suggestion that she ought to take her romantic drive around the estate with Violet. But Penelope had since decided not to believe that yet.

A knock at the door preceded Liam poking his head into the room. "I have remembered something encouraging." He stepped inside and closed the door behind him.

Penelope rubbed at her weary face. "What have you remembered?"

"Why Mr. Layton and I did not attend the same schools and why the one time I participated in the London social whirl, we hardly moved in the same circles." He seemed excited about whatever it was he had suddenly recalled. "Even before I met him, I heard whispers regarding his parents."

"I do not care to participate in gossip," Penelope said. "And I've not known you to do so either."

"Ordinarily, I wouldn't. But this is more than empty tittle-tattle. And it is helpful in our current predicament."

"I find that difficult to believe." The situation was complicated but not in a way that involved her runaway groom's friend's family.

"Hear me out, Penelope." To his credit, Liam didn't appear to be relishing Mr. Layton's unfortunate position as the focus of gossip. "He has his own estate, one that produces a very comfortable income," Liam said.

"Yes, he does."

"So he would not need his wife to have a dowry, which you do not have, other than Fairfield." Liam spoke quickly, something he did when particularly excited. "But Mr. Layton would not need Fairfield because he already has this estate, which would make him less inclined to object to your retaining ownership of it. That would make him an excellent choice for you."

Penelope shook her head. "I have already told you that I do not think he would cross his friend that way. And further, he would want to live *here*. I want to live at Fairfield. That is not an 'excellent choice' for me."

"That is, in actuality, what makes him nearly perfect," Liam said. "Mr. Layton's parents, according to every discussion of them, never lived together. Not at any point in their marriage."

She hadn't allowed herself to hope more than fleetingly for a husband who would like her, even love her, but marriage to a man who didn't even want to live in the same house as her sounded awful.

"There is every chance Mr. Layton would have no objections to you making Fairfield your home." It was Liam's fastest sentence yet. "Such an arrangement is well-known in his family."

"Is his family happy?" she asked.

Some of his enthusiasm ebbed. "I—I don't know."

"Did his parents love each other at all?"

Liam looked immediately confused. "You gave me a long list of requirements, Penelope. Love was not on it."

Maybe it should have been. "The Laytons' family arrangements sound miserable. I hope I am not so desperate as to have to resign myself to that."

"Of course, I wouldn't want you to be miserable," Liam said. "But I also don't think we ought to abandon the possibility of Mr. Layton."

She didn't correct his use of *we*.

"I also mean to explore the possibility of Lord Aldric Benick."

Who was that? "To have that title, he must be the younger son of a duke or marquess."

Liam nodded eagerly. "The younger son of the Duke of Hartley."

"We don't even know the Duke of Hartley." Was Liam's worry over her future leading him to imagine connections he could not claim?

"Lord Aldric has just arrived at Pledwick Manor." Liam smiled broadly. "We will be well-acquainted with him soon enough."

"Could you allow the gentleman one evening's respite before attempting to tie him to your sister?"

"I am contenting myself with simply meeting him," Liam said. "If there seems a chance of turning his head in your direction, then I'm prepared to do so."

"I imagine he will be civil and gracious, but we are far beneath the notice of a duke's son."

"Were you and I to go to London, we would not even cross his path." Liam's enthusiasm was returning. "But we have a unique opportunity here. I don't intend to squander it."

"I am still hopeful that Mr. Greenberry will choose to proceed with the match," Penelope said. "Antagonizing his friends will undermine that possibility."

"In the end, we may discover that none of them is interested, and you will leave here as single as you arrived." Liam didn't appear to mean the blunt observation unkindly. "But if I can leave here as even bowing acquaintances to these gentlemen whose station in Society is so enviable, that would change everything, Penelope. I could attend the London Season with hope of success and of making other very beneficial connections. I hope you would not begrudge me that."

"Of course not." She didn't want him to continue feeling the sting of rejection he had endured during his one London Season. "Only, proceed with care."

"I don't—" He took a tight breath. "I am fully capable of navigating social situations, Penelope. And far more experienced than you are. It is unfair of you to lecture me on that."

"I hadn't meant to lecture." She offered a quick smile. "I am simply anxious. A great deal is riding on our success here."

"I know." He looked entirely uncertain. "And we will only be successful if we try. I am going to try, Penelope."

"So am I."

Liam left with an air of determination mingled with a nervousness she could relate to. Nothing had seemed to go their way since arriving in England. She needed that to change, especially since she was attempting to sort such an unsolvable puzzle entirely on her own.

She pulled on a shawl, still a little chilled from her soaking, and went in search of the closest thing to an ally she had. She found Violet in a small, cozy sitting room facing the back lawn. She also found her *not* alone. Sitting beside her was an elegant lady, their same age, with impeccable posture and a fashionably tidy appearance. When the unidentified lady's eyes fell on Penelope, her gaze turned immediately searching. Penelope would wager this was a person best not underestimated.

Violet waved her over.

"Nicolette," she said to the other lady, "this is Miss Penelope Seymour of Ireland. Penelope, this is Mrs. Nicolette Fortier, late of France and now residing in Sussex."

"And married to one of the Gents, if my memory serves," Penelope said as she curtsied in greeting.

"*Oui. J'ai* épousé *le plus beau d'entre eux.*"

"Though it pains me to admit as much," Penelope said, "I speak almost no French."

Mrs. Fortier colored the tiniest bit, her eyes darting to Violet. "Was I speaking in French?"

Violet smiled. "You have been mixing French and English ever since your arrival."

Mrs. Fortier shook her head at herself. "I have spoken only French for weeks and weeks. My mind seems to be struggling to remember that there are other languages."

Penelope leaned a little closer, working to keep her expression solemn. "In case you aren't certain, *that* was English."

A corner of the Frenchwoman's mouth tugged. "What a relief."

"Do sit," Violet insisted. "I'm curious to know how your ride with Niles went this morning, aside from the downpour, of course."

Penelope eyed Mrs. Fortier as she sat, unsure what the lady knew or how she felt. Her scrutiny did not go unnoticed.

"Violet has informed me of your current efforts to court him," Mrs. Fortier said. "She has further assured me that you will honor his feelings on the matter when all is said and done."

"I could not, in good conscience, do otherwise." The declaration emerged more fervent than she'd intended. But the thought of anyone being unkind to Niles Greenberry pricked at her heart. "He has shown himself to be kind and considerate. I will not mistreat him."

Mrs. Fortier raised an inquisitive brow. "This is the same Niles Greenberry who, in essence, jilted you in Cornwall?"

"And lied about his reasons?" Violet added.

Her ally was clearly not entirely convinced. "Will you think me utterly lacking in judgment if I told you that even with all those things arguing against his character, I still think he is a good person?"

Mrs. Fortier shook her head. "Niles is one of the very best of men, and his behavior in this matter is very much out of character for him."

"Is complete indifference to a lady who asked him to go for a ride with him and with whom he discovered a mutual love of horses and who has an estate that would be his home, which he expressed a great interest in having, *also* out of character for him?"

Violet watched her closely. "He didn't swoon over you during your ride?"

"Do gentlemen swoon?" Penelope asked, only half-jesting.

"They do sigh romantically now and then." Mrs. Fortier was difficult to sort out. She might have been jesting with that observation. But she might just as easily have been in earnest.

"Niles certainly didn't sigh or swoon today." Penelope needed to proceed with caution lest they decide that her efforts at courtship ought to already be declared a failure. "He enjoyed talking about horses, and I do think he enjoyed riding with me. I'm not certain what else to suggest. Playing another round of ground billiards or driving a pony cart around the estate did not pique his interest. I am hoping to come to know him better, but because I don't know him well, I cannot seem to stumble upon an activity that he would eagerly participate in."

"All the Gents are excessively fond of parlor games," Violet said.

Parlor games. Penelope wouldn't have thought of that. "I enjoy games."

"We will insist that is settled upon for our evening entertainment," Mrs. Fortier said.

"Does this mean you are willing to help me with my courtship, Mrs. Fortier?"

"You may call me Nicolette," she said. "And I am of the same mind as Violet on this courtship. Getting to know Niles Greenberry better is something more people ought to do. And you two might actually prove well-suited." Nicolette's posture and expression grew more firm. "I would not be at all accommodating of your efforts, however, if not for your promise to accept Niles's decision if your courtship does not prove successful."

"Have the two of you placed a time limit on my efforts?" Penelope hadn't the first idea how long their support would last.

Violet shook her head. "I suspect Niles will make that clear in his own way."

"I don't know him well enough to know what that way might be."

A smile tugged Violet's mouth upward. "We do mean to help you, Penelope. We adore our Gents, but they can be terribly confusing."

"I am discovering that."

"We aren't hoping you will fail," Nicolette said. "We want Niles to have a fair chance of determining what he actually wants, with all the information he needs to determine that. Helping you navigate that will help him."

She had two supporters. They were helping her only because they cared about Niles, but they were still helping. Penelope was grateful for that. She hadn't managed to make much headway. With Violet and Nicolette even a little bit on her side, she had a far better chance of succeeding.

Chapter Thirteen

By the time the houseguests had gathered in the drawing room after the night's meal, Niles was feeling a little more on firm ground. Wilson had done a fine job fixing his hair after the soaking he had received, so he looked like less of a mess. His own valet had chosen a comfortable but fashionable ensemble for him to wear. And the Gents were all unified in their determination to be obnoxious countercourters, or whatever it was Aldric had called them. Regardless of the title, Niles was grateful for their assistance.

Within moments of being in Nicolette Fortier's company once more, Niles was reminded of why they'd all come to like her so much so quickly. She was intelligent and clever, personable and thoughtful. And she had brought inarguable happiness to Henri, who had known more unhappiness than he deserved.

Niles kept that in mind as he watched Nicolette and Violet interact with Miss Seymour. There was a friendliness between the ladies that Julia would almost certainly have embraced as well if she were there. It complicated his need to keep the lady at bay, but he couldn't fault them for being welcoming and kind.

He could, however, find great hilarity in Mr. Seymour's overly pointed efforts to win over Digby, who was doing an admirable job of not making his annoyance obvious, as well as in the interest with which he watched Aldric. This was a brother on the hunt.

"Shall we undertake a parlor game?" Nicolette suggested, shooting the Gents a look that warned of dire consequences should any of them not agree.

"Impromptu performances would be enjoyable," Violet said.

"'Tisn't one I'm familiar with," Mr. Seymour said, a rare moment of unmistakable Irish flavor in his voice that had been trained to sound as English as any of the Gents during his British education, no doubt.

"This game is a great deal of fun," Violet said. "All participants' names are written on slips of paper and placed in a hat or bowl. Two are drawn at a time, and they form a team. Once everyone is paired up, all the teams are given a set amount of time in which to decide upon a performance—a musical talent, a reading, things of that nature. Everyone gathers once more and enjoys the impromptu performances. If there is time and desire, the entire thing can be repeated with new pairings."

"That seems enjoyable," Mr. Seymour said.

Parchment was quickly acquired, cut into slips, and names scrawled on them. Violet drew the first two names.

"Nicolette," she read, "and—*me*."

"*Magnifique*," Nicolette declared.

The two ladies looked delighted. Digby didn't look reassured.

"Our next team—" Violet pulled out another slip of paper. "Kes." She smiled at her husband, then selected another slip. "And Digby."

"*Magnifique*." Digby repeated Nicolette's declaration but with decidedly more flare.

Violet read the next paper. "Niles." She pulled out another. "And Penelope."

Oh, lud. He'd not given any thought to the possibility of being teamed with Miss Seymour. Violet and Nicolette looked intrigued.

"I had hoped the Seymours would be teamed together," Kes quickly said. "We might have been treated to something very Irish, which I think we would all enjoy."

The other Gents quickly adopted the line, attempting to undo the predicament Niles found himself in.

Miss Seymour's eyes had narrowed the tiniest bit as Kes had finished his declaration. That narrowing eased into a look of realization as the Gents' continued their championing of the change in partners. Niles was certain he saw embarrassment touch Miss Seymour's expression. She had, it seemed, recognized the ruse for what it was, and she was hurt by it.

Confound it. He'd not intended for her to be wounded.

"Perhaps we'll have an Irish performance in the next round," Niles said, making certain his smile was easy and pleased, with no hint of the panic he was feeling. He met Aldric's eyes for the briefest of moments, but he felt certain the General understood what he hoped to communicate. Countercourting was well and good, but hurting Miss Seymour was not part of the strategy.

"Draw the next team, Violet," Aldric suggested. "Perhaps Mr. Seymour will find himself partnered with someone who has a deep appreciation for Irish performances." The redirection was well managed; the focus was off *Miss Seymour*, and the tone was kept light.

The next name Violet drew was Mr. Seymour's, leading to enough light titters to further ease the tension in Miss Seymour's expression. Then she drew Aldric's, which sent the group into full, deep laughter.

"I hope you have a deep appreciation for Irish performances," Miss Seymour said.

"I suspect I soon will," Aldric answered seamlessly.

There was no need to pull from the hat the remaining names, as only Lucas and Henri had not had their names drawn. With the teams determined, the planning began.

Niles walked beside Miss Seymour to a far corner of the room, unsure how to begin a conversation. Ought he to acknowledge what he'd seen in her expression? Apologize for the embarrassment she'd endured? Ignore it all entirely in favor of moving forward on good terms?

She saved him the trouble. "I realize your friends do not actually long for an evening filled with Irish-themed entertainments. But I suspect they *would* appreciate something genuinely enjoyable. That leaves us with the question of what we are able to plan and execute together."

It was, in fact, the challenge of two randomly selected individuals attempting to find something both could equally participate in that made the game enjoyable.

"Unfortunately," Niles said, "I don't think Digby would permit us to ride horses in the drawing room. We share that talent."

"Even with the drenching, it was an enjoyable ride, wasn't it?"

He nodded. "It was." And he found he meant it. Yes, he was uncomfortable with her pointed efforts at courting him, but he couldn't deny that he'd enjoyed riding with someone who was good at it. That part of the morning had been nice. "Though we did end our race without a winner."

"You will think me odd, but that was one of my favorite aspects of our morning ride. I have not lost a horse race in five years. Continuing that run of luck without actually winning was unexpectedly delightful."

Niles wasn't certain which aspect of that declaration he found most intriguing: that she was undefeated for a half decade, that she was not upset to have not been victorious, or that she took genuine delight at having lost a race without truly losing a race. Too many people who shared his enjoyment of athletic pursuits were so focused on victory that they didn't enjoy the oddities that occurred from time to time.

"Since Morwenna and Midnight can't join us, what ought we to do instead?" Niles asked.

"Do you draw?" she asked.

Niles shook his head.

"Neither do I." Playfulness twinkled in her eyes. Miss Seymour liked to tease, that much had become clear early on.

"I also don't sing," Niles said.

"Neither do I."

A quick glance around the room revealed very different interactions. Nicolette and Violet were smiling broadly, clearly enjoying each other. Aldric and Mr. Seymour appeared to be having a very stilted conversation, one punctuated by how intimidating Mr. Seymour seemed to find his partner.

"I incompetently play the pianoforte," Niles said to Miss Seymour.

She laughed lightly. "A perfect description of my ability on the instrument."

"We could subject the others to a painfully inept duet," he suggested.

"That *is* the most entertaining variety." She brushed her hand against his, though in a way that he didn't think she even realized she'd done. Or did she? It might very well have been more of her courting efforts. He would do best to remain on his guard. "We should go see if Mr. Layton has any music broadsheets we could fumble our way through."

Their trek from the room took them past Lucas and Henri.

"Abandoning the competition already?" Lucas tsked. "We promise to say flattering things no matter how mortifying your performance is."

"We not only aren't quitting," Miss Seymour said, "but we also intend to hold you to that promise no matter that you don't realize how impossible a task you have set yourself to."

"*Ce sera une performance douloureuse?*" Henri had slipped into French more often these past few days than he usually did.

Miss Seymour looked to Niles, a question in her eyes. But there was no flirting in her gaze, which eased his worries from a moment before. "I don't know what he said," she whispered.

"He asked if our performance will be painful."

"Ah." She turned to face the others once more. "*Horribly* painful, which makes it an absolute shame that there will not be a prize for the worst performance. We would be sure to win."

"I don't know about that," Niles said. "I spied another team who looked to be struggling with their collaboration."

"My brother and Lord Aldric?" Miss Seymour guessed with a grin.

"Perhaps standing about in uncomfortable silence will be their offering." Niles chuckled.

"What are you two planning to offer?" Henri asked.

Miss Seymour shook her head. "You'll have to wait, just like everyone else."

"Have you at least told Puppy?" Lucas asked.

"It was his idea," was her answer.

And for reasons Niles couldn't explain and did not choose to explore, he was inordinately pleased that she'd acknowledged that.

She hooked her arm through his and gave Henri and Lucas a look of cheeky challenge. All Niles could manage was a look of worried confusion. He tried to silently ask his friends if he was now on shaky ground, if this was more of Miss Seymour's attempts to turn his head.

Were they going to intervene? Stage a daring rescue?

"Off with you two," Lucas declared, shooing them away.

Apparently, Niles was on his own. He took that to mean he didn't need to be concerned. He *was*; he simply told himself he didn't *need* to be in that particular moment.

"They are fun to tease," Miss Seymour said as she and Niles walked into the music room.

It was a nearly exact echo of what Stanley always used to say when Niles would ask him why he bantered so often with the Gents. "Because the lot of you are fun to tease," he would answer.

"Perhaps they will choose being teased as their performance this evening," Niles said.

The smile she tossed at him, a simple and fleeting one, had a most unexpected effect. His heart hopped a bit in his chest. But he was quick to shake that off. It was just that he was wholly unaccustomed to ladies smiling at and favoring him. His inexperience might lead him to believe foolish things when he knew perfectly well that her smiles earlier had been part of a scheme.

They looked through the few bits of music Digby had. Niles wasn't certain why Digby had a pianoforte at his house. He didn't play, and he lived alone.

"I don't know that I could play any of these without weeks of practice." Miss Seymour looked up from the parchment and at Niles once more. A hint of embarrassment tiptoed over her features, and just as it had earlier that evening, the sight tugged at him.

"I would need time as well," he assured her. "It seems we both understated our ineptitude."

"I think we should insist that Mr. Layton simply didn't provide enough variety in his musical broadsheets."

Niles nodded. "I like that strategy: blame Digby."

Miss Seymour put the music broadsheets back in the drawer where they'd found them. "What should we do for our impromptu performance now?" she asked, turning back to him.

"I suppose we had best gather the horses."

She smiled at him again, and his heart reacted once more. That foolish organ had no idea it needed to be on its guard. "You are funny, Niles Greenberry."

He didn't think anyone beyond the Gents had ever said that about him.

"Perhaps we could tell a few jokes for our performance," Niles suggested, laughing a little in spite of himself.

"I suspect that is what Lord Jonquil is going to do."

He acknowledged that likelihood with another nod. "We do call him the Jester."

"Do you have names for the ladies in your group as well?" she asked.

"Julia—Lady Jonquil—is called Our Julia, and Violet is sometimes called Lily. Nicolette has become known amongst us as *Le Capitaine*."

"You are so fortunate to have such wonderful friends." She tapped out the first five notes of a scale. "I'd love to have that." She finished the scale, then began another.

"You remember your scales." Niles moved to stand next to her and, two octaves below where she was playing, tapped along with her, getting only one note incorrect.

"You remember too," she said.

"Mr. Donovan would be so pleased." It had been many years since Niles had thought of his oft-frustrated music instructor.

"An Irishman, was he?"

"He was, in fact."

A moment later, the entire house party entered the music room, Digby at their head.

"Since your performance involves this room," he said, "we're beginning in here, with you two."

Niles looked at Penelope in the exact moment she looked at him. Without speaking, she widened her eyes and shrugged almost imperceptibly, the message clear: what ought they to do?

A quick thought revealed an answer. He closed the space between them and whispered, "Scales?"

She laughed. "Perfect."

Chapter Fourteen

PENELOPE AND NILES STOOD BESIDE the pianoforte, facing the gathering. The other two ladies were seated. The Gents stood near them. Liam stood among them, but he didn't appear to be succeeding in getting a foothold in this group of socially significant people.

"Shall you introduce our performance?" Penelope asked Niles. "Or shall I?"

"When given the option," he said quietly, "I will always choose *not* to be the spokesman."

Why was that? He was articulate and entertaining and personable. That was a mystery she fully intended to sort later.

To the gathered group, she said, "Ladies and the Gents"—her adjustment of the usual form of address brought grins to the onlookers—"our impromptu performance will be a piece on the pianoforte that both Mr. Greenberry and I remember well from our long-ago years as very impressive students of music."

Liam looked perplexed, no doubt owing to his memory of her participating in her music lessons under extreme duress. Niles's friends watched in apparent anticipation of being very entertained.

She turned to Niles. "Shall we?"

Niles offered a very solemn nod, which she returned.

They stood next to each other at the instrument, Penelope positioned in front of the treble clef and Niles in front of the bass clef.

He whispered out of the side of his mouth, "We didn't choose which scale to play."

"C major?" she suggested just as quietly. "'Twas the simplest, after all."

"Once up, once down?"

Undertaking such an absurdly brief "performance" would be particularly funny. She nodded.

They both hovered their right hands over a C key, two octaves apart from each other. At his nod, which they didn't have to communicate ahead of time to each other, they began. From C to the next C, then back to the start.

With a flourish that matched each other despite, again, no prior discussion, they turned to the room and offered a bow and a curtsy respectively, both so overdone that one would think they were in the presence of every king and queen, emperor and empress in the world.

"Remarkable!"

"Bravo!"

"A triumph!"

Their audience offered their praise with an enthusiasm every bit as exaggerated and unwarranted as Penelope and Niles's show of pride. Even Liam smiled. He was not an inherently unhappy person, but his worries over their standing in this group and her future had rendered him heavy of mind.

"We should call off the remainder of the impromptu performances," Penelope said to the group as a whole. "This first one cannot possibly be outshone."

"As true as that may prove," Mr. Layton said, "we would not be very sporting if we refused to try." He looked to the others. "Can everyone else's performance be undertaken in this room, or do we need to relocate?"

Each of the duos indicated the music room would suit.

"Let's move, then, to Lord Aldric and Mr. Seymour."

All the Gents usually spoke of and to Lord Aldric without his title, but Penelope suspected Mr. Layton used it in this instance because the duke's son was being referenced alongside Liam, who was not on such informal terms with the extremely high-ranking gentleman.

Liam either didn't notice the change or wasn't bothered by it. He simply looked nervous as he followed Lord Aldric to the front of the group.

"The skill we will be displaying"—Lord Aldric spoke very directly and with very little indication of his feelings on the impending performance—"is the ability for Mr. Seymour to list the counties of Ireland and I to list the provinces of France in alphabetical order."

"France first," Mr. Fortier requested. "I am anxious to see if you manage it."

Did Lord Aldric know France well enough to impress the French-born couple?

"*Comme vous le souhaitez*," Lord Aldric said to the Fortiers. Then he began his list. "Alsace. Angoumois. Anjou. Artois. Aunis. Auvergne. Béarn. Berry. Bourbonnais."

Penelope watched the Fortiers as Lord Aldric continued his list. They conferred now and then but always ended the whispered discussion with nods. No doubt they didn't know the provinces in alphabetical order by rote memory and were debating if one had been missed.

She turned her gaze to Niles, who stood beside her chair. He looked at her in the same moment.

With a quick smile that seemed a little embarrassed, he whispered, "I couldn't list all the French provinces, so I have no idea how he is doing."

"Neither do I, but I think we ought to accuse him of missing one, just to see his reaction."

Niles's fleeting smile returned, this time lingering. She enjoyed knowing that she'd brought a smile to his face. He was not an unhappy person, nor were his smiles necessarily infrequent. But there was something about the way he smiled at her that she had come to treasure and long for. It was not necessarily a step forward in the courting she needed to do, but it felt like progress just the same.

"Poitou. Provence. Roussillon. Saintonge. Touraine." Lord Aldric offered no flourishing bow or words of acknowledgment as he finished his list. He simply stepped back and indicated that Liam should take his turn.

Penelope didn't think Lord Aldric was an unhappy or impersonable gentleman. And she also didn't think he was lacking in social graces. Yet his aloofness didn't appear to trouble the Gents any more than Niles's reticence. This was an interesting group, to be certain.

Liam took a step forward. Her heart went out to her brother. He was so overawed as he looked over the gathering. Liam wanted to lay claim to these circles, but the Seymours were comparatively unimportant.

Before Liam could begin, Lord Jonquil turned and looked at Penelope. "I'm afraid you're the only one present who'll be able to tell us if his list is correct."

She knew all the counties, to be sure, but she'd never tried listing them alphabetically. "I'll not be making a whipping post of my fellow Irishman in front of a bunch of English neddies."

"Penelope." Liam's eyes pulled wider than she'd seen in ages as he all but gasped her name.

The rest of the room, however, burst into uproarious laughter at being called English donkeys.

"She's put us in our place," Lord Jonquil declared.

"Not all of us," Mrs. Fortier retorted, a broad smile on her face. "How do you feel about *French* donkeys, Miss Seymour?"

"I've never met a French donkey . . ." She let the sentence dangle.

"That you didn't like?" Mr. Layton supplied.

"No. I've simply never met a French donkey."

And the laughter began again. Liam joined in but with more trepidation than mirth.

From directly beside her, Niles whispered, "Your brother doesn't seem to know what to make of us."

"I hardly know myself," she answered, no louder than Niles had spoken.

"We can be a little daunting when taken as a whole."

"I think he does feel a little daunted." She turned to Niles. "I—"

He was so close. There were brown flecks in his blue eyes. And a slight crookedness to his nose. And one side of his mouth seemed to sit higher than the other. She had the oddest, strongest urge to trace her finger from one corner to the other, to test what she was seeing.

Good heavens, she needed to get her thoughts sorted out. She looked forward once more. "Best list those glorious counties, Liam," she said. "My heart longs to hear them."

With the eyes of the gathering on him once more, Liam seemed to find his footing, abandoning his obvious struggle between scolding his sister and impressing their companions. "Antrim," he began. "Armagh. Carlow. Cavan. Clare. Cork. Donegal."

Niles looked at her a couple of times as the list continued. He likely was checking to see if her brother had made any errors. But meeting his eye on the second glance, she saw a little surprise in the moment before he returned his gaze forward. Had something of her thoughts regarding his lips shown on her face? She'd not thought so.

Was he studying her, noticing the color of *her* eyes or the tilt of *her* mouth?

Could it be that her efforts at courting him had begun to bear fruit? That he'd started taking note of her, started feeling at least some interest? The possibility ought to have rested on her mind as relief. But where she felt it most acutely was in her heart. That organ pounded harder, beat faster.

Liam finished his list with Wexford and Wicklow. Applause and congratulations were offered as the two gentlemen ended their performance. Lord Aldric returned to his seat with unwavering nonchalance. Liam took a moment to soak in the approval he was receiving. He wasn't exactly subtle about it.

Penelope took a few deep breaths. She needed to keep her head, not lose her heart.

Violet and Nicolette sang a song in French—the only French song Violet knew, by her own admission.

Mr. Fortier and Lord Jonquil recited a poem they had composed during the extremely brief preparation period, one that was both ridiculous and, Penelope had to acknowledge, a little impressive.

Mr. Barrington and Mr. Layton ended this round of performances with the former untying his cravat and the latter retying it with his eyes closed. When pressed on what exact skill Mr. Barrington was demonstrating, Mr. Layton insisted his partner's offering was "the rare ability to admit when one's cravat knot is a travesty."

The group agreed to a second round of impromptu performances. Even Lord Aldric seemed not displeased to continue. He was an intriguing mystery, in neither a romantic nor dangerous way. He was, more than anything, confusing.

Penelope's name was drawn with his.

"I *also* know all the counties of Ireland," she told him as they settled into a corner of the music room to discuss what they would offer when their turn arrived. "In case you fancy an encore."

"I suspect we can think of something else." Lord Aldric still didn't sound displeased, but the indifference he had displayed with Liam had been exchanged for subtle misgiving. She didn't openly acknowledge it, but she was entirely aware that it was there.

"How is it you know so much about France?" Penelope asked.

"My mother was French. We often visited France while she was still living. During those years, France felt almost as much my homeland as England."

"I am sorry you lost your mother," she said.

A look of unmistakable sorrow passed very quickly through his eyes. In a quieter voice than she'd heard him yet use, he said, "It has been a very long time since anyone has said that to me. I think people forget that such a loss doesn't stop aching."

More than three years had passed since Penelope had lost her father. She missed him, and that often ached.

"May *I* ask *you* a question now?" Lord Aldric requested.

She nodded, attempting to predict in her mind what he might ask.

"Why do you want to marry Niles?"

She could not have predicted that.

"Before you answer," Lord Aldric said, "I should warn you I will not be satisfied by variations on 'because it is all arranged.' You would have been *less* inconvenienced had you abandoned the arrangements upon realizing he had defected, and you could have found someone else. Traveling this far, making efforts to convince him to change his mind back, doesn't make sense if you were simply looking for any husband. So, my question, in reality, is why do you want to marry *Niles*?"

"You are very direct, Lord Aldric."

"You will find, Miss Seymour"—his tone was solemn but without anger— "that in the matter of my friends' happiness, I do not shrink when I feel something needs to be understood or addressed."

"You've said that you consider 'because everything has been arranged' to be an insufficient reason, but 'tis a significant part of it. My circumstances are odd, and I'd very little hope of finding a gentleman who would agree to a marriage contract that took those circumstances into consideration. That he did, that he agreed to terms that would help my otherwise very difficult situation, was something of a miracle. I'll not find that again, I'm all but certain."

He was listening, but he offered no indication of what he thought of her admittedly vague explanation.

"Ladies have little power over our own futures, Lord Aldric. And marriage agreements more often than not take away even that. I found myself one of those rare lucky few who had a chance of a marriage on footing closer to equal than is ever seen or heard of." She was keeping her voice low, knowing she didn't dare allow this to be overheard. Lord Aldric gave her no reason to believe he would be satisfied with an incomplete or less-than-honest answer. "I wanted to meet the gentleman who'd agree to allow his arranged-for bride to have a say in her own future and afford her a bit of hope to cling to. And I wanted to see if there was a way to get that back."

Lord Aldric nodded. "Allow me to quickly, seeing as we are running out of time to choose a performance, tell you something about Niles Greenberry. He is stronger than he often seems, more capable than he is often given credit for, and more deserving of sincere connections than he is generally afforded. Making him think he is cared about when he is merely convenient would be even more cruel than you likely realize."

Was she being warned not to hurt Niles? Had no one warned him not to mistreat her? Had anyone thought how his refusal to even face her in Cornwall, leaving her to pick up those pieces, would hurt and humiliate her?

But those defiant thoughts quickly ebbed. He hadn't acted as he ought, but she didn't begrudge him that. Perhaps someday, she would understand his reasons. For now, she would be content with simply understanding *him*.

"No matter that he lied to and abandoned me and has not yet offered an explanation or an apology," she said, perhaps not as entirely magnanimous about that as she had insisted to herself that she was, "I do think he is deserving of sincerity, as you have said. And I cannot imagine anyone who truly knows him thinks he lacks capability or strength. No doubt, people make such a grave error in judgment because he is quiet, which is utter ridiculousness. Being quiet does not make a person weak. I saw him rush to the rescue of the poor young man who fell in the lake. He can ride as well as I can, which is, I assure you, impressive. And he verbally spars with the lot of you with ease, which I suspect is a rare enough thing. Strong, capable, and deserving—I challenge anyone to say otherwise."

Lord Aldric responded to her vehement declaration with nothing more than a dip of his head. "And what would be your reaction if you learned that someone was lying to him?"

"Who is lying to him?" She looked around the room. Certainly no one here would do so.

"Lying holds, perhaps, too harsh a connotation. *Misleading* or *manipulating* hits a little closer to the mark."

Penelope shook her head firmly. "That would be a horrible thing."

"I agree." The edge that had crept into his voice a mere moment ago was gone. "Now, what is it we are going to do when our turn to perform arrives?" She didn't think he was now pretending to be on friendly terms with her. He had warned her against hurting his friend, but he didn't seem to truly think ill of her.

She was so very confused.

"We could list the *English* counties in alphabetical order," he suggested.

"I wouldn't be much help. I don't know all the English counties." With a little effort, she kept her tone light. The confusion she felt was beginning to inch toward something uncomfortably close to guilt.

"We could attempt to place everyone here in order of age, from youngest to oldest." Lord Aldric apparently liked lists.

She did as well, truth be told. Perhaps not quite as much as he did but enough to agree to this easily performed "talent."

They had mere moments to confer before the group was assembled once more and the second round of performances began.

Lord Jonquil and Violet performed a rather silly rendition of a nursery rhyme. Mr. Layton and Nicolette performed a portion of the allemande. Mr. Barrington and Liam recited the declension of several words in Latin, which caused Lord Jonquil to insist he was reliving the horrors of his early education, which, in turn, led the Gents in the room to laugh in shared misery at having been required to learn the language. Liam laughed along with them and beamed at having found something they inarguably had in common.

Niles and Mr. Fortier were next. They announced their performance as a feat of agility.

Mr. Fortier invited Lord Jonquil and Lord Aldric to join them at the front of the group, which they did. In turn, he challenged them to attempt to catch a wood-cased pencil he held above their hand, perpendicular to the ground, by closing their hand around it before it dropped below their grasp.

Both gentlemen tried.

Both failed quite spectacularly.

"Now, assembled friends," Mr. Fortier said, "I will do the same with Puppy, but *he* will catch it."

The Gents were quick to toss out words of teasing doubt. Liam didn't seem to know if joining in their taunting would be considered uncouth or presumptuous.

The trick was undertaken, and Niles did catch the pencil. It was repeated three more times, and he was successful twice more.

As the applause for this display sounded, Lord Aldric and Penelope were invited to the front. Lord Aldric explained their performance. Everyone looked both intrigued and interested in hearing what their guesses of everyone's ages were.

Lord Aldric, of course, knew the ages of the Gents. The ladies, he'd been a little less sure of. Penelope was able to provide her and Liam's ages. In the end, the only true demonstration they were providing was whether or not they could guess Violet's and Nicolette's ages.

"Lucas. Henri. Niles. Myself. Digby. Kes." Lord Aldric saw them through the Gents portion. Next came the tricky bit.

They'd thought it best if Penelope guessed the ladies' ages, as it would be seen as less of a slight if an incorrect guess came from her, so she took on the remainder of the list. "Myself. Nicolette. Liam. Violet."

A quick conference among the audience indicated they had guessed all positions correctly. The congratulations would have led Penelope to make as grand and deep a bow as she had after the scales on the pianoforte, if not for the briefest of moments when she met Niles's eye. Wariness flickered there in the moment before he settled into a smile. Wariness and hesitation.

Making him think he is cared about when he is merely convenient would be even more cruel than you likely realize.

Misleading.

Manipulating.

Lord Aldric's words had stung, and she was beginning to realize why. Because there was some truth underlying his accusation. And Niles Greenberry knew it.

Chapter Fifteen

PENELOPE RODE OUT THE NEXT morning on Midnight, needing distance from the house and quiet in which to attempt to sort out her thoughts. Liam intercepted her on a borrowed mount of his own and joined her on the ride, eliminating her chance for self-reflection. All the Seymours were excellent riders, and Liam was no exception. Even if Penelope had decided to gallop off and leave her brother behind, he would easily have caught up to her.

"Mr. Layton is not interested." Disappointment flavored the unexpected declaration.

"I've told you that any number of times," Penelope said. "Why have you suddenly decided to believe me?"

"It is not *your* word I am depending on in this matter." There was a stiffness to his posture that was strange for him, especially on horseback.

"Then, *whose* word?"

Liam angled his chin upward in a show of confidence that rang hollow. "I asked Mr. Layton."

Penelope pulled back on Midnight's reins, the horse stopping on the instant. "You asked him directly if he wanted to marry me?"

"I needed to know the truth of our situation."

"Liam, are you mad? We will be seen as ridiculous and uncouth. We are already terribly far beneath the touch of our current companions; behaving in such an impertinent way will highlight that, not reduce it."

Her brother's jaw tensed. "I made headway with the gentlemen last evening."

"I was present last evening. Nothing that happened would lead me to believe Mr. Layton would welcome such a bluntly personal discussion." Good heavens, she couldn't believe Liam would make such an enormous misstep.

"I watched you last evening as well, Penelope." His brows rose in anticipation. She didn't take the bait.

She didn't need to.

"I don't know what you and Lord Aldric spoke about," Liam said, "but it was obvious even from across the room that there is no chance of the duke's son being interested in you."

"Another thing I told you myself before last night's gathering." Midnight skittered a little beneath her, most certainly sensing her growing tension. "You don't intend to ask him to marry me, do you?"

"Why are you being so confrontational?" Liam turned his mount a little.

"Liam, you asked a gentleman we barely have the standing to speak to if he wanted to marry me. That blunder will undermine everything I am attempting to do."

His gaze dropped away. He winced. But the moment of regret didn't last. "And what exactly are you attempting to do, Penelope?"

"To know Mr. Greenberry better and give him a chance to come to know me," she said. "I am attempting to salvage the arrangements you worked so hard to bring about."

"I don't need you to do my work for me," he muttered petulantly.

"I am trying to work *with* you."

The petulance turned to frustration. "I am the head of our family. Why do you never let me be the head?"

Where was this coming from? "I have never undermined you."

Liam motioned vaguely all around them. "The fact that we are here is proof that you browbeat me with alarming regularity."

"*We* agreed that discovering Mr. Greenberry's reason for defecting was worth the effort of coming here."

Liam shook his head. "*You* insisted he ought to explain. *You* insisted we make this journey. All this after *you* insisted I search the world over for a gentleman who would agree to the terms you demanded. And I capitulated every time."

He wasn't just frustrated; he was angry.

"The situation was bad enough in Cornwall," he continued. "A gentleman being unsure of a match his family arranged on his behalf to a lady he had no acquaintance with is understandable. It doesn't reflect poorly on her. But for him to actually make her acquaintance, come to know her better, and then be *even less* enthusiastic about the match is . . . humiliating. For everyone concerned."

"There are worse things than being embarrassed."

His mouth tightened into a sharp line. "That is an easy declaration to make when one is not the person constantly being humiliated." He set his horse to a slow walk once more. Penelope nudged Midnight with her knees, and the mare began walking as well.

"I was jilted by a gentleman in a very public manner," she said. "I assure you that was inarguably humiliating."

"You are intelligent and personable. You are adept at all the social niceties. You are beautiful. You have a very fine estate. Gentlemen should be lining up for the chance to secure your hand." He looked increasingly frustrated. "Yet you are spending an inordinate amount of time trying to convince one to accept your hand who clearly doesn't want it."

She winced. "You do not have to be cruel."

"I am not being cruel," he insisted. "I am being *reasonable*. The only one of us who is, I would add."

"I do not think it so unreasonable that Mr. Greenberry might decide that he would, in fact, like to marry me."

Liam looked over at her. "I can't justify remaining more than two more days. Though I do believe I made progress in forging something of a connection to the gentlemen, it will never be enough to warrant outstaying our welcome."

"Mr. Layton hasn't seemed truly upset about our visit."

"Do not mistake civility for acceptance, Penelope." Liam's sigh was one of embarrassment every bit as much as exasperation. "Two days is all we can justify."

"Two days isn't enough time," she insisted.

He set his shoulders. "Do not make the mistake of assuming you are the only one disappointed by how this visit has played out. You did not win the regard of a gentleman who had already rejected you. I did not gain any degree of connection to a group of people who could have given me a place in Society, a better chance of making a good match myself, and a less rocky future for the family estate."

"Is something the matter with the estate?"

That was apparently the wrong question to ask. He prickled up on the instant. "I am the head of our family," he repeated. "And it is my estate. Please stop knocking my legs out from under me."

"I wasn't—"

He set his horse to a canter that sped into a gallop, leaving her behind.

She and her brother had certainly had disagreements in the past, even a few rows, but Liam had never seemed this angry with her before.

He was angry. Lord Aldric was issuing warnings. Violet and Nicolette were helping her but with firmly worded caveats. Niles watched her with suspicion.

How had everything gone so wrong?

"I'm not a horrible person," she whispered. But her assertion didn't reassure her. She wasn't cruel, but being disingenuous was not precisely the behavior of a kindhearted person.

"I'm not lying to him." But giving an impression one knew was deceptive was not very honest. "I'm not horrible, and I'm not a liar." Her whispered words broke a little. "I just need him to believe me enough to—"

There it was. The unvarnished truth. She needed him to believe whatever it was he needed to believe in order to move forward with the match that had been arranged.

Not precisely a paragon of sincerity, am I?

She had ridden, without truly noting it, back to the stables. Liam didn't appear to have done the same.

A groomsman met her and assisted her in dismounting before leading Midnight away.

As Penelope turned to go, she spotted Niles at the edge of the silver-gray filly's pen.

He looked over at her. She held her breath. He put a finger to his lips and held his other hand out to her. She set her hand in his.

"The filly has been inching closer to me for a quarter of an hour," he said in a whisper as he tugged her over to the fence.

"Employing the same volume, she said, "The head groom told me this morning that the filly won't approach anyone."

"Not yet." He kept her hand in his as he watched the little horse out of the corner of his eye. Though he probably didn't mean for the gesture to be significant in any way, she was affected by it just the same. It was trusting and kind. There was a softness to it that she very much needed after such sharp conversations with her brother and herself.

"The stable staff said she skitters off anytime they approach her," he said, "which gave me an idea."

She pieced together that idea in an instant. "Allow her to approach you."

"Precisely."

The filly took a single step toward the fence. Niles didn't move, and he didn't look directly at the filly. It was precisely the approach she would have taken.

"If the little girl can find the courage to come make my acquaintance," Niles said, "she might be willing to approach the staff as well."

"You are very patient with her."

"She's in an unfamiliar place, and she's alone. I think that warrants some patience."

He was a very genuine person, open and sincere. She'd not realized that at first, but it was undeniable now.

Niles met her eye. He didn't seem upset to have found her watching him. He simply smiled a little, the asymmetry of his mouth adorably apparent. "Did you have a good ride this morning?"

"A short one," she admitted. "I suspect Midnight wishes I'd let her gallop."

"Do you also wish you'd let her gallop?"

Did she? "I was unusually distracted this morning. It is for the best that I didn't give a fiery horse her head while I wasn't paying enough heed." Niles released her hand as he turned enough to lean a little against the fence.

She missed the warm reassurance of his touch. She, who had always prided herself on being so fiercely independent, missed that connection.

"Is your horse in Ireland as feisty as Midnight?" he asked.

"Which one?" She moved a little closer.

"How many do you have?" He seemed genuinely curious.

"Three that are mine in particular. Though they are no longer in Ireland. They have been moved to Fairfield."

"Your estate in Surrey."

Her heart thudded for the briefest of moments as she contemplated telling him the entirety of her situation there. Hadn't she just been chastising herself for being dishonest?

"My hope is to make Fairfield a horse-breeding establishment. One of my horses is a stallion: strong, intelligent, and rather beautiful. And I've two very good brood mares."

"One of them is a true-white horse." He looked back toward the pen, though still not directly at the filly.

"You remembered." They'd discussed it so briefly that she'd not expected him to recall that detail.

"I have only seen an actual white horse twice in my entire life," he said. "The fact that you have one is not something I would easily forget."

If she explained her ambitions for her estate, would he find that equally intriguing? "With the addition of another stallion and a couple more brood mares, I could have what I think would be a very successful venture at Fairfield."

He nodded as he listened. "The reason, no doubt, you wished to retain your ownership of the estate even after you marry."

"And the reason I more or less have to marry." She sighed. "A lady living alone is frowned on. A lady living alone *and* overseeing a business venture would be scandalous to a destructive degree. Not to mention, essentially no one is willing to do business with an unmarried lady."

"Hmm."

She didn't know if that was a sound of contemplation or an unspoken wish for her to leave him alone. "I'm talking too much, aren't I?"

He looked back at her. "Was I giving you that impression?" That he seemed surprised set her mind at ease.

"I like talking with you," Niles said. "And I would wager I'm not the only one."

"Most horses like talking with me."

He returned his gaze to the pen. "Horses are very good judges of character."

The young horse currently evaluating *his* character had come nearly all the way to the fence. That spoke well of him.

"If you marry a man who doesn't agree to you keeping control of Fairfield," he said without looking back at her, "then you will have no ability to make your dreamed-of equine venture a reality."

"And a man who won't agree to my keeping Fairfield is unlikely to allow me to keep my horses or the money I have earned thus far breeding them." She shrugged a little. "I would lose everything."

"It is miserable, isn't it?" He held his hand out the tiniest bit, palm up, toward the approaching filly. "Feeling like you have no control over your life and future?"

"Do you feel that way as well?" she asked.

"I haven't had much true control over my future until quite recently. But I'm not sure I know how to keep hold of that control."

"'Tis also a miserable thing, that," Penelope said, "feeling your hopes are at last within reach but you don't know how to actually seize them."

It was such a personal conversation, and seemingly out of nowhere. Here was an opportunity to know him better and he her. She didn't dare waste it.

"What is the hope you are attempting to take hold of?" she asked.

His eyes returned to her face, and his features pulled in that wary expression she saw far too often on his face.

In a nearly strangled voice, she said, "Please don't look at me that way, Niles." Her misstep struck her immediately. "*Mr. Greenberry.*" What a mess she was making of this. "I have met so many Misters Greenberry in the last while that

I've needed to think of you by your Christian name simply to keep everyone straight. I hadn't ever meant to address you so informally."

"There are an awful lot of Misters Greenberry," he acknowledged. It was very gracious of him. "How was I looking at you that upset you?"

Niles was proving a remarkable gentleman. He'd not been offended by the inappropriate liberty she'd taken with his name. And he sounded legitimately interested in knowing what had upset her. All of this while knowing that she had been trying to convince him of a future she wanted without knowing if it was what he wanted. He deserved to be treated better than she had been treating him.

"I am not cruel." She could not entirely ignore the pleading quality in her voice. "Not truly. And I'm not dishonest, at least not intentionally. I do try to be a decent person." She released a breath.

"And I looked at you in the way one would a cruel, dishonest, not-decent person?"

"You look at me like you don't trust me."

He didn't answer, but the hesitation in his eyes was answer enough.

Penelope pushed down a surge of misery. "I've been trying to snatch hold of some of those elusive hopes. But in doing so, I know I have made you uncomfortable."

"I have been confused and uncertain but not truly uncomfortable."

Her doubt could not possibly have remained hidden.

Niles, good-hearted person that he was, smiled again. "Perhaps *a little* uncomfortable but not enough to justify your current level of self-castigation."

"Your face has said otherwise."

"I wouldn't listen to it if I were you." The absurdity in Niles's brown-flecked blue eyes undercut his earnest tone.

"You don't mind that I'm here?" she asked.

"When any of the stablehands have wandered anywhere nearby, this nervous filly has backed away. But she didn't when you approached. She still hasn't." He glanced at the horse, which was within a breath of nudging his hand with her nose. "That says something about you, Penelope Seymour."

"I like animals," she said.

"As do I." His eyes narrowed. "Except for cats. Cats are terrible."

Penelope burst out laughing. Niles had offered his excoriation of cats with such an overdone tone of disgust that there was no doubt he hadn't meant a word of it.

"Nothing in your family's letters prepared me to discover that you are so funny," she said.

He smiled ever more broadly. "I can't imagine most people describing me as funny."

"Do you spend time exclusively in the company of thick-headed people?"

He shrugged. "The Gents are known to be exceptionally bacon-brained."

That set her laughing again, and he joined in. The filly looked at them, quite as if she felt they had taken leave of their wits. But she didn't back away.

"I do wish we'd met under different circumstances," Penelope said. "I would greatly enjoy being your friend."

"Is it inevitable that our difficult beginning means we cannot move forward as friends?" he asked.

Heaven help her, he was making her hope for things she ought not. Her disappointment would only hurt that much more. "I have imposed on you in many ways. I cannot expect you to continue any sort of acquaintance with me."

"You overstate the situation, Miss Seymour. You tracked me here and have attempted to turn my head a bit in order to push forward the originally proposed connection between us."

She blushed at hearing her efforts stated so bluntly by the one on the receiving end of them.

"I refused to return home at the previously determined date and left you to face the humiliation of a missing groom," he continued. "Had the two of us been undertaking a sporting competition, the contest would currently be considered a draw."

He didn't mean to hold her schemes against her, schemes Lord Aldric had disapproved of, Liam had condemned, and both Violet and Nicolette had been hesitant to participate in until after they had been assured Penelope didn't mean to truly impose on Niles.

"Could we begin again?" she asked. "Start fresh—or as much as we can; there is no way of truly dismissing all that has happened—and be friends?"

"I would like that."

Her heart thudded a bit against her ribs with a quiver of something a little less hopeful than she would have expected. It was as if her heart were rejoicing and weeping at the same time.

"There you are, sweet girl," Niles cooed.

When the filly didn't pull back, Niles rubbed her nose gently. His smile was so tender, and there was pride in his expression. But that pride was directed at the nervous little horse who had chosen to be brave.

She had gained the hope of his friendship but realized in the very moment he had offered it that her heart wanted more. In her efforts to convince him that he could be happy in a match with her, she had begun falling in love with him.

Chapter Sixteen

AFTER CHANGING FROM HIS RIDING clothes, Niles sauntered toward the library, where he'd been informed the Gents had congregated. A sudden burst of laughter echoed from the room as he approached, confirming their presence even before he stepped inside.

You are so funny. Penelope's words echoed in his mind, pulling his lips upward. Few people even noticed him, let alone credited him with a sense of humor. He very much liked that she had done both.

"You look pleased, Puppy," Digby said, watching Niles's entrance from a comfortable chair.

"I saw a hedgehog during my ride this morning. And the weather held until I was almost inside, saving me from a miserable soaking. I negotiated a truce with Miss Seymour, won over Digby's reluctant filly, and went yet another morning without receiving a letter from my grandfather telling me what a horrible grandson I am. All in all, I would say I have ample reason to be quite pleased."

All the Gents were watching him now, except for Lucas, who sat at the desk, writing what was likely a letter. Their Jester was a prodigious letter writer.

"Was this hedgehog on its own or with its prickle?" Kes asked in the same moment Digby asked, "Why did your valet decide on this particular pairing of jacket and waistcoat?"

Aldric looked a little annoyed with both of them and posed his own question in the next instant. "What is this truce with Miss Seymour? Did she say she considered the two of you to be at odds?"

Not at odds as much as she considered herself to have ill-used him. But Niles found himself reluctant to share that. It was an admission that had clearly pained her.

I do try to be a decent person. She'd been trying to convince herself as much as him.

Her pursuit of him, undertaken as it was with an aim in mind rather than the result of actual affection or unbiased interest, had made him uneasy. But he'd not ever thought she was cruel or heartlessly dishonest or any of the things she'd applied to herself.

"She asked if we could start over again, this time as friends," Niles said.

"How precisely did she phrase her request to be . . . friends?" Digby posed the question in a way that told Niles there was significance to the answer.

"She acknowledged that the beginning of our acquaintance had been uncomfortable and suggested we should make a new start."

Aldric didn't seem to entirely believe that. Or perhaps he disapproved of the changed approach.

"Do you—Do you think this is simply a new courting strategy of hers?" Niles hadn't thought that before, but he was wondering a little now.

"I don't know," Aldric said. "But I think we all ought to pay attention in case that is precisely what this is."

I'm not cruel. And I'm not dishonest, at least not intentionally. She'd seemed to him to be entirely sincere.

"If she *is* in earnest about beginning over," Niles said, "do you think I'd be unwise to accept her friendship?"

Aldric shook his head without hesitation, which was reassuring.

"Are you certain friendship is actually what she wants?" Kes asked.

"Do you think she doesn't? She seemed honest in her request."

Digby dropped a hand onto his shoulder. "When a lady suggests she be *only* your friend, that can mean a few different things, Puppy, especially if she was interested in something more."

"Like Miss Hanover changing her tune so suddenly a few years ago?"

Far from embarrassed by the memory, Digby raised a single eyebrow in a show of palpable pride. "I will have you know, she was *devastated.*"

"No, she wasn't," Aldric said.

"She traded the possibility of Digby Layton for the reality of Wilbur Garner." Digby twisted a pearl cuff link. "How could she be anything but devastated?"

"The Garners seem very happy," Henri countered.

"She is bravely soldiering on," Digby insisted.

From his writing table, Lucas snorted.

"Monarchs execute jesters with alarming regularity." Digby's threat might have held more sway if not for the laugh he was clearly stifling.

Kes was generally a source of reliable information, so Niles turned to him. "What was Digby initially trying to warn me about?"

"A lady saying she wishes to claim merely friendship when that did not previously seem to be her wish can indicate she no longer has any romantic interest, or she never did and has grown weary of pretending otherwise, or that she does not actually wish to be a fellow's friend but hasn't thought of a kind way to say as much."

Niles swallowed. "That's a long list."

"Or," Kes continued, "she actually does wish to be something more than friends but is hoping that by being a little coy or by being less obvious in her wishes, she'll have greater success."

"Oh." Niles tried to sort it in his mind. "So, either she does, in fact, wish to be my friend, or she doesn't *even* want to be my friend, or this might simply be more of her attempts at courting but is disguised as a truce?"

They all nodded. *Oh bother.*

"Which do you hope it is?" Aldric asked.

"Does it matter?"

"Of course it does. How we proceed will be guided by what you want."

What did he want? He liked Miss Seymour. He would very much like her to continue being his friend. And based on the way that final word stuck uncomfortably in his mind, at least some part of him would like something more than friendship.

"Have you enjoyed spending time with Miss Seymour?" Niles asked, looking at the others. "She's really rather delightful, and no matter that she concocted an uncomfortable scheme, I think she's been a good addition to the group."

"Oh, certainly," from Kes.

"*Très agréable*," from Henri.

"She is," from Aldric.

"How 'delightful' do *you* find her?" Digby wiggled an eyebrow.

Lucas kept at his letter, but he grinned as broadly as the others. Even Aldric wasn't hiding his amusement.

"I can't imagine why all of you are inferring something far more . . . amorous in my words," Niles said.

"I don't believe any of us mentioned *l'amour*," Henri was quick to say.

"But how very telling that *Niles* was so quick to mention it." Kes was wearing his "I have made a startlingly intriguing discovery" expression.

"And so quick to insist there is no romantic element to any of this," Aldric added, looking every bit as intrigued.

"I was simply trying to get ahead of your imaginations."

With an air of palpable dignity, Digby said, "Methinks he doth protest too much, Gents."

"Speak more slowly, everyone," Lucas said. "I can't write as fast as you talk."

"You are writing all of this down?" Niles wouldn't put it past him.

"Julia would never forgive me if I didn't relay every word of this to her."

Blasted blazes. And yet, Niles couldn't even be truly upset. The Gents were forever pestering each other, and it was always good-natured.

"That's how you know you're one of us now," Stanley had once explained to Niles. "Just make certain you give it back as well and as often as we toss it at you."

To Lucas, Niles said, "Make certain you include in your report of this moment how ridiculous Digby looks. She'll want to know that."

Just as Niles knew it would, that comment sent Digby into a veritable tidal wave of dramatic declarations of offense. The rest of the Gents joined in the teasing, some taking Digby's part and others insisting Niles's pretended disapproval was accurate. Their propensity for laughing together had seen all of them through incredibly difficult times.

Wilson slipped silently into the midst of this entertaining bit of chaos and crossed directly to Lucas. "This has come for you, m'lord." He held out a letter.

Lucas took it and flipped it over to the wax seal. "It's from Lampton Park."

"Julia again?" Henri guessed.

"Based on the handwriting"—Lucas studied the address on the front—"it appears to be from my father."

Niles hoped that meant Lord Lampton was feeling better. His health had been poor, and that weighed on Lucas's mind.

Wilson turned to leave but seemed to change his mind. He spun around once more and whispered something to Lucas.

"Of course you can talk," Lucas said. "In more formal settings, you'd be expected to scrape and bow and such, but when it's only us, you need simply ask Mr. Greenberry if you can drop a word in his ear."

Niles couldn't help but be intrigued. Why did Wilson want to speak with him?

The young man approached, his posture a mixture of the expected deference and an undeniable confidence. Wilson would, no doubt, prove to be a very interesting sort of valet. Perfect for Lucas, truly. "Mr. Greenberry, might I drop a word in your ear?"

"Of course."

"While I was salvaging your hair yesterday—"

"Best to not use the word *salvaging*," Digby said. "You make him sound like a castle ruin or a shipwreck."

Wilson shrugged the tiniest bit, holding his hands up and lifting his eyebrows. The message was clear: he felt his word choice was quite accurate even when explained the way Digby had just done.

That set the Gents laughing again.

"I overheard you saying that you could have the estate you want if you could gather a bit more money." Wilson looked to Digby once more. "I know I'm supposed to pretend I couldn't hear any of the things that were being said, no matter that I was standing among all of you."

"Well, you *are* supposed to pretend you don't hear anything," Digby conceded.

"Leave Wilson be, Your Majesty," Lucas said, eyes on his letter but apparently also following the conversation being had nearby. "I like having a valet with the skills of a spy."

Wilson beamed with unmistakable pride. He continued addressing Niles. "I thought you might like to know that the fair in Hamblestead will include a pugilistic tournament. All the gentlemen in and around the village are planning to wager on the various matches. Might be a chance to gain a bit of those funds you're looking for."

That set the Gents to discussing what they knew of the fair, which pugilists were likely to come to Hamblestead to participate. None of them was an inveterate gambler, but neither was any of them morally opposed to the occasional, reasonable wager. What constituted "reasonable" varied among them, according to their circumstances, and they all made a point of never pressing each other toward uncomfortable forfeits.

But Niles was intrigued by something other than the unavoidably risky gambler's method of lining one's pockets.

To Wilson, he asked, "Did you happen to overhear what the purse for the tournament will be?"

"The winner will receive £150. The one who loses the final match will win £50."

That was an enormous purse for so small a village. A fighter of significance must have been expected to attend. Or hoped for, at least. That £150 would give Niles what he lacked to purchase the property in Essex he had his eye on.

Wilson took his leave, and Aldric stepped up beside Niles. The other Gents were in conversation with each other, except for Lucas, who had given his full attention to the letter he had received.

"You're thinking of fighting?" Aldric seemed to already know the answer.

"The idea is crossing my mind." Lud, was he truly considering this?

"Talk it through," Aldric said. They'd taken this approach for years: Niles spilling his often jumbled thoughts, and Aldric helping him make sense of it all.

"The Green Badger is clearly expecting someone significant, else the purse wouldn't be so large." Niles rubbed at his tense neck as he spoke. "That makes fighting riskier."

"When was the last time you pugilated?"

Too long. "I spar when I'm in London."

Aldric shook his head. "I mean an actual bout. You know better than any of us that sparring and fighting are different things."

"I'll confess, it's been some time. But if there's even a chance of winning . . ." His voice trailed off. Claiming a £150 purse would change everything. He would have his property. He could return to his family without fear of being forced into a future that would steal that hope from him. He would have independence and the ability to pursue the dreams he had. "Even if I can make it to the final round and lose, I'd come away with £50, which will cut more than a year off the time I need to get my property. More than a year."

Aldric watched him intently but made no further arguments.

This was a decidedly unexpected turn of events. And the path ahead was strewn with risk.

"If I don't at least try," Niles said as much to himself as to Aldric, "I think I'll regret it."

Aldric didn't hesitate nor try to dissuade him. Instead, he addressed the group. "Gents, dust off your fists. Niles has a tournament to prepare for."

Chapter Seventeen

Violet and Nicolette were in the sitting room, chatting amiably.

"May I join you?" Penelope asked from the doorway.

She was invited to do so and took a seat among them. Not one of the Gents was present. "Do you worry that the Gents are up to mischief when they are nowhere to be found?"

"I don't *worry*," Violet said. "I *assume*."

"They have not yet realized that they ought to make the same assumption about their ladies," Nicolette added.

Penelope very much liked the idea of a group of ladies who enjoyed a bit of mischief. "Does Lady Jonquil join you in these bouts of devilment?"

"She instigates most of them," Violet said.

"Oh, I would so very much like to meet her." Penelope understood why the newly delivered mother could not make the journey, but she grieved the missed opportunity to make the acquaintance of a lady she suspected she would thoroughly like.

"You will be pleased to know," Nicolette said, "that Our Julia without question knows all the counties of Ireland and could recite them in alphabetical order."

"Does she have connections to Ireland?"

Nicolette shrugged. "What she has is a deep and abiding love of learning and a mind that can recall most everything it has ever been presented with."

"She's very intelligent, is she?" Penelope didn't know whether to be impressed or intimidated. Likely both.

"I would wager she is a genius." Violet didn't seem cowed by her friend's astonishing intelligence. "Julia is also delightfully fun and personable. You would adore her instantly."

"I suspect she would find me rather too thick for her to endure." Penelope raised a sardonic eyebrow. "I've done nothing but make a mull of things ever since arriving."

"I wouldn't say that," Violet reassured her. "Julia would applaud your decision to sniff out your absentee, would-be fiancé rather than simply shrug and accept the implied rejection."

"The rejection was not merely *implied*." Penelope's pride had been hurt by the initial rejection. It was her heart that ached most now.

"And what do you think of our Niles now that you know him a little better?" Violet didn't pose the question in casual tones.

"I suspect he likes horses as much as I do. He is interesting to talk with. And he's kind and patient." She truly was beginning to fall in love with him. "He is wonderful."

He was undeniably wonderful, and she was quite suddenly running out of time. Liam had said they would remain for only two more days. The truce she had negotiated with Niles was a way of beginning again, but starting over when her time was so short seemed rather hopeless.

"How does Niles seem to feel about you?" Nicolette asked.

Her heart dropped a little.

Before Penelope could explain about her impending departure, the sound of men's voices bursting into laughter at a distance down the corridor pulled all their attention to the doorway. A moment later, the Gents strolled into the room, grins on every face, mischief in every pair of eyes.

"We are off to Hamblestead, ladies," Lord Jonquil declared. "I am afraid your time will be absolutely empty without us. Consider yourselves warned."

"I suspect we will survive." Nicolette waved off the pretended concern with a graceful swipe of her hand.

Mr. Fortier crossed to his wife and took her hand, raising it to his lips. "I will bring you back a sweet, *ma chérie*."

"Bring back yourself, and I will be entirely pleased."

They continued their conversation in French.

Mr. Barrington pulled Violet into an embrace. "I would offer to bring you sweets, Lily, but I don't know that it is the best bribe."

"Why do you need to offer a bribe?" Violet asked. "Are you planning to do something you will get in trouble for?"

"She sorted you quickly," Niles said, laughing.

He had a very nice laugh. And his eyes lit up when he did it, a sight Penelope enjoyed immensely. Indeed, she couldn't look away from the light in his expression.

Lord Jonquil set an arm around Mr. Layton's shoulders. "I'm afraid there'll be no tender farewells for you, my friend. You'll have to content yourself with the Gents' assurance that we think you're quite a catch."

The Gents were quick to good-naturedly tease their friend. Mr. Layton seemed to enjoy the humor swirling around, no matter that it was at his expense.

"We want to return in time to change for supper," Lord Aldric said. "So, we had best be on our way."

Lord Jonquil snapped a salute. "As you command, General!"

The gentlemen were soon on their way, clearly looking forward to their outing. Penelope suspected she would have enjoyed going with them. But she also knew she would enjoy spending the afternoon with the ladies. All her life, she'd imagined finding friends with whom she could simply be the person she was and be liked and appreciated for it. She got along well with the people in Dublin but had nothing beyond a friendly acquaintance with any of them. Her neighbors thought her odd. To have a group such as this—friends who were family to each other and who liked each other as they were—would be a dream come true.

"Though we like to joke about their tendency toward the ridiculous," Violet said, "they are good men, every last one of them."

"Why did they give you the nickname of Lily?" Penelope asked.

"Because they can't spell *Violet*." Violet offered the answer with perfect seriousness, but that lasted only a moment before being replaced by laughter. "I acquired the nickname during an evening parlor game. My sweet Kester, not realizing how much of his heart he was revealing, compared me to a lily-of-the-valley flower and waxed long and eloquent about how delightful he thought I was. I have been Lily ever since."

Penelope turned to Nicolette. "Niles told me you are called Le Capitaine."

Nicolette nodded. "A name also acquired during a game."

"What name do you suppose they would give Penelope?" Violet asked Nicolette.

Penelope answered. "Whatever they are able to spell, I'd wager."

Violet's smile grew. "Perhaps they would choose to call you Kitty."

"Kitty?" Penelope repeated, unsure of the reason for the guess.

"On account of your connection to Puppy."

"He said we weren't to be enemies," Penelope objected. "Cats and dogs generally are."

"I didn't mean it that way," Violet said. "Cats and dogs don't get along. But kittens and puppies, when brought together while still young, can actually be very good friends."

"I am hopeful that we can find a friendly connection."

"Would it surprise you, Penelope," Nicolette asked, "to hear that we are increasingly hopeful of the same thing?"

"It would, a little." Her mind and heart were heavy where Niles was concerned. "I should have been more sincere with him."

"Posh." Violet shook her head. "I've watched the two of you interact the last two days, and everything I saw appeared entirely genuine."

"It didn't feel genuine, not on my part." Penelope was embarrassed to admit as much, but she felt she owed it to her integrity to be honest about her behavior.

"You'll not convince me that the look on your face when Niles laughed a moment ago was anything but *genuine* tenderness."

"I have come to realize what a lovely person he is," Penelope said. "He is kind and considerate. Just being in company with him makes me happy in a way so few people do. But the feeling is not mutual. He is content to call our connection a potential *friendship*. I've only two days left here as it is. Nothing more could come of my increasingly tender feelings, so I think it best not to impose upon him further."

"Why only two days?" Nicolette asked.

"My brother has said that Niles's continued disinterest is embarrassing and we are to depart for Ireland the day after tomorrow." Penelope released a tense breath. "I ran out of time."

"And if you don't wish to leave?" Violet asked.

Penelope shrugged. "I don't have a choice."

Her new friends both leaned forward.

"If Julia has taught us anything," Violet said conspiratorially, "it is that we *always* have a choice. Let's sort out what choices you actually have."

"Earlier this year, I found myself in a similar situation to yours now," Nicolette said. "I had fallen entirely in love with my Henri when my brother declared that I was to leave England, and he would hear no objections. Leaving Henri was impossible for my heart to accept, but like you, I was very much at the mercy of my brother's whims."

"What did you do?"

Nicolette smiled in obvious satisfaction. "Julia and I concocted a plan."

That was both intriguing and promising. "What was the plan?"

"Julia declared that I would remain in England as her lady's companion," Nicolette said. "She didn't need one, but I required a situation that allowed me to not bend to my brother's edicts. It worked brilliantly."

"I don't suppose either of you is in need of a companion?" Penelope asked with a laugh.

"In need of?" Violet repeated. "No. Willing to *say* that I am? Absolutely."

"Truly?" She had in no way earned such an enormous kindness from them. "My courtship of Niles has, thus far, been a failure. I promised you I wouldn't keep trying if—"

"It hasn't been a failure," Violet said. "He's intrigued, and you have managed to see him more clearly than even his own family does. What you need isn't to abandon your efforts. You need time."

Penelope might be able to stay. Hope bubbled anew. To stay here, where Niles was. To enjoy his company. To see him smile. To hear him laugh. To perhaps discover something deeper growing between them. Her heart swelled at the possibility.

Chapter Eighteen

"Sir Punchmuch?" Niles shook his head as he repeated the name Digby had invented while in Hamblestead.

"We couldn't put your actual name on the roster, now could we?" Kes said in all their defense. "And you were reluctant to take up your previous sobriquet once more."

The Gents had returned from the Green Badger and were following Digby to an outbuilding on the grounds of Pledwick Manor.

"I still think you should have chosen Marmaduke Fisticuffs," Lucas said.

"Do not discount the brilliance of Monsieur Poing." Henri looked thoroughly pleased to repeat his suggestion. "Or Lord Punchington." He motioned toward Aldric with a twitch of his chin.

In the end, Niles had decided it did little good not to use the name he'd been known as during his active years fighting for purses. They'd had no difficulty getting the Cornish Duke on the list of fighters for the tournament. Aldric had realized their difficulty—placing Niles on the roster while neither giving away his identity nor raising suspicions by having the famed fighter's name put forward by a group of gentlemen with no established connection to him—and had, as always, devised a brilliant plan.

The Cornish Duke, he'd told the proprietor, was rumored to be in the area, and the whispers were that the pugilist, who had not fought in some time, was game for a new bout. Should his name be added, Aldric had further added, the man himself would, no doubt, send confirmation.

It had proven enough, and quick as anything, Niles had committed himself to stepping once more into the pugilists' ring.

As the group reached the outbuilding they were aiming for, Digby pulled a key from his pocket and unlocked the door. The interior was dark and the air a bit musty. Henri, Lucas, and Digby pulled down the dingy fabric hanging over the windows, allowing light to spill inside.

"I still cannot countenance that you are returning to your duke-ness rather than taking up any of our suggestions." Digby sounded nearly horrified. "That shows an unforgivable lack of creativity."

"But a far greater chance of remembering what my false name is," Niles reminded them all.

Aldric's expression turned excessively somber. "Are you arguing that Lord Punchington is not memorable? I should call you out for that."

"Do," Lucas said eagerly. "It would be excellent practice for Puppy's upcoming matches."

Digby shook his head. "I am relatively certain dueling pistols are not used in prizefights."

"And I," Niles jumped in, "am even more certain the General would never actually shoot me, no matter that I did not decide to enter the pugilists' ring as Lord Fisticuffington."

"Lord Punchington," Aldric repeated. "Let's not be ridiculous."

One of Niles's favorite things about the Gents was that every so often, they would be in a mood of utter ridiculousness that would grow and expand for days on end. He cherished those times. To have that happen while he was dealing with a crisis was proving an utter godsend.

The outbuilding was a decent size. A traveling coach could fit inside with ample room to spare. It was also entirely empty aside from a generous layer of dust.

"What was this building used for previously?" Niles asked.

Digby eyed the space with a barely-held-back look of underlying disgust. "My father put things in here that he was hiding from my mother."

"There's room enough to hide a lot of things," Kes said, looking around as well.

With a tight sigh, Digby said, "Yes, there is."

He almost never spoke of his family, but the Gents had filled in a great many blanks. All of Society knew Digby's parents had hated each other. It was also general knowledge that the in-fighting in the broader Layton family made the Capulets and Montagues look like the friendliest of neighbors. What no one seemed to know was how it had all begun or the details of what it looked like among them now. The only thing the Gents knew for certain was that Digby's mother was dead, his father was not, and Digby permitted very few questions about any of it.

"Tell us what would be most helpful in here, Puppy," Aldric said. "We can begin the work of finding all the things you need."

That was their General: quick to get back to the task at hand, always ready to strategize their next endeavor.

"Sacks of grain." Niles had often used those for practicing delivering punches at force. "Fabric strips." He mimed wrapping his knuckles in the fabric. "Chalk to mark off the size of the ring on the floor."

"Heavy things to lift," Aldric added. "That'll build your fortitude, add a few muscles to your scraggly frame."

"I haven't fought in a true bout in some time," Niles acknowledged, "but I'm not a dandyprat, by any means."

Lucas swung a lobbing fist in Niles's direction, the sort never intended to actually land. "I'm afraid you'll have to prove that to us, Puppy."

Niles took up the pretend sparring. "I've blackened your eye in the past. All of your eyes."

"I only have two, you dunderhead." Lucas swung again.

"I meant all *the Gents'* eyes, muck brains."

"No, no, no." Kes shook his head. "*Digby* is muck brains. Lucas is stupid head. Henri is, of course, most reverend sir."

That set them all to snickering. Henri's moniker was, after all, Archbishop.

"Best decide what we mean to call Violet and Miss Seymour," Digby said from one of the windows. "Both ladies will be here in a moment."

Pugilistic matches were fought not only bare-knuckled but also bare-chested. Thank the heavens they hadn't trekked that far down the practice path yet.

Just as Digby had said, Violet and Penelope arrived in the doorway a mere moment later. When Niles had begun thinking of her as Penelope, he wasn't certain. But it somehow fit her so much better than the more staid and sedate Miss Seymour.

"We were told we would find you here," Violet said.

"Who's whispering our secrets about?" Digby said with mock offense.

"We've been sworn to secrecy," Penelope declared. "Torture us if you must; we'll never reveal our source."

The Gents looked at each other and, in unison, said, "Wilson."

"Wilson? Wilson who?" Violet said innocently. *Too* innocently.

"Never heard of anyone by that name," Penelope added. She was somehow even more gorgeous when laughter filled her intoxicating brown eyes. They twinkled when she was enjoying herself; he'd noticed that time and again since meeting her.

"So, why did you seek directions from this unnamed teller of tales?" Kes slipped an arm around Violet. "I'm not complaining, mind you."

"I should hope not." Violet kissed Kes's cheek.

Niles turned to Penelope. "I know the Gents and their ladies well enough to be certain that this"—he motioned to Violet and Kes's embrace—"could go on for some time. If Julia were here, we'd hardly have a coherent sentence out of Lucas."

"It's kind of a lovely thing, though, isn't it? Couples who love each other that much?" Penelope said.

It was entirely lovely. And it was exactly what Niles wanted. But that was not a conversation he was ready to have with Penelope Seymour, of all people. "If your business is of a pressing nature, you'd do best to take the reins at this point, seeing as how Violet is currently quite distracted."

"Yes, one would think she were attempting to win over a hesitant filly," Penelope said.

Niles shook his head solemnly. "Kes is not nearly as interesting as a horse."

"I heard that," Kes objected.

Penelope leaned closer to Niles and, in an overly loud whisper, said, "He's a grumpy horse."

Niles sighed dramatically. "Alas, grumpiness is an inseverable aspect of his character."

"Not unlike the remaining hints of my Irish accent."

"Except," Niles said, "your accent is beautiful. His grumpiness is tiring."

"Do you truly like m' accent?" Penelope asked. "So few in England seem to think well of it. We're taught from so young to affect an English manner of speaking, though I never entirely managed it."

"Few in England care for a Cornish accent, so I can empathize."

She smiled softly. "You don't have a Cornish accent."

"I do now and then."

"Truly?" Her eyes pulled wide. "Could I hear it sometime?"

"You want to hear me talk West Country?" He couldn't imagine why.

She set her hand lightly on his arm. "I would love to. I really would."

The touch of her hand sent a tingle of awareness through him. Ladies had set their hands on his arm before—when being led out for a dance or when taking a turn about a room with him—but the experience had never resulted in anything but indifference. He didn't think poorly of those young ladies, nor did he think them unworthy of being thought well of. He'd simply discovered as a young man that he was not the sort of person who grew infatuated easily. He sometimes wondered if he was doomed to never fall in love. He wanted to. He knew he could be happy if he finally met someone his heart could be that wholly attached to. But he'd never even come close.

Until now.

A lifetime of feeling lonely and a little broken, then this Irish whirlwind arrived in his life, upending everything and making his hands tingle and his heart pound. It was exhilarating, yet somehow terrifying.

"I'm sorry there's nowhere for you to sit," he said, falling back on civilities while his mind was spinning. "This outbuilding is entirely empty."

She shook her head, still smiling, though no longer touching his arm. "No matter. I like being on my feet."

"So do I."

"So do I," Lucas enthusiastically called over to them.

It was both funny and a timely reminder that there were other people around. Niles said to Penelope, "Lucas is far less obnoxious when Julia is with him."

She laughed as she turned to Violet. "We should explain why we're here."

"Yes, of course." Violet stood with Kes's arm around her, though she spoke to them all. "Mr. Seymour has declared that he and his sister will depart for Ireland the day after tomorrow."

Though Niles felt certain he kept his expression neutral, the only way to describe what he felt in that moment was panic. He'd waited all his life to feel even an inkling of what the Gents had described when they'd experienced various adorations over the years, a tenderness that, according to those among them who were now married, had intensified and deepened as they'd fallen ever more in love with their now-wives. After a lifetime of wondering if he ever would, he felt the first minute whispers of that, and the lady who'd inspired it was leaving.

Violet continued on, oblivious to his anxiety. "Penelope has decided she doesn't want to go to Ireland; she would like to remain. But being a woman and laws and expectations being what they are, she can't simply stomp her foot and refuse to go."

Penelope wanted to stay. Hope began to glimmer once more.

"So, to give her time to sort everything out, we decided to borrow a page from Julia's book of ingenious strategy and utilize the same approach that kept Nicolette from being required to return to France when *her* brother made a similar declaration." Violet was one of the most enthusiastic people any of them had ever known. She was genuinely happy and optimistic, even more so now that she and Kes were building a life together. "As Julia is not here to make the offer, I would like to do so." Violet looked at her husband. "This impacts you, so we've come to ask if you have any objections. It wouldn't be a permanent arrangement, only until she can determine what is needed for her to take up residence at her property in Surrey."

"Of course," Kes said. "We'll do whatever we can to make certain her options remain open."

Violet turned to Penelope once more. "Shall we move forward with our plan, then?"

Penelope nodded eagerly. "Thank you," she said to Violet and Kes.

She was remaining for a time. Shifting from unspoken panic to soul-deep relief was proving exhausting. Niles had long bemoaned his lack of infatuations and adorations, but he was now beginning to suspect he'd unknowingly avoided years of swinging on an emotional pendulum.

"We also came in search of you all," Violet continued, "because this has arrived." She produced a letter from the small bag hanging from her wrist.

"Lucas," the Gents said in near unison.

"Actually," Violet said, "it's for Niles."

And the pendulum swung once more.

The letter was handed from Violet to Kes to Aldric to Niles, who didn't take a single breath as he watched it draw closer. Once it was in his hands, he eyed the inscription, and his heart dropped to the soles of his feet.

"*Est-ce que ça vient de ta famille?*" Henri guessed.

Niles nodded. "Grandfather's handwriting." Laws, this was going to be painful. "I've been expecting to receive word from him. The only real surprise is that it took him so long to write."

"What are the chances," Lucas asked, "that taking as long as he did means he was in a better mood when he wrote than he would have been otherwise?"

Niles gave him a dry look. "What do you think?" There was no avoiding the missive or the words contained therein. He took a quick breath and squared his shoulders. "Do excuse me," he said and walked out of the outbuilding.

He'd not gone far when he heard Penelope call after him. He turned and saw her rushing toward him.

"Niles." She reached him, her features pulled in concern. "Is your grandfather terribly angry, do you suppose?"

"He is far more likely to be disappointed. That has always been his way."

She looked ever more worried. "My father was like that as well. I hated when he was disappointed in me."

"I hope he would have been proud of you these past few weeks," Niles said. "You've done some remarkably brave things in pursuit of the future you deserve."

"So have you," she said firmly.

But he shook his head. "Hiding here instead of facing my family was a cowardly act."

"No. You were attempting to maintain some control of your own life, which should never have been something you were required to give up or fight for."

"Another of the Gents, Stanley—he's no longer with us—used to say something very similar to me. 'It is a travesty how many people have to fight so very hard simply to be granted the right to live the life they ought to have been permitted all along.'" Niles eyed his letter again. He didn't know what precisely it contained, but he would have to address it either way.

"Would it help if I sat with you while you read it?" Penelope offered. "I won't peek, I promise."

His first inclination was to reject the offer in favor of privacy. But his heart pleaded with him too loudly to be ignored. Having her nearby would help. It truly would. "I would appreciate that." He tentatively held out his hand, unsure if she would take it.

But she did. And the same tingle up his arm and to his heart that he had felt before returned, accompanied by a feeling of relief and peace and reassurance.

"There's a walled garden not terribly far from here," he said. "And there's a bench in there that we can sit on."

She nodded.

They walked hand-in-hand to the spot he had in mind. But one thing he hadn't thought of rendered the arrangement untenable. This being England, the bench was terribly wet from repeated bouts of rain that day. Her dress would be ruined and his trousers decidedly worse for the experience should they sit.

"We can just walk," she suggested. "We do both like being on our feet, after all."

"Yes, we do," he said, smiling despite the worry still clutching at him.

She walked at his side. But breaking the seal on the letter and opening it required both his hands, necessitating he release hers. He'd heard the other Gents say that letting go of a lady's hand was sometimes a very difficult thing to do. He understood that better now.

Niles,

It was an abrupt greeting, lacking in friendliness or nods to social niceties.

I am certain I needn't tell you the reason for my letter. But as you have not written nor returned to Cornwall, I suspect I <u>do</u>

need to express the utter disappointment and frustration we are all feeling. Embarrassment does not begin to touch on what we have experienced as a result of your foolishness and disloyalty. Your mother and grandmother are heartbroken. Your father is confused. I am simply disappointed.

When the late Mr. Cummings first argued in favor of granting you additional time before requiring you to marry, I was hesitant, fearing you might set your heart on someone unsuitable in the interim or miss an opportunity for a particularly good match. Never in my most vivid imaginings did I believe for a moment that you would take my generosity and burn it to ashes as you have done.

I took seriously my role in finding you a suitable match, even going so far as to find a lady who would bring property to a marriage so you would not be homeless and one whose interest in horses matched your own. I moved forward only once I felt hers was a disposition that could blend well with yours.

And this is how that effort is repaid.

Let us all pray Mr. Seymour and his mother do not bandy about the details of this fiasco. Our family name would be dealt a blow, and you, Niles, would find yourself with far fewer options moving forward.

—RG

He lowered the letter, thoughts spinning, his feet following the path of the garden without his mind paying the least heed. Grandfather had signed the letter with his initials, something Niles didn't think he'd ever done in their previous correspondences.

"Is it as horrible as you feared?" Penelope asked softly, still walking beside him.

In some ways, it was worse. His family was disappointed, yes, but not exclusively in his decision not to return to Cornwall. They had gone above and beyond what even he had realized in an attempt to find a match for him that they felt would bring him the most happiness and contentment. It hadn't been done out of convenience or a desire to be rid of him. Neither had the decision been made without giving consideration to his needs and wishes.

That he seemed not to appreciate that was what disappointed them.

And the fact that he hadn't even realized all that they had done for him left him disappointed in himself.

"I suspect I have a great deal of mending to do when I return to Cornwall."

"You are going back?"

"At some point, I have to." But leaving now meant missing the tournament that might see him able to obtain his land. And leaving Yorkshire also meant abandoning these first whispers of affection, which he'd waited for and longed for all his life.

Delaying his reckoning in Cornwall would make things worse with his family, but he knew he couldn't go now. He couldn't simply walk away when he felt the way he did about Penelope. He couldn't toss aside this unexpected possibility of love. He couldn't.

He *wouldn't*.

Chapter Nineteen

"I NEED TO SPEAK WITH you, Liam." Penelope had been trying to have a private conversation with her brother all afternoon, but he had proven impossible to pull aside. She wanted to talk to him about her decision to remain in Yorkshire before he heard about it from the others.

It had been only that morning that he had told her of their impending departure. So much had happened. So much had changed.

Liam stepped into her guest chamber, she having come upon him in the corridor, and motioned for her to say what she wanted to say.

"I have given thought to your plans to return to Ireland in two days' time," she said, "and I'm choosing to remain in England." Liam blinked a few times, his mouth turning downward. She pressed onward. "Fairfield is in England, and 'tis well past time I began establishing myself in this country."

"There are arrangements that must be made before you can live and travel in a country without your brother's presence to lend propriety to the situation."

"I have taken that into consideration," she said. "I am to act as Mrs. Barrington's lady's companion."

Liam looked undeniably confused. "How is being a lady's companion in another household meant to aid you in establishing yourself at Fairfield?"

His was a point well made, though she didn't mean to let it deter her. "As you said, there are arrangements that must be made. While I am deciding how I mean to set up my household at Fairfield, I will have a pleasant and proper situation without having to make the return journey to Ireland."

"Ireland is your home," he objected.

"Fairfield was always meant to be my home. I can't finish my preparations for living there from so far away."

He didn't appear the least convinced. "We have managed it thus far."

"Receiving quarterly reports on the property is not at all the same as preparing it to become a home and a functioning estate." She didn't mention her plans to make it a profitable horse property. The one time she'd hinted at that intended venture had resulted in a somewhat heated argument between them. Now was not the time to revisit the topic.

"This is an inexcusably impulsive decision." He moved as if to leave the room.

"We have always known I would make this move from Ireland to England," Penelope said, blocking his departure. "Until Mr. Greenberry's change of plans, I assumed the move would be made as part of the life adjustment of getting married. The order of things is simply being changed now."

"Simply?" He repeated the word. "A single lady cannot *simply* uproot and relocate at will without repercussions."

"Thus, my decision to begin the relocation to England with a temporary tenure as a lady's companion. There is nothing objectionable about that. I'll not be frowned on nor seen as bucking the conventions. And you have said yourself that this group of ladies and gentlemen are of the highest standing in Society. This arrangement will not be detrimental to my acceptance in England. It would actually elevate my standing."

But Liam shook his head all the more fervently. "You should not have imposed this arrangement on them. We aren't—"

"It was not my idea, and I didn't suggest it. The ladies do not wish for me to have to leave, and the gentlemen are pleased that I won't have to depart. I didn't impose myself on anyone."

He blinked a few times. "They want you to stay?"

Why should that surprise him so much? She wasn't in demand in Dublin society, but neither was she an outcast. "We've become friends."

His mouth twisted a little. "The gentlemen all went to Hamblestead today."

"I know."

"I wasn't included." A flash of embarrassment pulled at his expression. "I am never included in any of their excursions or even conversations outside of the evening entertainment."

"They have been friends their whole lives," Penelope said. "That is a brotherhood one doesn't join very easily."

Liam shook his head. "I wasn't expecting that. I had thought I'd made some progress toward being someone they at least acknowledged. Obviously, I was wrong."

She knew how it felt to be rejected. Her heart ached for him.

"We haven't been here very long. If you were to change your mind about leaving the day after tomorrow, you might make more headway."

Annoyance pushed much of the embarrassment out of his eyes. "You are already being invited to make your home with the Barringtons. But with more time and effort, *I* might have some hope of not being forgotten the moment I am out of sight?"

"That isn't what I was saying."

"It is." His mouth tightened. His entire demeanor dripped with irritation. "And it is always what you are thinking."

She couldn't even begin to make sense of that.

"If I tried a little harder, my estate could be more profitable again. If I had put in more effort, I could have found my footing in London. If I just put in the effort, I could find any number of gentlemen who would accept what you demanded in a potential husband." It wasn't mere annoyance in his eyes now; he was angry again. "If I made the journey to Yorkshire, the marriage arrangement I worked so hard on wouldn't come to naught. And now, if I will only endeavor to be patient, these exalted people who have already embraced you might minutely accept me."

Penelope couldn't manage a response. She'd not anticipated this at all.

"I have my own estate, acceptance in Dublin society, an English education, a sufficient income." He shook his head with tense movements. "But you continually manage to make me look and *feel* like a failure."

"I have never thought of you that way."

He looked away. "You treat me that way. You have for far too long, and I am not going to bear the brunt of your judgment any longer."

This difference of views was different from anything they'd experienced before. A chill crept down her spine, crawling over her skin like the icy fingers of an unexpected frost.

"It sounds to me like it is for the best that you are leaving," she said. "You'll not have to endure your interpretation of my opinions. Perhaps in time, you will realize that you are wrong about that."

He didn't appear to entertain even the slightest doubt in his judgment of her. If anything, his expression hardened all the more. "I know what it is you want in a husband and a future, and I have always known how slim the chances were of you finding it. But your stubborn refusal to accept that will see you only more deeply disappointed in the end, no matter the fine friends you have made."

"I choose to believe that I will find someone who will accept what I'm hoping for."

"The law is an odd thing, Penelope." He stepped around her and to her door. "You have your estate. Your trustees can see to the legal aspects of running it, sign contracts for you, that sort of thing. But they cannot sign marriage contracts on your behalf." He stepped into the corridor, then tossed back at her, "Only I can do that."

"What are you saying?" She followed him out.

"Marrying without a specific contract means the law applies with its defaults. Without a marriage contract that specifically bars your future husband from ownership of Fairfield, it will be his, legally and entirely. And without me to sign on your behalf, there can be no marriage contract preventing that."

"When the time comes—"

He stiffened his posture and squared his shoulders. "Penelope, you cannot simply say, 'Go away, Liam, I don't need you' until the day having me around would suddenly be terribly convenient for you, then twitch your finger and expect me to do your bidding."

"You, as you pointed out this morning, are the head of our family now. You cannot simply refuse the responsibilities that come with that."

"Family is more than a collection of people for you to use for your own benefit." Liam quite suddenly sounded very tired. "I keep waiting for you to realize that, but I'm beginning to think you never will."

Use for your own benefit. That was not what was happening between them. He had threatened to not sign a marriage contract should the need arise. *He* was turning his back on his family member, not the other way around. Yet he was attacking her.

He walked away from her. "Have the Barringtons decide what they mean to do about a lady's maid for you since Gracie is technically in my employ and, I suspect, would like to return to Ireland."

To her dismay, Penelope realized she'd not even thought of the impact of her decision on her abigail.

"I wish you luck, Penelope," he said as the distance between them grew. "Do what you feel you must. I intend to do the same."

Use for your own benefit.

Until the day having me around would suddenly be terribly convenient for you.

Do what you feel you must.

Penelope swallowed down the lump in her throat, pushing back with it a surge of unexpected emotion. She'd spent so much effort attempting to convince herself that she wasn't cruel or dishonest. Maybe her greatest shortcoming was selfishness.

Penelope had arrived for the evening meal that night more than a little nervous. She didn't know how Liam would behave or what he might say to her. But he had requested a tray in his room, sending the excuse that he wished to direct his valet in packing his belongings. Though no one in the group said as much, Penelope felt certain they all realized that not only did Liam's valet not need help doing his job, but he also didn't need to begin packing two nights before departure. No one was looking at her with disapproval, so Liam likely hadn't shared with any of them his evaluation of her character.

But he had told her, and that was enough. The passage of hours hadn't lessened the impact of his accusations.

Family is more than a collection of people for you to use for your own benefit. I keep waiting for you to realize that, but I'm beginning to think you never will.

When she'd ridden out on Midnight that morning, it had seemed a perfectly ordinary day. It had proven, instead, exhausting in every way. She'd had to change every plan she had. Moments of worry had mingled with heartwarming friendship. Niles had held her hand more than once, and he seemed to have warmed to her. Liam had torn her to pieces.

She sat in the drawing room among the other guests at Pledwick Manor in a state of self-reflective crisis after supper that night. Again. *People for you to use for your own benefit.* Were Liam's words of accusation true here as well? Mr. Layton was making room for her in his home because she had imposed upon him. His friends had all arrived to support Niles after he had desperately fled from a match *with her* that he didn't truly want. Violet was taking Penelope on as a lady's companion despite having no need of one.

People for you to use for your own benefit.

She hadn't intended to be thoughtless. She hadn't even realized she had been, which only seemed to strengthen Liam's argument.

"You are very quiet this evening, Penelope." At some point, Nicolette had sat beside her.

"My brother was not best pleased with my plans to remain," Penelope said. "We had an argument, I'm afraid."

"That is a difficult thing." Nicolette spoke as one who knew. "I managed to part with my brother on relatively good terms, but that was in question for quite some time. *Mon Henri*, sadly, is not so fortunate. He and his brother do not speak, and their sister is caught in the middle of it all."

"That must be very hard on Mr. Fortier."

Nicolette nodded. "*Oui.* It is."

Nothing in Penelope's interactions with the Frenchman indicated he was anything but selfless and considerate. Clearly, being at odds with one's family didn't *always* indicate a person was selfish. But it did sometimes.

Violet moved to sit with them, smiling as she so often did. "Kester and I have decided that we ought to visit Lucas and Julia and their two little boys once they have returned to Brier Hill. Then you will be able to meet his family."

"I would not wish to cause you further inconvenience," Penelope insisted. "I am certain I have already disrupted your plans."

Violet brushed aside that concern. "We live nearer to Julia and Lucas than any of the other Gents, and we visit each other quite often."

At least in this, Penelope wasn't being selfish. But there was no avoiding the new difficulty she needed to acknowledge. "My lady's maid will likely be returning to Ireland. If she does, that will leave me without an abigail. I can send word to my solicitors to authorize the expense of hiring a new maid, but that will take time."

"I am certain Digby has someone on his staff who could fill that role for the remainder of your time here if need be. And we could make the journey back home by way of Newcastle. You would more easily find a lady's maid there than in our tiny corner of the kingdom."

Again, she would be inconveniencing people. Would she have even given that a thought before Liam's lecture? She certainly hoped she would have, but she couldn't be certain.

Her gaze wandered to where Niles sat, a bit apart from the others, his expression pensive. His mind was heavy as well. The letter he had received from his grandfather had dampened his spirits as he'd read it. The impact hadn't seemed to lessen over the hours since.

He had said he would be returning to Cornwall. In that moment, she'd thought of how much she hoped he didn't make that return trip too soon. She wanted more time with him. And she'd not even given a moment's consideration to how selfish that was. If he needed to return home to his family to make amends and heal relationships there, he ought to do so, and she ought to support that because it was what was best for him.

Twitch your finger and expect me to do your bidding. 'Twas another of Liam's descriptions of her behavior that was hitting too close to home. She had made arrangements to stay in England, in part so she could get everything in place to begin her time at Fairfield but also because she hadn't yet given up on the possibility that she and Niles could make a match of things after all.

Her heart had grown tender toward him, and she didn't think he entirely disliked her. She'd made certain she could remain on the assumption that he would stay as well.

So many of the things she had assumed and depended on were crumbling all around her. She needed a surer foundation but hadn't the first idea anymore how to create one.

Chapter Twenty

A MAID FROM THE PLEDWICK Manor staff attended Penelope the next morning. Lucy was her name, and she showed herself to be both competent and friendly. Penelope was certain to thank her, the absence of Gracie reminding her of her failure to take her abigail's concerns into consideration before making a significant life decision. Lucy seemed pleased, though, so at last, Penelope had managed to do something right.

And she had decided during the course of a rather restless night that she meant to do something else right as well.

Dressed and ready for the day, she made her way not to the breakfast room but to Liam's guest chamber. He ought to know that she appreciated all he'd done and how hard he'd worked to bring about the match with Niles, no matter how it ended. She needed her brother to know that she loved him and that she would do better from then on to show him that she did.

But he was not there. Nothing was in the room but the furniture. The dressing table was empty. Nothing sat atop the bedside table. Penelope opened the clothespress only to find it bare as well. Every drawer in the lowboy was also empty.

It didn't make sense. Liam wasn't leaving until tomorrow. She knew that for a fact.

She knew well his tendency to be rash when he was upset or frustrated. She'd seen it time and again. But she hadn't expected this.

In that moment, an upstairs maid slipped inside the room, freezing on the spot when she saw Penelope.

"Beggin' your pardon, Miss Seymour. I'd not realized you were in here. I'll come back later to see to the room." She turned to go.

"Wait, please." Penelope took a single step toward her. "Is my brother . . . ? Has he gone?"

"Yes, miss. Left early this morning."

He left. Her gaze turned toward the window and the rain pelting the glass. "He left in this downpour?"

"Yes, miss."

He left. He left a day early in inclement weather rather than waiting. He left . . . without even bidding her farewell. Without giving her a chance to say goodbye.

How could she put things right now? Did he even want her to?

"Please, do step inside and see to your work," Penelope said to the maid still hovering in the doorway. "I'll not delay you in it."

"Thank you, miss."

Penelope stepped from the room her brother had abandoned with such alacrity. He was on his way back to Ireland while she had no idea where she was headed.

At home, when she was overwhelmed or upset or confused, she would choose whichever of her horses seemed most anxious to expend energy, and she would ride furiously for as long as they both could endure. She could do so even in a light rain. But a torrent like the one currently falling often led to disaster. She was a fearless rider but not a reckless one.

There would be no escaping the house to find respite in nature today.

Respite in nature.

There was but one way to claim that in horrible weather, and that was in a conservatory. Fortunately, she knew Pledwick Manor had one, though she'd not visited it yet. She slowly wound her way there, her thoughts growing heavier with each step.

Liam had abruptly left. It was a far more drastic action of protest than he'd ever taken before. How had the disagreement between them led to such a complete and horrible rift? It didn't make sense. How could she possibly fix this?

She wasn't the only one inside the conservatory when she arrived. A man she guessed was a gardener was tending to an orange tree. Penelope smiled at him as she passed, and he dipped his head before returning to his work.

The air was pleasantly warm and scented with the fragrance of flowers and citrus. And the space was quiet. Even the sound of the gardener's shears was soft and somehow soothing. Underneath it all was the patter of rain on glass.

Penelope released a breath and made a point of relaxing her shoulders. She could find a few minutes' solace here.

Liam had left, but she could write to him in Ireland. She could tell him in a letter all the things she'd intended to say that morning. Then he would at least know she hadn't wanted them to be at odds. He would know she cared about and appreciated him. And perhaps when he wrote back, he would express some sorrow at having not even said goodbye. Perhaps he would acknowledge how rash this current action was.

If he wrote back. That one word—*if*—pulled her spirits low once more. How had everything gone so very wrong so quickly?

Returning to Ireland would have cost her the chance to claim a future of her choosing and any hope of winning Niles's regard. But remaining in England, she was beginning to fear, might sever her connection to her family.

She needed something to give her some hope, to buoy her spirits. The peacefulness of the conservatory was helping, but she was struggling.

Her wanderings brought her to a section with bulb flowers, ones seldom seen outside of spring. On any other day, she would have thought it a nice bit of luck. But today, in this moment, the sight of snapdragons proved almost miraculous.

They were Niles's favorite flower; he'd told her so. But he'd also said they were all but impossible to find this time of year. Did he not realize Mr. Layton grew them in his conservatory?

Feeling a surge of excitement that at least momentarily lifted her heavy thoughts, she made her way back to where the gardener was working.

"Excuse me," she said.

He looked away from his trimming. To her relief, he didn't seem annoyed by the interruption.

"Might I have a small sprig of snapdragons, please?"

"Of course, miss." He stepped down from his short ladder and set his shears on the soil beneath the orange tree. "Only tell me which color you'd like."

It wasn't a question she'd pondered before. "Which is your favorite?" she asked as she walked with him back to the planter where the flowers were growing.

"I'm fond of the dark-purple ones," the gardener said.

"Then, that's the one I'd choose."

He allowed a quick smile as he walked very businesslike directly to the patch of snapdragons. He studied the various stalks for a moment before pointing to a petite sprig on one plant. The flowers were beautifully formed in miniature and were a gorgeous shade of deep purple. "How about this'n, miss?"

"Perfect."

He took a small pair of gardening scissors from a pocket in his work apron and, with combined gentleness and speed, snipped the delicate sprig of flowers, then handed it to her.

"Thank you," she said, taking it carefully. "This will brighten Mr. Greenberry's day. Snapdragons are his favorite flower."

"An excellent choice, that." The gardener glanced back at the many bulb flowers growing nearby.

"And thank you for taking such care of this conservatory. It's a lovely place."

His shoulders squared, and his chest puffed a bit. "I work hard at it, and I think it shows."

"It does."

He gave a quick nod. "I'm happy you've enjoyed it, miss."

"I'll let you return to your work." Penelope raised the sprig of snapdragons. "And thank you again for this."

Another quick nod.

Penelope slipped from the conservatory. Alone in the corridor, she carefully removed one of the straight pins along the neckline of her dress that held the tucker in place. There were ample others, so removing this one would not wreak havoc.

Having accomplished that, she went in search of Niles, or at least in search of someone who could tell her where he was. Her path crossed with a footman, who was able to point her in the direction of the library, where she found Niles.

Excitement added a bounce to her step as she crossed to him at the cherrywood desk. He looked up from the sheet of parchment he was writing on, smiled fleetingly, then looked back down.

She was interrupting. Again. And she hadn't even given a moment's thought to the possibility. Again.

"Forgive me. I shouldn't have interrupted you." She turned to go, horrified at her own lack of thoughtfulness.

But his voice stopped her. "Please don't leave, Penelope."

Penelope. Hearing him use her given name brought an unexpected burn of tears behind her eyes. Not scandalized or sad tears, but the sort that, if allowed to fall, would bring relief. Unfortunately, they would also bring a wave of embarrassment.

She didn't turn back, desperate to get herself under control once more, but she also didn't leave.

Behind her, she heard the scrape of chair legs on the wood floor. His steps were quiet. In the length of a breath, he had moved to where she stood, stepping around to face her.

"Please don't leave," he repeated softly.

She swallowed down the lingering emotion and smiled. "I brought you something." She held up the sprig of tiny flowers.

His brows shot upward. "Snapdragons."

"They are growing in the conservatory. They are your favorite, so I asked the gardener if I could have a sprig."

"You remembered."

"The first time in ages I didn't win a horse race? Of course I remembered."

"You also didn't lose," he said, "so I'm not owed a forfeit." He didn't laugh or really smile, but she'd come to know him well enough to realize he was enjoying himself.

"It's not a forfeit." She twirled the sprig of snapdragons. "I thought it would make a lovely buttonhole flower."

He looked down at his frock coat, then back up at her. "I think you're right."

She held it up, pointing with the sprig toward his lapel. "May I?"

She was all but certain she heard him swallow even as he nodded.

She slipped her fingers around the top edge of his coat and carefully threaded the stem through the buttonhole. Heavens, why were her fingers shaking? With great care, she pinned it in place.

"There are several varieties of snapdragon in the conservatory." She ran a fingertip over the topmost bloom. "I daresay you could find a different color to complement every frock coat you have."

She raised her eyes once more to find him looking not at the deep-purple blossoms but at her. His gaze was both soft and intense. Her heart raced but in a rhythm of eager anticipation. Dared she trust that? Dared she trust herself?

"Why do you like snapdragons so much?" she asked, her voice barely a whisper.

His sea-blue eyes didn't leave hers. "The blossoms are so tiny." He didn't speak any louder than she had. "If one doesn't look closely, each flower blends in with every other, and there seems nothing remarkable about any of them. But they are beautiful and unique. One need only be willing to make the effort to truly see it."

Penelope's heart swelled as he spoke. Her arms ached to wrap around him and lean into the quiet, unobtrusive strength of him, to tell him that *he* was worth the effort to truly see. It was not an impulse she had felt for any gentleman before.

"I should allow you to return to the letter you were working on." She tried to sound as though the ground beneath her were steady, no matter that it had felt less and less so all morning.

"I wouldn't object if I were entirely prevented from finishing it." He shook his head, seemingly at himself. "I am attempting to pen a response to the letter I received from my grandfather. Thus far, it is proving a very daunting task."

"Family can be a difficult thing," she said with a sigh.

Niles took her hand. That simple touch soothed her battered soul. "Yes, indeed."

"My brother left this morning." Again, a lump of emotion formed in her throat.

"I thought he was leaving tomorrow." That he appeared surprised was some reassurance that she hadn't entirely misunderstood Liam's plans.

"So did I."

Niles wrapped his other hand around the one of hers he already held, cocooning it in warmth and comfort. "That must have been a difficult leave-taking."

"He has done imprudent things before when he was upset, but this is different." She swallowed against the thickness in her throat. "He left without a single word, without telling me he was going, without bidding me farewell. He just left, as if saying goodbye to me didn't matter at all, as if I wouldn't want to say goodbye to him."

"Oh, Penelope." It wasn't pity that filled his voice but kindness and concern.

And with that simple response, he broke the dam that had been holding back all the overwhelming emotions she'd felt for days. Tears spilled over as her heart cracked painfully open.

Niles pulled her into his arms, and she clung to him. For the first time in memory, she simply let herself fall apart.

Chapter Twenty-One

"I HUGGED HER." NILES LOOKED around the sack of grain hung from the joists of the outbuilding Digby had given him use of. Aldric stood on the other side, stopping the bag from swinging. "I realize that's a pathetic thing for a gentleman of thirty to be both new at and exhilarated by, but—"

"Niles, I've known you for sixty years now—"

"Thirteen," Niles corrected with a laugh.

Aldric waved that off. "Semantics. The Gents have all known for as long as we've known you that you aren't one to feel an inclination toward physical shows of affection without a deep and abiding emotional connection. That does not and has not ever made you anything resembling pathetic."

"The *ton* would disagree."

"Pummel while you talk, Niles," Aldric said. "You need to be ready for this tournament."

Niles raised his fists once more. "I never ignore an order from the General."

"Rubbish. Every one of the Gents has ignored orders from the General over the years. To your cost, I would add."

Aldric resumed his braced position on the other side of the grain bag. Niles returned to his series of punches and jabs, repeatedly changing the angle and force in an effort to make certain his muscles remembered how.

"Do you suppose Penelope let me hold her because she . . . feels . . . ?" Niles couldn't bring himself to finish the question, so he focused on his punches once more.

"When you were holding her," Aldric asked, "did she pat you awkwardly on the back while pulling away? Or look at you the way one would a cut of venison that had gone off?"

Niles paused and looked at his friend. "Does that often happen when a man hugs a woman?"

"Apparently." Aldric preened a bit. "Personally, I've never had any complaints."

"I remember quite a few complaints from Céleste Fortier." Niles landed a solid blow with his left.

"Those complaints were lodged against our idiot brothers," Aldric pointed out.

"I am going to tell Henri you said he's an idiot."

Aldric shook his head. "You know perfectly well I meant Jean-François."

"But you said, 'Céleste Fortier's brother is an idiot.' Henri is her brother. Therefore . . ."

"People looking in on the Gents from the outside insist you are a quiet, sheepish person," Aldric said dryly.

Niles laughed again. "They'd never believe I was the only one amongst all of us who campaigned to be included in the group and the one most able to beat the others to an absolute pulp."

"Far too many people have underestimated you, Niles. Let us hope your opponents at the pugilistic tournament do as well."

"I heard it whispered in Hamblestead that there is some hope that Sam Martin will be among those vying for the purse," Niles said.

The revelation had precisely the impact it ought. Aldric looked both impressed and concerned. "Blazes, Puppy. He'll murder you."

"He's a clean fighter." Niles landed two successive punches at just the angle and force he wanted. "I might very well get pulverized, but I'm highly unlikely to actually die."

Aldric stepped away from the grain bag.

"Did I mention that my likelihood of death decreases significantly if I work very hard in the time I have left before the fair?" Niles watched his friend, unsure what strategy the General could possibly have in mind that involved halting the exercises prematurely.

"I wasn't going to suggest you give up," Aldric said. "I just thought it would be a good idea for you to practice swinging at something that's moving."

"And that something would be you?" Niles grinned. "I may not be Martin's equal, but I did win a decisive victory against Will Ward."

"I was there for that fight, Niles," Aldric said. "Absolutely brilliant. You were also young and spry then, not the aged Puppy you are now."

"I'm barely older than you are."

"But still, you *are* older." After tossing him a pitying look, Aldric grabbed two small horsehair cushions Digby had managed to procure. Knowing a good valet needed to be skilled with a needle and thread, Digby had talked Wilson through the logistics of sewing strips along the back that hands could be slipped under, allowing the one holding the cushions to do so with palms extended.

"Jab at the one I hold up," Aldric instructed.

It was one of Niles's favorite exercises, focused as it was on improving his speed and dexterity. He was not large, and though he felt he could land a fearsome blow, he was also well aware that he hadn't the bone-crunching power of fighters such as Humphries and Johnson. But Niles was quick, and that had seen him emerge the champion in what ought to have been easy victories for his opponents. He needed to make certain that aspect of his methodology was polished to a shine.

While holding cushions for Niles to hit, Aldric took up the topic Niles thought had been abandoned. "So, during this hug you were inflicting on Penelope—"

"Surely *inflicting* is not the right word." Niles was nearly certain the General was joking.

"She seemed to welcome the embrace, then?"

Niles jabbed at a cushion. "She was sobbing at the time, so it is a little"— he jabbed again—"difficult to say."

"Was she sobbing because you were hugging her, or were you hugging her because she was sobbing?"

"The latter." Another jab. "But also because I really, really wanted to."

"And she didn't object?" It did Niles's pride a great deal of good that Aldric didn't seem to believe Penelope had been repulsed by the embrace.

"I think she felt better afterward." Sensing he'd just opened himself up to a bit of Gents-style teasing, he quickly added, "And during."

Kes, Lucas, and Henri came bounding into the outbuilding in the very next instant.

"The talk at the Green Badger is focused exclusively on the tournament." Lucas gave Niles a shove as he passed, then mimed punching him a few times. "Word has spread that the Cornish Duke will be fighting for the first time in years." They all gave Niles a knowing look. "And the innkeeper has confirmed that the Bath Butcher *will* be fighting."

Sam Martin, the Bath Butcher. The man was a legend, though not an undefeated one. However, he also hadn't gone as long without fighting competitively as Niles had.

"My best hope," Niles said, "is that if Martin does join, he and I won't meet until the final match. Second place comes with prize money. Being knocked out of the tournament early does not."

A look passed between the three new arrivals. There was more they hadn't told him.

"What is it?" Aldric had clearly seen the unspoken exchange as well.

Kes spoke for them all. "With word that both the Duke and the Butcher are vying for the purse, all the other fighters have withdrawn. It's not to be a tournament any longer but a single fight."

"And the purse has been increased," Henri said. "It is now £200 for the victor, £100 for the one he pummels."

Niles nodded. "I can endure a pummeling for £100. It would be enough that I could try to negotiate to buy the property I've had my eyes on."

Aldric studied him. "Why are you so certain you won't win?"

"I've seen Martin fight. He wasn't felled by blows far more forceful than I am able to deliver. And he blocks blows very efficiently. Not to mention he's bigger than I am."

"Humphries is smaller than Mendoza," Lucas said, "but he was the victor in their last bout."

That wasn't the reassuring argument Lucas seemed to think it was. "I have a chance of not being killed by Martin; Humphries would annihilate me."

"I've seen Martin fight as well," Aldric said, "and he isn't as fast as you are. I think speed is the Cornish Duke's greatest asset."

"Even if I were quick enough to evade his blocks," Niles said, "I cannot hit as hard as most of the opponents he has defeated."

"But land enough blows and you'll have the same impact," Kes said.

"I do not intend to simply not try." Niles began to get the impression that his friends feared he had abandoned hope altogether. "I've learned over a great many matches that approaching the ring knowing what my disadvantages are decreases my chances of being carried away limp and lifeless."

"Best watch yourself, General," Lucas said. "Puppy is vying for your role as master strategist."

Though Aldric could give the impression of being hardened and distant, those who knew him best were well aware that he was thoughtful and considerate and not easily offended. To Niles, he said, "Add this to your stratagem: knowing your disadvantages is helpful in avoiding an unmitigated beating, but knowing your *advantages* is helpful if you want to win."

Niles emptied his lungs in a woosh of breath. "I wouldn't mind winning."

Aldric gave a single, almost curt nod, then held up one of the horsehair cushions again. "Hit the one that's up."

Chapter Twenty-Two

NILES THOUGHT IT A GOOD sign that he was neither exhausted nor sore when his afternoon's exercise ended. Experience told him the aching muscles usually made themselves known the day *after* a particularly strenuous return to pugilistic practice, but he usually felt at least a little of it after the passage of a few hours. This time, however, he mostly felt invigorated.

A good sign, indeed.

And as if fate wanted to make amends for the misery of the past few months, he was handed another good sign as well. Penelope sat beside him on a settee in the drawing room when everyone gathered there after supper, and she did so with such natural ease that he felt certain her motivation was simply that she enjoyed his company.

"You appear to be in better spirits this evening," he said.

"I am feeling a little less despondent. I followed your lead and decided to send a letter." She smoothed her skirts but not in a nervous or uncomfortable way. "Of course, I had to guess which inn my brother will be stopping at for the night. There is every chance my letter will not reach him, but I had to at least try."

"You, then, are doing better than I am. I never did manage to finish my letter."

She turned a little, facing him more directly. "Is it that you don't know what to say or that you're afraid what you wish to say will only make the situation worse?"

"A little of both."

Penelope set her hand atop his. "I am sorry, Niles. I am sorry this is all so painfully complicated."

He turned his hand enough to properly hold hers, then did his utmost to ignore how his heart pounded at the simple connection. His inexperience with such things was rendering him rather pathetic, no matter that Aldric had insisted otherwise. "That our situation is so messy isn't your fault, Penelope."

He held his breath, waiting to see if she would object to his use of her given name. She had just used his, so he felt himself on firm footing, but he was still nervous.

"It isn't entirely *not* my fault though." No dismay or disapproval touched her face or words, so she must not have been upset at his informality. "Perhaps if you wrote to your family and told them that I hold no ill-will over all that has occurred, they might breathe a little easier. Had there been any indication in the letters sent to Liam that you were not eagerly accepting of the arrangement, I'd not have chosen to move forward. So, truth be told, we might lay quite a lot of this mess at *their* feet."

She offered the olive branch with just enough impishness to bring a smile to his face. A bit of teasing, he had learned early in his years among the Gents, went a long way toward easing worries and burdens.

"I shall toss out what I have started in my letter and begin anew. My second attempt will read simply, 'Grandfather, this is all your fault.' That ought to tidy things up nicely."

How was it that the mere sight of her smile tied his stomach in such pleasant knots?

Her gaze dropped for just a moment, then her eyes widened a bit. "What happened to your hand?"

That pulled his attention to their entwined hands. His right, sitting atop hers, sported a cut on one knuckle. It wasn't long or deep, but it was that angry shade of red that indicated a relatively new injury. He'd wrapped his hands in strips of muslin that afternoon to reduce the bruising and such, not wanting to go into the upcoming fight with hands already in horrible condition, but he'd still managed to split the skin over one knuckle.

How did he explain the injury to her without confessing to what he'd been doing and why? A gentleman taking up boxing for prize money was unacceptable, the very reason he fought under a false name and even took pains to disguise his appearance as much as was permitted. If his exploits were known, it would ruin him.

"I cannot say with certainty precisely when it happened." That was entirely true. "But I can say I was with the Gents when it did."

She laughed lightly. "That I believe."

"We tend to get into mischief when we are together."

"From what I am discovering," she said, "so do the Gents' ladies."

And easy as that, the topic was turned. She didn't press for a larger explanation, didn't insist she disapproved of whatever he might have been doing that resulted in an unsightly gash. She simply sat beside him, leaving her hand in his, looking entirely content with the arrangement. And he, who had never felt a significant draw toward any lady, wanted nothing more than for her to stay precisely where and as she was. He wanted to hold her hand, to listen to her talk, to watch her eyes dance when she was stifling a laugh. All the while, the scent of the sprig of snapdragons he'd asked his valet to move from his morning coat to his evening one reminded him that she thought of him even when they were apart. Unlike so many others, she didn't forget him when he wasn't nearby.

"Friends." Digby stood in front of the group. "Tonight, I propose we play a parlor game."

"We always play parlor games," Kes pointed out.

"This time, though," Digby said, "it will be one of my own invention."

Oh, lud.

"We will divide into two teams. I will then draw two slips of paper containing concepts or things that must be incorporated into a poem composed by each team. The best poem will be declared the winner of that round. We will play as many rounds as we choose, and those with the most wins will be granted the right to choose tomorrow night's after-supper entertainment."

Penelope leaned a bit closer to Niles and asked in a whisper, "Do the Gents often compose group poetry?"

"This is the first time that I know of." He glanced at Henri and saw a nod pass between him and Digby, confirming Niles's suspicions. Henri was secretly a published poet and, it seemed, either wanted to practice composing or was looking for something to inspire his next poetic effort. Penelope was the only one in the group who didn't know of Henri's occupation. It wasn't Niles's secret to share.

"Is the expectation that the offerings be silly or that they be impressive?" Penelope asked Niles.

"Both."

She smiled at him. *At him.* He didn't think he would ever grow tired of that. "I suspect I can manage ridiculous poems that show no aptitude. Fortunately for me, that is apparently acceptable."

"And expected," he added.

Her hand was still in his. He'd not yet been certain of Penelope's feelings, but he was getting an inkling. *Please don't let me be mistaken in this.*

Digby drew from a crystal bowl one name after another, creating their two teams. Aldric, Henri, Kes, and Digby constituted one. The other consisted of

Lucas, Violet, Nicolette, Penelope, and, to Niles's delight, himself. That meant Penelope could continue sitting beside him. They could talk. He would be able to hear her laugh, see her smile. She wasn't holding his hand any longer, but she hadn't left his side. And he truly didn't want her to.

"Now that we have our teams," Digby said, "let us obtain our first poetic prompt. Our poems must include"—he drew a slip of paper from a different bowl, this one white porcelain with blue designs—"a cat and"—he drew from yet another porcelain bowl—"a tricorn hat." He shook his head. "Best of luck, all."

Niles and Penelope's group had all gathered around the settee, Lucas on Niles's other side and the two ladies in chairs that had been procured for them.

Nicolette spoke first. "I daresay the suggestion of a cat and a tricorn has led us all to think of the same thing: *Le Chat botté.*"

Remembering Penelope had said her French instruction had been virtually nonexistent, Niles leaned closer and translated for her, "The Puss in Boots."

"Ah." She nodded emphatically. "That is precisely what came to my mind. He is nearly always depicted as wearing a tricorn hat."

"Our question, then," Violet said, "is whether we wax poetic about this fairy-tale feline or take a different approach altogether."

Lucas jumped in. "I, for one, can now say that if we don't get to use the phrase 'fairy-tale feline' in our offering, I will be forever disappointed in us."

They all laughed. But though it was Lucas who had offered the quip, Penelope smiled at Niles.

The evening continued on that way. Someone in the group said something funny or entertaining, and Penelope exchanged a look of delight with Niles. Not once did she give so much as a fleeting indication that she was displeased or disappointed in his relative quietness. He had never felt pressure from the Gents to be more outgoing or talkative than he was. That had helped him not feel hurt when he'd been overlooked or forgotten about when they were in public. Those who knew him best liked him as he was.

He'd lived decades in fear of his family choosing for him a wife who didn't accept or comprehend the person he was. In the end, Grandfather had managed to find a lady who was proving very nearly perfect, and Niles had rejected and abandoned her.

What a muttonhead I am.

"I believe this had best be our final round," Digby declared after two hours of alternately impressive and ridiculous poetry. He drew forth two slips of paper. "Cheese. And . . ." A laugh sputtered from him. "Cornwall."

"Unfair!" Kes called out. "They have Puppy on their team."

"And you have Archbishop on yours," Penelope said. "He has shown himself a more adept poet than the rest of us combined."

That had them all laughing again, though she most certainly did not realize the entire reason why.

That felt a little unfair, but fortunately, Nicolette was in their group and knew the extent to which Henri was comfortable with his situation being known. "Henri's course of study at Cambridge was poetry," she told Penelope. "It seems, after so many years, he still remembers some of what he studied."

"Ah." Penelope nodded, then stood and, in a dramatic posture, pointed at the other team. She declared in thunderous tones, "Unfair!"

That sent uproarious laughter through the room once more.

In the midst of it, Lucas leaned closer to Niles and said, "I wish Julia were here. She and your Penelope would be instant friends and mischief makers."

"She's not *my* Penelope," Niles insisted.

"Then, you, my friend, are not paying enough attention."

"To her or to myself?"

"To either one."

Penelope sat once more, grinning broadly and looking as though she couldn't have been happier with life. "This had best be the greatest poem ever composed on the topic of Cornish cheese," she warned them all in laughing tones. "I believe I have just staked all our reputations on it."

"Cornwall does produce some very delicious cheese," Niles said. "But I cannot say we are particularly famous for it."

"So, a poem about Cornwall's lack of famous cheeses?" Lucas suggested.

Nicolette nodded solemnly. "Such a tragic thing *must* be immortalized in verse."

After the allotted time had expired, the team elected Niles to be the one to share their offering, he being so closely connected to the subject matter.

> *Listen friends to my tale of woe,*
> *When down to the southern coast I go,*
> *Through towns and villages alike,*
> *I seek in Cornwall a tempting delight.*
> *But no lesson have I ever learned better:*
> *I must go to Somerset when searching for Cheddar.*

He took a sweeping bow amid the cheers and laughter of the group. This game Digby had invented would, perhaps, not actually prove helpful in Henri's professional endeavors, but it was proving an absolutely delightful way to pass an evening.

"With our final offering of the night . . ." Digby motioned to Aldric, which was almost as much of a shock as Niles being the representative of his team. Aldric was many things, but he was not a performer.

> *In vain I have tried to dismantle*
> *My love for Pont l'Eveque and Cantal,*
> *Gloucester and Cheddar, Wensleydale and Gruyère.*
> *Though many things try, none can compare.*
> *So let us embrace and pay true homage*
> *To the joy that we glean from delicious le fromage.*

As the room applauded, Penelope leaned closer to Niles. "Am I right in remembering that *fromage* is French for 'cheese'?"

He nodded, and her attention returned to the group. How easily and naturally she turned to him with questions and conversation. Niles was very unaccustomed to that.

Try as they might, a winner for the evening could not be decided on. The Gents could be competitive when they chose to be, but most of the time, they played games purely for the enjoyment of it. That night proved the same. They shrugged at their lack of a victor and declared the evening an unmitigated success.

The exertion of the day began to catch up with Niles, and he reluctantly excused himself for the remainder of the evening, intending to drop exhausted on his bed.

Penelope, however, followed him and pulled him aside at the edge of the corridor. It was empty at the moment, but enough people were still awake and still wandering about that it wasn't so private as to be scandalous.

"Thank you," she said.

"For what?"

"I'm certain that when I arrived here, you wanted nothing so much as to see me depart. But instead, you've allowed me to be part of this group, to be able to call them friends, and to know you better. I . . ." She seemed momentarily at a loss for words. "I have been lonely for a long time, Niles. I don't feel that way anymore. And I am so glad to know you—actually *know* you, not merely know the list of things I was told about you. So, thank you."

"I'm glad you came, Penelope." The sincere, heart-deep declaration spilled from him unbidden. "And I'm glad you stayed."

"So am I." She rose on her toes and pressed a feather-light kiss to his cheek before turning and slipping inside her room.

Niles didn't move for what felt like hours.

She'd kissed him. *She* had kissed *him*. And his world had tipped on its axis. He'd been hemming and hawing over his seemingly conflicted feelings. Then she'd kissed him, and there was no sense denying it any longer. He had fallen in love with Penelope Seymour.

Chapter Twenty-Three

LUCY ACTED IN THE ROLE of Penelope's lady's maid again the next morning. She was good at it and seemed to enjoy the assignment. Penelope meant to ask Mr. Layton if she could make an offer of employment to the young woman. It was possible Lucy had family nearby or didn't wish to leave Pledwick Manor, and Penelope didn't mean to try to force anyone's hand either way.

The weather was wet once again, and she was delayed in taking her daily ride. She didn't mind, which was a rare thing. The rain afforded her the opportunity to spend the morning gabbing amiably with Violet and Nicolette and blessing fate once more for this unexpected opportunity to make two new friends. And the two of them told her enough about Lady Jonquil, whom they insisted would want Penelope to call her Julia, that she felt as though she knew the lady already and had gained a *third* friend. The Gents had begun to feel like friends as well.

And Niles . . . Well, Niles felt like something more. Something even better.

By early afternoon, the rain had ceased falling for a couple of hours. The grounds would be dry enough for a not-too-miserable ride. With Lucy's help, she changed into her emerald-green riding habit and quickly made for the stables. She hadn't ridden at all the day before, and she was anxious to be on horseback again.

Upon reaching the stables, however, she was distracted as she so often was by the filly. The little horse was standing in the midst of her small pen, being brushed by a stablehand.

"She is doing so much better," Penelope said, indicating the arrangement.

"She ain't so afeared of us as she has been," the stablehand answered.

There was something so heartwarming in watching an animal learn to trust people who were worthy of that trust. It was a connection that wrapped the soul in hope.

"Has she a name yet?"

The stablehand shook his head. "Haven't come upon one that suits her."

"She needs an elegant name."

"That she does."

The groomsman who had ridden out in search of Liam to deliver Penelope's letter happened past in the next moment.

"Did you find Mr. Seymour?" she asked him.

He doffed his hat. "I did, Miss Seymour. You guessed right on the inn he stopped at."

"And you gave him my letter?"

"I did, miss." He reached into the pocket of his coat, still muddied from the road, and pulled out a sealed letter. "He asked me to give you this."

Liam had sent a letter back. That had to be a good omen, didn't it? She took the letter, nervousness and excitement warring inside. This was likely similar to how Niles had felt upon receiving the letter from his family—hoping it contained words of reconciliation but fearing the letter held only more rejection.

"Mr. Greenberry doesn't happen to be out for a ride just now, does he?" Niles liked to ride as much as she did, after all, and the weather was finally clear enough.

"I don't know, miss."

But from the filly's pen, the stablehand chimed in. "I saw him aiming for the outbuilding he and the other gentlemen have been making use of, miss."

The Gents would be there. "Thank you."

She hurried in the direction of the outbuilding. She held fast to Liam's letter, unable to convince herself to feel relief at having received word from him. The possibility that he had written to denounce her again felt far too heavy.

But one thing she was certain of: she would feel better if Niles were with her while she read it.

He'd held her hand so tenderly. It had taken all her self-control not to simply curl into him and plead with him to hold her as he had when Liam had abandoned her. There had been such comfort in his embrace. She'd felt safe and cared about, and her heart had all but burst out of her chest. But the drawing room, surrounded by all the other Pledwick Manor guests, was not the place for throwing herself into the arms of a gentleman who wasn't related to her. An outbuilding in full view of the Gents wasn't either. But they couldn't object to Niles being at her side while she read a letter.

As she approached her destination, she heard the oddest sound: a repetitive thud, almost like the sound of carpets being beaten. Why such a thing would be undertaken inside a building, she couldn't say. The Gents indulged in some odd larks, to be sure, but this didn't seem like one of them.

Afraid that whatever it was would stop if they were alerted to her arrival, Penelope walked slowly and quietly to the door of the outbuilding, deeply curious. She peeked inside, then froze on the spot.

Niles was alone, standing in front of an enormous burlap bag hanging from the ceiling, punching it. That was not the most shocking bit though. He was stripped to the waist, revealing more rippling, glistening muscles than she even knew existed.

Good gracious.

Upon first glance, under ordinary circumstances, most everyone would describe Niles as small, and not merely because he was the shortest of his friends. He gave the impression of slightness. But heavens, seeing him shirtless, his muscles flexing as he delivered one crushing punch after another, she knew he was anything but flimsy.

Good gracious.

As she stood there, too astonished to speak or move or make sense of anything, Niles happened to look over at the door.

"Penelope." His eyes pulled as wide as hers must have been. He began frantically looking about, likely searching for his shirt.

The blush of embarrassment that inched up his neck pulled her out of her stupor. She turned away a little, setting her eyes on the doorframe. "I hadn't realized this outbuilding had been converted into a boxing salon, otherwise I would have . . ." What would she have done? "Knocked, I guess. Except the door was open."

Over the sound of his frantic footsteps, Niles said, "I would have kept the door closed, but it had grown overly warm in here."

"My brother once told me he enjoyed a bit of boxing while at school." Penelope kept her eyes diverted as she spoke. "Pugilism is, apparently, not unpopular amongst gentlemen, young and old. Not that I'm saying you are old; you just aren't a schoolboy any longer, clearly. I don't mean 'clearly' to indicate that I was studying you and came to that conclusion. I—I simply—I need to stop talking." Merciful heavens, she was flustered.

"It is certainly a popular sport, though *actual* bouts fall outside the bounds of acceptable gentlemanly pursuits." Niles took an audible breath. "I suspect I would, nevertheless, have an impromptu bout with your brother on my hands if he knew I'd appeared in front of you bare-chested." His voice grew louder as he drew nearer. "I am sorry about that."

He wouldn't have moved to stand by her were he still without his shirt-sleeves, so she hazarded a glance. He was dressed once more, though only in his pantaloons and untucked shirt. It was entirety possible he didn't have anything else there, having had no reason to expect company.

"You are not the one needing to apologize," she insisted. "'Twas I who intruded on your privacy."

"Then, let us agree that our moment of awkwardness was neither of our faults and we both are to be considered utterly blameless."

"I think that is a brilliant strategy." Her panic began ebbing. She took a breath, the first full one she'd drawn since stepping inside. "How often do you box?" Curiosity was quickly replacing her befuddlement. "A lot of effort was put into transforming this space, and at least at the moment, you are the only one taking advantage of it."

"Quite often, when I am able. I have a similar space to this at my parents' estate in Cornwall, and I patronize an establishment in London." He wiped at a trickle of sweat making its way down his chin. Doing so drew attention to the strips of fabric wrapped around his knuckles.

A realization landed on her mind. "This is how you hurt your hand yesterday. The cut on your knuckle."

He nodded. "Probably. I don't remember it happening specifically, but I was in here most of the afternoon."

He really did enjoy the exercise, then. "You told me when we first met that you enjoyed athletic endeavors. I could tell you meant it in the context of horse riding, and you clearly enjoyed the game of ground billiards. I am beginning to suspect you are more of a sportsman than most people would guess."

Niles snatched up a rag and wiped the perspiration from his brow and neck. "I am small and tend to be quiet. People make a lot of assumptions based on that."

"Believe me, I understand."

"You are tiny; I won't argue with you on that score. But—" He seemed to suddenly think better of the remainder of his comment.

"You were about to insist that I am not, in fact, quiet."

His lingering blush turned furiously red once more.

Penelope set her hand on his arm. "I am the one who told you about my nickname of the Little Banshee. I am not unaware that I am far from silent. I am also perfectly and wonderfully content to simply be at peace when I am able."

"You fight when you need to," he summarized, "and cherish times of serenity all the more, as a result."

She had never known anyone who seemed to understand her as well as he did. Even her father, who had been the one in her family to comprehend most the person she was, had struggled. "I suspect you are the same, Niles. Peace and contentment are important to you, but that doesn't mean you won't fight when that is what is needed."

He set his hand atop hers. It felt odd, wrapped in fabric as it was, but there was still such comfort in his touch. "We are proving more and more alike, you and me." He then adjusted his hand so he was holding hers, pulling it away from his arm. "What was it that brought you out here looking for me?"

She had all but forgotten. "The letter I sent to Liam reached him last night at the inn."

"You guessed right, then." He sounded genuinely pleased for her.

"And he wrote back."

"Did he?"

She glanced at the letter once more. "But I'm nervous about what it might say, so I came here, hoping you would hover nearby while I read it."

"You did the same for me when my family's letter arrived," he said. "I'd be honored to return the favor." He motioned her toward two well-worn chairs under one of the small windows.

Already feeling more equal to discovering what her brother had to say, Penelope took a seat and waited for Niles to do the same. With him beside her, soothing her nerves, she turned the letter over and broke the wax seal. She unfolded the parchment and read.

Penelope,

No "Dearest Sister" or "My Dear Penelope." When he'd written to her while away at school, he'd begun his letters with variations on those two tender greetings.

> *I am not certain what to write in response to your letter. I do appreciate that you made the effort, and I am grateful that you have acknowledged the effort I have expended and the frustrations I have endured on your behalf these past weeks and months. But you also insisted you will not abandon your current course.*
>
> *I am now charged with explaining to our mother why you have abandoned Ireland altogether without so much as a farewell to her. When Dublin society wonders where you have disappeared to, I will be required to formulate some explanation*

that does not portray me as a browbeaten brother or that would undermine Mother's standing.

More worrisome than those consequences, though, are the ones you are courting for yourself. Mr. Greenberry might not have chosen to move forward with the arranged match, but your choice to move forward with your ill-advised requirements for Fairfield will all but guarantee that no one who is worthy of you will ever consider you again. And that, Penelope, is an utter shame.

Something in the hint of kindness with which he ended his otherwise painful summary of her difficult situation brought a thickness to her throat.

Should you have a change of heart before moving forward with this folly, I will be returning to Ireland by way of first London, as I have friends there whom I have not seen in some time, and then Cornwall, wishing to offer my gratitude to the Greenberrys for their hospitality and my apologies for the way things ended.

I wish you luck in the path you have chosen, Penelope. And I will endeavor to formulate a version of events that will neither alarm our mother nor give her reason to think poorly of her daughter.

Write to me now and then and let me know how you are faring. We may not be in agreement about this, but I do not wish to be forever at odds.

Yours, etc.
Liam

Chapter Twenty-Four

PENELOPE HAD HOPED TO DISCOVER words of reconciliation in Liam's letter but had been mentally preparing herself for utter rejection. That what she'd received was a little bit of both and a tremendous amount of what felt like unshakable resignation hurt even more than she'd anticipated. If Liam had been boiling mad at her, there would have been some hope that when his anger cooled, they could mend the current breach.

"Your expression matches how I felt reading my family's letter," Niles said softly, still sitting beside her, "which worries me."

She let the letter rest on her lap. "I wrote to him with such high hopes, telling him how much I love him and want him in my life, how I didn't want there to be a rift between us. I pleaded with him to consider returning to Pledwick Manor, or staying at Fairfield for a time, so we needn't be separated by an entire sea. I offered an entirely sincere olive branch."

"And he rejected you?" Niles took her hand once more. He had unwrapped his hands while she'd been reading her letter.

"Have you ever read a letter that felt like a shrug?" she asked.

"He expressed indifference, then?"

"Worse even than that. Indifference with an ultimatum." Whatever she might have been expecting, it would never have been that. "He says no one will ever marry me so long as I retain ownership of Fairfield and that if I decide to be flexible about that, he might be willing . . . not to keep trying to find me a husband, necessarily, but to even just see me again." Her posture drooped; she couldn't help it. "My mother might refuse either way."

Niles rubbed her hands gently between his. "You don't speak of her often."

"She can be . . . difficult." Penelope shook her head. "Appearance and social cachet are everything to her. So long as I am bolstering her standing and contributing to the flawless facade she insists on, she's pleased with me. Otherwise, I'm a waste."

"You have never been a waste, Penelope. Not ever. And you never will be, regardless of what anyone, including your family, says."

She leaned her head against his shoulder. "I gave up on my mother long ago, I'm afraid. I keep the peace with her, but I have no expectation of affection. But I thought Liam . . . I never thought he would turn away from me so entirely."

"Would you ever consider giving up your claim on Fairfield in order to reconcile with him?"

The very idea struck painful fear directly to her heart. "I've known Fairfield was mine from the time I was a little girl. It was a source of strength and reassurance my whole life. Women have so little power over any aspect of our existence. Our residence, income, comings and goings, our very persons are, by law, not our own. Any and all of those things can be taken from us on a whim. We spend so much of our existence desperately trying not to upset those who have the power we are prevented from having, knowing our survival depends upon it. But Fairfield meant I always had something that couldn't be taken away. So long as I had that estate and the ability to make it what I chose, I could breathe. If I lose Fairfield, I will be holding my breath for the rest of my life. Liam doesn't understand that at all. I don't think the men of this country truly realize how chronically starved of air the women truly are."

"Do you know what I think, Penelope Seymour?"

The question was kindly worded, but she felt herself grow tense just the same. "That I talk too much and have too many opinions?" She'd certainly been told that before. Her mother had often made that very declaration.

"No."

She looked over at him at last, fully expecting to see pity in his expression. What she saw was mischief.

"I think," he said, "you need to hit something."

"I *what*?" A laugh bubbled without warning.

"You need to curl your hands into fists, think of all the things and people who are frustrating you, then hit something as hard as you possibly can."

"Are you volunteering?"

He grinned almost wickedly, which she found she liked very much indeed. "While I confess I would probably enjoy sparring a bit with you, I was going to suggest the bag of straw I was pummeling when you first arrived." He motioned to it hanging from the rafters.

The thought of him when she'd first arrived sent a wave of awareness over her that she quickly tucked away. Liam thought her scandalous for wanting to run Fairfield as she saw fit; he'd have apoplexy if he knew she was struggling not to swoon at the memory of Niles Greenberry shirtless and rippling muscled.

"Is there a trick to hitting a bag of straw?" she asked.

"There's some technique, but when undertaken for therapeutic purposes, the most important thing is vehemence."

"Will you show me how?"

He was still holding her hand, so it was easy as anything to walk with him back to where he'd been standing earlier.

She set her letter on a windowsill nearby, then stood facing the bag. "Do I just hit it?"

"Let's get you positioned first. Make a fist, and hold your arm out in front of you, as if you've just hit the bag."

She did as instructed, her right fist just barely grazing the edge of her target.

Niles stood behind her and set his hands on her shoulders. "You need to move a little closer to the bag." He nudged her toward it.

"But this close, my extended arm goes past the edge of the bag," she said.

From surprisingly near her ear, he said, "It's supposed to."

And before she could sort out why the tickle of his breath on her neck was so enjoyable, he stepped away, walking to where her fist hovered beside the bag.

He took her hand in his and tapped a finger on her thumb. "Your thumb needs to be outside your fist, not inside."

"Wouldn't it be safer, better protected like that?"

He gently extricated her thumb. "It's more likely to be broken if tucked inside."

"This is more dangerous than I thought."

He set her thumb atop the first knuckles of the neighboring fingers, then ran his thumb lightly over it. "Yes, it is," he whispered.

All thoughts momentarily fled her mind at the slow, lingering brush of his fingers. Something about having seen such irrefutable proof of how strong he truly was made the gentleness of his touch all the more upending.

He seemed to re-collect himself before she did. A quick breath and he was back on task. "Pull your right arm back now, bent at the elbow. And set your right foot a little farther back than your left. Not overly much—you don't want to throw off your balance—but a little."

She adjusted her feet, making changes as he suggested them.

"Your arm and shoulder position is important too." Niles set his hands on her shoulders and adjusted the angle so she faced the bag but with her left shoulder a little forward and her right a little back. His hands slid to her arms, tucking her elbows in and raising her fists up toward her face.

She tried to pay attention to his explanation, but his hands on her arms, even through the thick layers of her riding coat, were incredibly distracting.

His hand wrapped around her right fist. Heavens, it was difficult to even breathe.

"As you punch the bag, thrust your right shoulder forward with it, and twist your arm so your fist hits the bag straight on. And hit it with your knuckles, not the flat of your fingers."

Penelope nodded. It was impossible to actually speak.

Niles let go of her hand, much to her dismay. He placed himself on the other side of the hanging bag, his shoulder leaning into it and his hands holding it in place. "Whenever you're ready, Penelope. Think of everything and everyone who has cut off your air over the years, and hit the bag with every ounce of frustration you feel."

She closed her eyes for just a moment. She thought of those in Dublin society who had made her feel so unwelcome. Of being labeled the Little Banshee by her neighbors. Of Mother wishing aloud that Penelope's beauty hadn't proven an utter waste. Of Liam abandoning her and brushing aside her attempts to make things right.

She tensed her arms and shoulders and opened her eyes once more. She followed Niles's instructions as precisely as she could. Her clenched knuckles stung as they made contact with the rough burlap. But it was a cleansing sting. Invigorating.

A surge of excitement swept over her. "Niles!"

He stepped out from around the bag, grinning as if she'd just won some sort of pugilistic championship; she assumed such a thing existed. "It's very satisfying, isn't it?"

She bounced, something she hadn't done in ages. "Amazing. May I hit it again?"

He laughed as he returned to his position of keeping the bag from flying about. "Whenever you're ready, Penelope."

She hit it again, harder this time now that she knew she wouldn't miss. It really was tremendously satisfying. She spun around, laughing with delight.

"Careful," Niles said, a smile in his tone. "You'll find yourself a devotee of pugilism before you even realize it."

"Oh, Niles." She threw her arms around him. "Thank you."

He pulled her into a true embrace, tucking her close. She leaned into him, reveling in the warmth and strength he exuded.

"I probably don't smell overly nice at the moment," he said.

"If you let go, I'll utilize my newfound skills to pummel you."

Penelope felt him laugh, even though he didn't make a sound. She slipped one hand to his chest and laid it, open palm, over his heart. She'd felt him breathe and laugh, but she wanted to feel the rhythm of his heart, to know if it was beating as ardently as hers was.

He set his hand atop hers. Such strong hands but touching her so gently.

"I'm sorry I didn't go to Cornwall," he whispered.

She closed her eyes, breathing deep, *feeling* the moment. "And I am glad I chased you to Yorkshire."

His lips brushed over her forehead. Every inch of skin his lips touched tingled. Her heart raced, but the feeling was too distracting for her to be able to make out his pulse beneath her hand.

He lightly kissed her temple. "I'm glad, too, Penelope."

She turned her face just a little. Just enough. And he didn't need to be asked. Niles kissed her, a soft and tender tease of his lips on hers. His powerful arms held her fast, one hand splayed against her back as the other cupped the nape of her neck, keeping her head at just the right angle to continue kissing her.

She kept one hand pressed to his heart and wove the fingers of her other through his thick, silky, brown hair. His sigh told her he enjoyed her touch as much as she delighted in his.

She'd so often told herself that she could be content with a marriage that simply let her keep her estate. In this one kiss, she discovered the truth she'd not yet been willing to confess: she wanted—needed—to be loved. And in a rare bit of fortunate fate, she had found someone who might.

Chapter Twenty-Five

PENELOPE WAS WALKING ON AIR. She'd trekked to Yorkshire hoping to convince a stranger to go through with their wedding. The gentleman she'd come to know was proving everything she hadn't realized she'd been longing for. It was more than his love of horses and athletic endeavors, more than his enjoyment of nature and friendly interactions. He was kind and considerate, intelligent and thoughtful. His sense of humor so perfectly complemented her own. He knew of her difficulties with her family and her struggles to claim her future, and he not only understood, but he also wasn't condemning her for her missteps.

And he'd kissed her in a way that she would thoroughly enjoy experiencing every day for the rest of her life. And she'd not complain about the occasional boxing lesson either. Just the memory of his thumb brushing the length of hers sent shivers all through her.

She was smitten; there was no denying it.

Every time her eyes met his across the supper table that night, Niles smiled and even colored a little. That set her heart fluttering and hope shining ever brighter in her mind.

No sooner had she and the other two ladies settled into the drawing room than that very topic was taken up.

"Based on the looks passing between you and Niles," Violet said, "I am beginning to suspect we will be forgoing the fair next week and holding a wedding instead."

Though entirely pleased with the idea, Penelope shook her head. "You are seeing more in this than there is." *At the moment*, she silently added.

"You *don't* think Niles's thoughts have turned in that direction?" Nicolette seemed to think Penelope rather foolish to be as cautious as she was being, which only added to the hope Penelope felt.

"He kissed me."

Both ladies' eyes widened.

"Am I wrong to believe he wouldn't have done that on a whim?" Penelope pressed.

"You are not wrong," Violet declared at the same time Nicolette said, "*Il ne ferait pas* ça," which Penelope assumed also meant that there was every reason for her to see depth in Niles's show of affection.

A sudden commotion sounded in the corridor.

"That does not sound like the gentlemen abandoning their port," Violet said.

"I would say it sounds like an arrival at the house." Penelope rose and moved toward the door of the drawing room. She peeked out, curious.

It *was* someone only just arrived at Pledwick Manor: a lady, an infant, a child who appeared to be perhaps a year old, and a woman who appeared to be the nursemaid.

Penelope looked back into the drawing room. "Does Mr. Layton have a sister, by chance?"

"I honestly don't know," Violet said. "He doesn't speak of his family."

Then, this was not a relation of his.

She looked toward the entryway once more and realized the newcomers were headed toward her. The mystery would be solved soon enough.

Penelope stepped away from the doorway just as the lady, now holding the infant in one arm and, with her other, holding the hand of the older of the children, who toddled beside her, swept inside.

"Julia!" Violet and Nicolette exclaimed in unison.

Ah. The much-spoken-of Lady Jonquil. Though Penelope's curiosity had grown by leaps and bounds at having heard the lady mentioned so often and so glowingly, her nervousness at actually being faced with her quickly surpassed that curiosity. Whether or not the Gents or the ladies realized as much, Julia's approval and disapproval held tremendous sway among them. Suppose she decided Penelope was not to her liking?

Rather than face the possible answer to that question, Penelope slipped from the drawing room, giving herself a moment's respite in the corridor. But a moment was all she was afforded. The sound of the Gents' voices preceded their appearance by mere seconds.

"Let us hazard a guess which of your ladies has found herself missing you so desperately that she simply had to put an end to our post-dinner port." Lord Jonquil laughed. When he saw Penelope, he grinned. "It appears our culprit is Miss Seymour."

"'Twas not I," she said.

Mr. Layton took up the teasing. "Tell me, then, the one requesting our precipitous arrival, does she have a French manner of speaking?"

Mr. Fortier received a few elbow nudges.

"No," Penelope said, "but she did have something I was not expecting."

"What is that?" Lord Aldric asked.

Penelope let her gaze shift to Lord Jonquil. "An undeniable hint of red in her hair."

All the laughter left his face, replaced by a hesitant longing. In what was little more than a whisper, he asked, "My Julia?"

Penelope nodded. "And two absolutely beautiful children."

Mr. Layton dropped a hand on his friend's shoulder. "Your family is here, Lucas."

Lord Jonquil pushed out a shaky breath. "I've missed them."

"We know." Mr. Layton gave him a friendly shove. "Go hug them. You've been apart long enough."

Penelope watched through the door as Lord Jonquil stepped inside. No one seeing his face could ever doubt the all-consuming love he felt for his wife. And the tender way he'd said her name solidified that truth all the more.

Lady Jonquil turned at the sound of his voice. She smiled. "I grew tired of waiting."

As the family reunion played out in the drawing room, Penelope remained just outside the door. The Gents passed through the threshold, offering their greetings to "Our Julia" and her boys. Niles, though, stopped at Penelope's side.

He took her hand. "You look nervous."

She quit trying to hide it. "One thing has been clear since my arrival: Julia is extremely important to all of you. What if she doesn't approve of me?"

He pressed their hands to his heart. "She will."

"My neighbors never have. My brother currently doesn't. She might very well declare that I don't deserve to be part of your group."

"In that case, there would be but one thing to do." He closed most of the gap between them.

"What's that?" She managed a calm response despite the sudden fluttering of her heart.

He shrugged. "Hit something."

Oh, how she adored him.

"It is good to see you smile, Penelope." He raised her hand to his lips. "Now, screw your courage to the sticking place. It is time to go meet a lady who, I predict, will become a dear and lifelong friend."

"But what if she doesn't?"

He set his other arm around her, and she breathed again. "What happened to my bold Penelope who sniffed out her runaway bridegroom and arrived here demanding an explanation and a chance?"

"Bold as brass, I was." She leaned her head against his shoulder, the one that didn't boast a sprig of white snapdragons on the lapel. "But as Liam pointed out, it wasn't very thoughtful of me. I've caused a great many people far more inconvenience than I ought."

He held her close. "His censure has undermined you and left you questioning your own worth. I hate seeing it."

"I'm trying to be a good person." She brushed a finger along one tiny blossom.

"You already are a good person, Penelope Seymour. You need to find a way to trust that."

She looked up at him. "And you are a person worthy of having what you want in life, not merely accepting what is foisted on you. I hope you trust that."

"And the both of you need to realize that when a door is open, the threshold is entirely transparent." Lord Aldric stood just on the other side of that threshold, watching the both of them with a hint of a smile in his characteristically solemn expression.

Beyond him, the others in the drawing room were doing a poor job of disguising the fact that they had been watching the exchange prior to Lord Aldric's interruption.

Penelope's eyes darted to Niles, worried she had embarrassed him.

But though a hint of color stole over his face, he laughed. "Have I mentioned the Gents are troublemakers?" he asked out of the side of his mouth.

"I assure you, I sorted that out on my own."

Niles's arms dropped away. He motioned her into the room. That she saw levity on all their faces helped quell her own embarrassment. But Lady Jonquil watched her with unmistakable curiosity, which kept Penelope's uncertainty firmly in the forefront.

Lord Jonquil motioned her over with his head, both his arms being used to hold his infant son. "Julia, this is Miss Penelope Seymour. Miss Seymour, this is my wife, Julia, Lady Jonquil."

"A pleasure to finally meet you, Lady Jonquil."

"And I you. Nearly every person in this room has written to me about you, and that has made me very anxious to meet you."

They'd all written about her?

"I've made you nervous." Lady Jonquil reached out and set her hand on Penelope's arm. "Don't be. If I'd come intending to toss you out of the house, I'd have done so already." She sounded perfectly serious, yet if Penelope was not mistaken, there was laughter in her eyes.

"You're teasing me," Penelope said.

Lady Jonquil smiled broadly. "A specialty of everyone here. But I suspect you've discovered that already."

"I have."

Lady Jonquil hooked her arm through Penelope's. "Though Puppy will certainly object, I mean to kidnap you for the remainder of the evening."

"For the record," Niles said from just behind her, "I do object."

"And also for the record," Lady Jonquil tossed back, "I'm doing it anyway." She led Penelope away from Niles and toward the sitting area, where Nicolette and Violet were sitting.

"Now I'm confused," Penelope said.

"About what?"

"About why it is that *you* aren't the one they call the General."

"Because the name was already taken." Lady Jonquil sat. "But everyone knows who is *really* in charge in this group." She looked at Lord Jonquil once more, her gaze flirtatious and her smile besotted. "Isn't that right, my dear?"

"Sweetheart, I would agree to anything in the world you chose to say right now simply because I am so desperately happy that you are here." He passed behind the sofa on which she and Penelope sat, pausing directly behind his wife, then bent and kissed her. "Though I do hope you will allow yourself to rest tomorrow. That was a very long journey to undertake so soon after your confinement."

The tiny baby in his arms fussed a little at the change in position. Lord Jonquil adjusted the little one, who quickly stopped squirming. Across the room, Mr. Layton was pointing to various accoutrements, listing their names for the older of the two children. "Philip, this is a cravat," he said slowly and clearly. "Brass button. Emerald cravat pin." He spoke precisely the way one did when trying to teach a child a new word.

Lord Jonquil continued walking past the sofa, gently rocking his baby in his arms.

Niles and Mr. Fortier stopped Lord Jonquil when he approached them to have a better look at the baby.

"I hope it will soon be my turn to hold little Layton," Mr. Fortier said.

"Only after I have my turn," Niles countered.

Lord Aldric sat near Mr. Layton, giving the undeniable impression of hoping to have the older boy's attention at some point.

This was a different side of the Gents than she'd yet seen. While she'd always assumed there were gentlemen who weren't annoyed by children, she'd not personally had any experience with them. Her father had been an involved and interested parent but only after Liam had reached school age and Penelope had been approaching young womanhood. None of Liam's friends had ever shown any paternal or avuncular inclinations. And children were never present during society gatherings in Dublin, so she'd not ever seen her male acquaintances in that city interact with children.

"Now, ladies." Lady Jonquil glanced at them with a conspiratorial expression. "Please tell me the three of you are not still Miss and Mrs.-ing each other."

Violet waved that off. "Certainly not."

"Perfect." Lady Jonquil turned to Penelope. "I am Julia, and I hope I have leave to call you Penelope."

"I would like that very much." Another friend. She had another friend.

"And though it will feel odd to you, you ought to be on the same friendly terms with the Gents," Julia said. "Anyone who is welcomed into this group remains one of us forever."

Chapter Twenty-Six

NILES SAT BESIDE JULIA THE next day as a variety of outdoor games were set up on the back lawn. Lucas and Penelope, with the questionable "help" of little Philip, the Jonquils' eldest boy, were in the midst of setting up the pins for a game of lawn bowls. The group would have enjoyed themselves either way, but having Julia there—Julia and the little boys—made them feel complete again. Whole.

Julia had joked the evening before that she was the one "in charge" of the Gents and their ladies, but there was actually some truth to the assertion. She wasn't the leader of the group—there really wasn't one—and she didn't in any way dictate what they all did—everyone was granted full and intentional autonomy—but in the two years since Julia had married Lucas, she had come to be the thread that wove through them all, tying them together, much like Stanley had been.

"I must say, Niles," Julia said, "I didn't know quite what I would find when finally meeting Penelope."

"And now that you have met her?" Posing the question made him a little nervous.

"I think she is wonderful. I deeply enjoyed talking with her last night. She fits so well and so easily in this group, which is decidedly a point in her favor."

Relief trickled over him. "I am glad you like her. She was quite worried that you wouldn't."

"Truth be told," Julia said, "*I* was worried that I wouldn't. The most recent letter I received about the situation here led me to think our Puppy was growing a bit smitten. What was I to do if I arrived and discovered an adventuress had ensnared you?"

"What *would* you have done?" he asked, suddenly very curious about the answer.

"Tossed her out on her ear, probably. I can get away with that, you know. The Gents have to behave when interacting with a lady, but I am under far less obligation to do so."

"When have the Gents ever actually behaved?" He shook his head at the absurd mental image that conjured of them acting like sophisticated gentlemen.

"Never, I daresay," she answered with a grin. But her expression turned almost immediately contemplative once more. "Early in my marriage, when I was drowning in rejection and dismissal and a future in which I felt certain I would be all but forgotten, the letters that you and the other Gents sent me were like my first lungful of air in ages."

I don't think the men of this country realize how chronically starved of air the women truly are.

"You gave me reason to hope," Julia said. "And you helped Lucas and me find our way. I would never, *could* never stand idly by while any of you was rendered unhappy. I would try everything in my power to help you as you all helped me."

At the time, he was ashamed to admit, he'd thought Julia was being a little petulant, not recognizing that Lucas was trying so hard and wanted things to be happy between them. Only after talking with Digby, who had been entrusted with Julia's side of the situation, had the Gents realized how little of Lucas's intentions and thoughts and feelings had been communicated *to her*. Niles had, to an embarrassing extent, blamed Julia for not being able to read Lucas's thoughts. She had been left to guess, and when one was required to fill in gaps after one had been deeply hurt, filling them in ways that protected against future pain was entirely understandable.

Niles's significant misjudgment in that matter had only added to his reluctance to accept a marriage of his grandfather's arranging. How very wrong it could all go, and he didn't want himself or his future bride to be as miserable as Julia had been by the time she had nearly given up on Lucas.

"Mama!" Philip's little voice drew Julia's attention. He was toddling toward them, Lucas close behind. Philip toppled onto his backside a few times, but with his parents' encouragement and a bit of assistance from Lucas, he continued his slow journey through the short expanse of grass between himself and his mother.

Penelope skirted the little family and stood by Niles. He stood when she reached his side.

"I suspect this will not be the most competitive bout of bowls either of us has ever participated in," she said.

"For my part, I intend to make certain Philip ends this game knowing how much better I am at it than he is." Niles managed to keep his tone entirely serious right up until the last word, when Penelope's silent laughter undid him.

"You intend to utterly trounce a one-year-old in lawn bowls?" She laughed all the way through the question.

"The sooner he learns to recognize my athletic superiority, the better."

She bumped him with her shoulder. "How very cutthroat of you, Niles."

"Intimidated?" he asked.

"On the contrary." She offered a charmingly pert shrug. "I am now feeling extremely motivated to best you soundly."

They lined up beside Lucas, Julia, and Philip as the game began. Their littlest competitor was delighted with literally everything any of them did but quite obviously didn't understand what was happening.

Several throws into the game, Philip attempted to push the bowl and toppled over. Whether in frustration or surprise, he started to cry. Lucas scooped him up, kissing his round cheek, and encouraged him to try again. Julia watched the two of them with a look that spoke of absolute and utter peace.

My first lungful of air in ages. Julia had nearly missed out on this life she and Lucas were building because Lucas hadn't recognized nor prioritized what she'd needed to be and feel safe, loved, valued, seen.

If I lose Fairfield, I will be holding my breath for the rest of my life.

Penelope needed Fairfield. She needed the life there she'd been fighting for so many years to claim. That need had driven her to press her brother to keep looking for a husband who would agree to what would allow her to feel safe. It had pushed her to cross England on the chance that her runaway groom would see value in her. It had given her the courage to remain behind when her brother had abandoned her because she was determined to not lose herself to the version of her that Society wanted to impose upon her.

If I lose Fairfield . . .

She needed to build her life at Fairfield. She needed to fill her lungs every day with the freedom it offered her.

But he wouldn't be fully happy if he abandoned the life *he'd* been fighting for. He was quiet and overlooked, required for far too long to bow to the dictates of others, wanting to make a difference for others who were far more voiceless than he. He'd spent a decade studying the intricacies of Parliament and cultivating political connections so that he could one day be effective in that body.

Their dreams were in conflict. Watching Lucas and Julia's struggles, he'd seen the way losing dreams, feeling dismissed and discarded, ate away at even tender and loving connections.

"You look pensive." When had Lucas moved to stand by him? The ladies were a bit away, assisting Philip.

"Do you realize I have wondered over the years if I would ever fall in love? If maybe there was something inherently wrong with me that I didn't feel a pull to anyone when everyone else seemed to have their heads turned quite regularly?"

"Do you know what Stanley would say to that if he were here?" Lucas asked, then answered his own question. "'This careful and thoughtful approach is the way your heart chooses to love, Niles Greenberry, and there is nothing wrong with that.' And then he would applaud your heart for having chosen as well as it has now."

Niles's gaze remained on Penelope, who was now spinning in a circle with Philip in her arms. The sight made that careful and thoughtful heart of his skip a beat even as it dropped to his feet.

"And what would Stanley say once he realized how impossible this actually is?"

"What do you mean? I thought you'd decided she was to your liking after all, even if your grandfather did choose her."

"She is more than to my liking. She is . . . I couldn't imagine . . ." He pushed out a breath. "I have not ever been an orator. Perhaps I ought to remember that when I think on my parliamentary ambitions."

"For one thing, not all parliamentarians give speeches," Lucas answered firmly. "For another, being unable to put into words how deeply you love some-one is a sign of sincerity, especially for one who is, as you said, not an orator. Rest assured, Puppy, I have seen your feelings for her written all over your face."

"And what is written on my face right now?" He sighed.

Lucas studied him. "Heartbreak." He sounded surprised. "Why is that? She is your match, and you are hers, and she looks at you with the same expression of besotted tenderness with which you look at her. You ought to be elated."

Julia and Penelope were so engrossed with helping Philip that they weren't paying the least heed to Lucas and Niles. That was for the best.

"She needs to keep ownership of Fairfield. I didn't fully understand that until recently, but it's crucial to her. Julia needed you to be nearby, to not leave her behind, to not make plans without her, which you didn't fully appreciate at first."

"That is an understatement," Lucas acknowledged.

"Building a life in which she didn't have that would have been miserable for both of you."

"True." He nodded.

"That is Fairfield for Penelope. It needs to be hers in every real and tangible way."

"Sign the original marriage settlement, and it will be," Lucas said.

"Without property of my own, I would have to abandon what I have worked *my* entire adult life to achieve."

"The bout with the Bath Butcher will allow you to address that. Even the loser's purse would put you so close that you'd be months from claiming your own land."

"Away from Fairfield," he pointed out. "Representing an area of the kingdom where I don't make my home would not merely be unsatisfying; it would feel like selling my soul to become one of those MPs who doesn't actually care and doesn't do any good."

Understanding was dawning in Lucas's expression and with it, the same worry Niles had been feeling.

"I couldn't live apart from the lady I marry," Niles said. "I don't want that kind of marriage. I refused to accept it when the time came, and I can't resign myself to it now."

"But marrying Penelope and living *with* her means one of you loses what you've fought for."

"It makes me feel selfish, saying that those ambitions are important enough to interfere with . . . love. Admittedly, I am operating with no experience whatsoever, but poetry and theater and literature all insist that 'love is not love which alters when it alteration finds or bends with the remover to remove.' Abandoning love over something like contradictory residency requirements feels shallow."

Lucas shook his head. "You're not speaking of a mere preference for different counties. As things stand now, to move forward together, one of you has to abandon something that rests at the core of who you are. Either of you requiring that of the other is not mere alteration or a disinterested remover choosing to remove. I think the Bard would not mind if we added to his list that love is also not love which requires one person to disappear in the shadow cast by the other's pursuits."

"It's impossible, then?" Niles hadn't wanted to admit that to himself.

"Me ever regaining Julia's trust, *that* was impossible." Lucas looked over at his wife and oldest boy, both laughing together. "That's what miracles are for, Niles, for when crucial things feel impossible."

Penelope rushed over, her broad and beautiful smile restoring Niles's hope every bit as much as Lucas's reassuring speech. "It is your turn to bowl, Niles." She took his hand. "You are currently losing to Philip, so I suggest you do your very best." Still holding Niles's hand, Penelope looked at Lucas. "That son of yours thoroughly enjoys being the center of attention."

"I would say he gets that trait from his mother, but everyone knows that's not true." Lucas walked with bouncing step to his wife and son, taking the little boy in his arms and swinging him around.

"They are a very happy little family, aren't they?" Penelope said. "And they clearly love baby Layton every bit as much as Philip."

"Love is woven into the fabric of the Jonquil family." Niles looked away from them and directly at the lady he had fallen so completely in love with. "That's worth fighting for, don't you think?"

"I do."

He slipped his arm around her. "And do you believe in miracles?"

She set a hand softly against his cheek and whispered, "More every day."

Chapter Twenty-Seven

PENELOPE SAT NEXT TO VIOLET in the drawing room that evening after supper while the ladies awaited the gentlemen's arrival.

"I'm afraid I haven't the first idea how to be a lady's companion," she warned Violet. "But I'm willing to learn."

"And I haven't the first idea how to *have* a lady's companion," Violet answered. "But I'm willing to pretend."

Seated across from them, Nicolette looked to Julia. "I imagine you would have invented creative things had I taken on the role of companion."

"Creative?" Julia shook her head. "I believe the descriptor you were searching for is 'delightfully brilliant.'"

"I'm certain it was simply a mistranslation from French," Penelope said in very solemn tones.

"Undoubtedly." Julia managed to keep her expression earnest longer than any of the other ladies, who all quickly dissolved into the laughter so common among them.

The gentlemen arrived in the midst of the mirth.

"I always feel a bit worried when I chance upon the ladies and they're all laughing," Kes said.

Penelope hopped up and motioned for him to take the seat she had been occupying.

"You don't need—"

"Sit by your wife, Kes. Please," she said, cutting off his objection.

"Yes, please do," Violet said.

He clearly did not need any more prodding than that. And both husband and wife appeared utterly delighted to be in each other's company. Penelope made a mental note that providing opportunities for them to spend time together ought to be one of her aims as Violet's temporary companion.

At the moment, though, she meant to abandon Violet for the joy of Niles's company. He stood on the outskirts of the group and watched her with a small smile as she approached. That smile and the way her heart reacted to his nearness led her to believe her stint as a lady's companion would prove very short-lived.

"What had all of you so diverted?" Niles asked, taking her hand without hesitation.

"We were discussing the difficulties of having or being a lady's companion when one hasn't the first idea how."

"Will you be happy in that role?" His unwavering desire for her to be happy touched her.

"Were it anyone other than Violet or one of the other ladies here, I'd be less than enthusiastic. And if I'd no hope of the situation being temporary, that'd be quite dispiriting as well."

"Knowing a difficult portion of one's life won't last forever is reassuring, isn't it? Knowing over the past years that I would not always be dependent upon my family, that I could eventually pursue the life I wished to live and achieve the goals I'd set for myself was very motivating."

Penelope tugged his hand a bit, urging him to take a turn with her around the room. Her quick prodding was all he seemed to need, and they were soon undertaking a leisurely circuit.

"What goals have you set for yourself, Niles?" she asked. "I would very much like to know."

"I don't speak of them with many people," he said.

"And I have told very few of my dreams to establish a horse-breeding venture at Fairfield," she said, "but I shared that with you. Please trust me enough to tell me of your dreams."

"I assure you, it is far more a matter of my reticence than any lack of trust in you," he said. "I have long wished to have a seat in Parliament. Having a voice in the governing of the kingdom would allow me to make a difference. I wouldn't be the most well-known nor the most influential, but I could do some good."

The idea took immediate hold in her thoughts, growing more and more solid and real. "You would be an excellent addition to those hallowed halls, Niles."

"A hard-working one, at least."

"No, truly excellent." She squeezed his hand. "You are thoughtful and intelligent and compassionate. All those things would make you, in some ways, an oddity in politics, but those are the qualities that ought to be foremost in a member of Parliament."

He smiled at her, coloring a little. "I would like to at least try."

"I like this dream of yours, Niles. I think you should follow it."

He raised her hand to his lips and kissed her fingers.

From across the room, Digby announced, "I have chosen a game for this evening, friends. And I think it's an excellent one."

"Should we be worried?" Penelope asked Niles in low tones.

"Terrified."

"Our Puppy has taken to wearing buttonhole flowers in the evenings," Digby said.

Penelope couldn't hold back a smile. He had worn snapdragons in his lapel every evening since the day she'd first brought him a sprig.

"The flowers have inspired me." Digby stood tall and straight, watching the gathering with mischievous delight in his eyes. "I propose we play snap-dragon."

The suggestion brought excitement to the faces in the room. Penelope hadn't the first idea what the game was.

Lucas jumped up from his seat. "The boys would love this. We should bring them down."

Julia snatched hold of his hand, keeping him there. "Lucas, if you wake those boys, their nursemaid will murder you."

"But we're to play snap-dragon, sweetheart. It would be their very first time."

"They are too young to play with fire," Julia said. "We'll introduce them to the game when they're older."

He seemed to realize his wife was correct. "We could play snap-dragon when Adam next visits."

"An excellent idea."

Penelope turned a little to Niles. "Was Julia being literal when she said, 'playing with fire'?"

"Have you never played snap-dragon?"

She shook her head.

"Yes, Julia was being entirely literal. Snap-dragon is, at its most basic, playing with fire."

Penelope didn't know whether to be excited or nervous. She felt both in equal measure.

A footman brought a shallow bowl into the drawing room and placed it on a table. He sprinkled raisins inside and poured in a bit of rum. Everyone in the group moved to stand around the table, watching the bowl intently. Something interesting must have been about to happen.

A second footman came inside, carefully carrying a large cup from which steam was wafting. Digby lit a long, thin wooden spill in the low-burning embers of the fire. He reached the table just as the footman did.

The footman carefully poured some of the hot, slightly amber liquid into a very large spoon. He held it out near the bowl of raisins and rum. Digby touched the flaming end of the spill to the liquid in the spoon, and a burst of bright-blue flame emerged. The footman slowly poured the flaming contents of his spoon into the bowl, and the rum inside likewise erupted in blue flames.

The onlookers cheered. It *was* a dazzling sight.

"What happens next?" Penelope asked, mesmerized by the flames.

"The rest is a contest to see who can pull the most raisins from the fire and pop them into his or her mouth without getting burned."

Good heavens. "Is that even possible?"

"Something about the blue flames is not as hot as the more common yellowish flames," Julia said. "Don't be mistaken, it is still hot, but it doesn't burn as quickly."

"*As quickly.*" Penelope shook her head. "That is not as reassuring as you might think."

"The game ends when all the raisins are gone or everyone has been burned," Lucas added.

This game sounded absolutely ridiculous. But those who had played it before didn't hesitate. They gingerly snatched raisins from the bowl and popped them into their mouths.

"One!" Lucas declared in the exact moment Kes called out the same number.

Violet, Niles, and Aldric were next to call out "One!"

A moment after, Nicolette declare "*Un!*" Aldric called out, "Two!"

"You're all mad." Penelope half laughed, half gasped.

"Mad we might be," Lucas said from across the table, the blue flame lighting his face in slips of dancing azure. "But I would wager Niles is hoping you will emerge the winner." He flung a raisin into his mouth. "Two!"

Beside her, Niles popped another flaming raisin into his mouth, quickly chewing and swallowing. "Two!"

"Why would you want *me* to be the victor?"

"Tradition holds that the one to successfully eat the most raisins will be the next to fall in love," Niles said.

Penelope shot Lucas a defiant glance. "If you think Niles is standing about, *waiting* for me to fall in love, then you are astoundingly unobservant."

He received hardy and good-natured teasing from his friends and wife. All the while, the raisin snatching and eating continued, with numbers being called out.

"Do you not intend to try?" Niles asked her.

"You really haven't burned yourself?" She had significant doubts.

"I'm very quick." He snatched another raisin and popped it into his mouth. "Five!"

Penelope Seymour had never been accurately accused of being a coward. She didn't mean to give anyone reason to call her one now.

"I just snatch it right out of the flames?" She eyed the shallow bowl.

"Decide on the one you want, and grab it," Niles said. "You don't want to be searching around for it."

That made a good deal of sense. "What if someone snatches the one I'm aiming for?"

"That's part of the challenge."

Penelope set her sights on a raisin very near her in the bowl. Pulse pounding a nervous rhythm, she took a deep breath. Then another. *I am really going to put my hands in fire.* 'Twas a truly mad game, this.

She reached in and grabbed the raisin, pulling it out as quickly as she could. It was on fire.

"Pop it into your mouth," Niles instructed. "It'll put the flame out."

She did as instructed and bit down, just as she'd seen the others do. The heat of the fire was immediately replaced by the rush of juice. Her mouth was a bit warm, and her hands as well, but she wasn't burned.

She wasn't burned.

"One!" she called out, too excited to prevent the word from emerging as a shout.

The group enthusiastically cheered her accomplishment even as others snatched more raisins and ate them.

Henri burned himself, and his run was over. The others continued their attempts.

"Well done, Penny." Niles tucked her up against his side, neither moving away from the table.

Penny. She smiled at the nickname, wondering what had inspired it. No one else had ever called her by anything other than her full given name. "Penny," she repeated. "I like it."

He pressed a kiss to her temple. "Then, I mean to call you that quite regularly."

"And if I have a nickname, that makes me very much one of the group, as all the ladies have one." Though successfully snatching a raisin had been exhilarating, she far preferred standing there with Niles's arm around her and was content to simply watch the rest of the game play out.

Soon enough, the raisins were all gone and the flame left to extinguish itself as the rum burned off. The group made an accounting.

Penelope's one raisin put her in the very last position, though she could not possibly have been less bothered to have lost.

When it was revealed that Aldric, no doubt unknowingly, had claimed the top spot with twelve raisins snatched and eaten and no burns, the room absolutely erupted.

"Who's the lucky lady?" Lucas asked, giving Aldric's shoulder a shove.

"Or *un*lucky, as the case may be," Digby drawled.

Aldric remained as unshaken as ever. "You are meant to be mercilessly harassing Niles and Penelope. I'll not be lampooned when it is not my turn."

"But the raisins have spoken," Kes insisted. "You're next."

"Find a lady who'll have me, and I'll gladly take my turn." He didn't seem the least worried that such a thing would come to be.

Henri eyed the other Gents and, in very confident tones, said, "We have our assignment, *mes amis*. Find a lady who can endure the General."

Everyone, including the ladies, joined in the teasing as the night wore on. While Aldric made a show of being annoyed, Penelope didn't believe for a moment that he wasn't enjoying bantering with his friends.

Who were now Penelope's friends.

She leaned into Niles's embrace. For the first time in too many years, the future looked bright.

Chapter Twenty-Eight

"Have I ever told you that I enjoy watching you ride?" Niles felt a little foolish expressing the sentiment, but he couldn't deny it was true.

"You do?" Penelope seemed pleased.

He watched her a moment longer, riding beside him, making such a lovely picture atop Midnight. "You are so tiny, and yet this powerful and enormous animal obeys your slightest nudge. It's impressive and remarkable."

"And according to my mother, a bit too masculine." Penelope shook her head but smiled. "I think she wishes I would act as fragile as my appearance makes me seem."

"I, for one, like that contradiction in you."

"Probably because you are also a contradiction," she said. "You do not, on first acquaintance, give the impression of an athletic and physically powerful gentleman, neither would most people guess that you're clever and funny. That's not to say that you give the impression that you are weak or dull or somber."

"I am well aware that I don't make much of an impression at all. I would be more concerned about that if I didn't prefer to receive little notice."

They rode across the land bridge to the lake island with its natural beauty and elegant gazebo. Niles had always liked it on his previous visits to Pledwick Manor, but it had grown particularly special to him on this visit. And that had everything to do with it having been part of every ride he'd taken with Penelope.

"Why?" she asked without warning as they reached the island.

"Why *what*?"

"Why do you prefer to be unnoticed?"

His mind was wandering, which was unusual for him. Penelope had pulled them back to the topic they'd been discussing.

"There is a certain freedom," he said, "that comes with not being the center of attention." He dismounted, then gave Morwenna a quick pat. "When people forget I am present, they're far less likely to expect me to be a certain person or act a certain way. I've learned to appreciate that."

Penelope allowed him to help her dismount as well. Holding her, even for the brief time needed to lift her to the ground, sped his pulse. It was a heady feeling, one he didn't want to lose.

"Do you think, perhaps," she said once her feet were firmly on the ground, "that you've tucked yourself away as much as you have in the hope that your family would forget you were there and stop trying to force you to live the life they have chosen for you?"

"Stanley once asked me the same question." He took her hand, then walked with her along the gravel path.

"What answer did you give him?" she asked.

"I assured him that if I disliked being relegated to the shadows, I wouldn't keep returning there. But I honestly prefer having a bit of space in which to think and be myself. And I enjoy watching people more than I enjoy being watched and listening more than doing the talking."

"Then you have *chosen* your quiet corner rather than having been banished to it."

He looked at her. "Do you find that pathetic?"

"Not in the least." She leaned her head lightly against his upper arm. "I appreciate that you've decided who you are and what you want, and you aren't allowing people to force you into being anything else."

"You're doing the same," he reminded her.

"Peas in a pod, you and I."

Water lapped the edge of the island a few yards from where they walked. An early evening breeze rustled leaves and rippled the lake. The horses seemed quite content to remain where they were, nibbling at grass and standing about at their leisure. The setting was perfect for heartfelt confessions. He was still nervous though.

"I could not be more grateful that you made the journey to Yorkshire. Because of that, I was able to meet you and know you, despite having abandoned the original circumstances under which we were meant to meet."

"I am choosing to believe that this isn't leading to you saying you'd rather I left now."

His stomach dropped. "Is that what it sounds like I'm about to say?"

She nodded.

He sighed. "Lands, I'm horrible at this," he muttered.

"At *what*, Niles?"

He stopped their forward progress and stepped in front of her, taking both her hands in his. "You have laid claim to the entirety of my heart, Penelope. I find myself thinking of you when we are apart and counting the hours until I'll see you again. And when we are together, it's all I can do not to abandon politeness and decorum and simply beg you to let me hold you regardless of who might be nearby. When I thought you might be returning to Ireland, I have seldom felt so dejected. And when you insisted you meant to remain . . ." He was struggling to find the words to express how he'd felt when she'd chosen to stay. "I wondered if I was a fool to have imagined the connection I felt between us. But you stayed, and I think—I *hope*—you did so, at least in part, because you felt that connection too."

Her hair was a bit windswept from their ride. Her smile was small but tender. "I do feel it. And I treasure it."

"I have fallen wholly and unchangeably in love with you, and I couldn't let another day go by without telling you that, without confessing to you how completely you have captured my heart." Saying the words brought some relief but didn't entirely ease his nervousness.

"I love you, too, Niles Greenberry." She wrapped her arms around him as she spoke the words he had hoped to hear but hadn't dared let himself expect. "Wholly and unchangeably."

He held her, just as he so often wished he could. Breathed in the scent of orange blossoms that she wore, allowing himself to simply enjoy the feel of her in his arms. He would eventually have to ruin the moment by sharing the rest of what he needed to say.

"May I tell you a secret, Niles?"

"Of course."

"I also find myself wishing, even when there are far too many people milling about, that the expectations of polite behavior would allow me to simply melt into your arms like this. I wish for it all the time."

For so long, he'd feared he would never find a person with whom he could share this connection or have these feelings. He'd hoped to build a marriage like the ones he saw among his friends, though he'd not truly believed it possible.

He had that chance now, but fate had been cruel in the offering of it.

"You deserve to breathe, Penelope."

"I can breathe," she said with a little laugh.

"I don't mean literally in this moment. You said Fairfield was air to you, freedom to breathe in a society that offers women so little air. Hearing you speak of the dreams you have for your future there, I came to understand how crucial it is. And I want that for you. I want you to be happy, and I know you wouldn't be if Fairfield were snatched away. No matter what other happinesses you might have, losing that would leave a wound that would not truly heal."

She seemed to sense the growing somberness in his words. She pulled back a little, looking up at him. "My brother would sign the original marriage settlement, I'm certain of it. That allows me to keep Fairfield."

How to explain the complications that were there? "I would despise myself if anything I did prevented you from having it."

"What has you so solemn of a sudden?"

He took a breath. "I told you yesterday of my ambition to be in Parliament."

She nodded. "You would be wonderful there, working to do good and help people. Too many pursue the position purely for prestige or to further their own desires. You would do an entire world of good."

He adjusted so he was once more holding her hand and walking beside her. He'd do better at explaining things if he weren't holding her, knowing full well he might not be able to do so for long. "To hold a seat in the House of Commons, a man, among other things, needs a minimal income and must own property. He must own it himself. It cannot belong to a father or brother or friend or—"

"Or wife."

He nodded hesitantly. "Precisely."

"Are you suggesting we change the marriage settlement so that Fairfield would be yours after all?" He could not tell if the stilting quality of her question indicated she felt herself correct and was trying to endure the hurt of it or if she felt certain that was *not* what he was suggesting but couldn't think what else it might be.

"Not at all," he insisted. "Not ever. Fairfield is yours and always, always should be. I would never suggest otherwise."

She looked relieved but still didn't seem to have the least idea what he was attempting to say.

"I have known since I was young about the land requirements for an MP. As such, I have been saving what I could for years. I nearly have enough to buy a small, humble property in an inexpensive area of the kingdom."

"Oh, that does make more sense. And how wonderful that you are so close to your goal." Hope returned to her eyes, hope he would be extinguishing in a moment.

"An MP's income doesn't have to come from the estate he owns, which means with the income from Fairfield, I would have what I need in that regard, but I still have to *own* the property that qualifies me." He needed her to know how specifically impossible their current situation was. The estate ownership matter was not a minor one. "The property I am hoping to purchase is in Essex, not anywhere near Fairfield."

Her brow pulled as she contemplated that. "Though I would, by law, be the owner of Fairfield, it would still be our home. There is no reason we wouldn't both live there. And though I hope you would enjoy being part of the equine pursuits I have imagined for the estate, there is also no reason you couldn't be the wonderful member of Parliament you have always wanted to be."

"There is though." He pushed out a breath. "If I were to represent constituents I didn't know and never saw, representing an area of the kingdom in which I didn't live, whose interests were not my own, I would not be fulfilling that dream I've worked toward. I wouldn't be the helpful and ethical member of Parliament I want to be. I would be like too many others, the corrupt and uncaring MPs I've so long held in contempt. I would have a seat in Parliament, but I would despise myself."

"I hadn't thought of that," she said quietly.

"But neither could I be the sort of husband who lives permanently and intentionally away from his wife. I couldn't build a life elsewhere while you were building a life at Fairfield."

Penelope paled, though she didn't speak.

"I have an opportunity, very soon, to be the recipient of money enough to either purchase the property or place myself within mere months of doing so. But though it would be the fulfillment of years of work and the beginning of a pursuit that I know would be fulfilling and important to me, I find myself feeling . . . discouraged."

"I'm feeling a little discouraged myself." Her soft words were barely audible over the sound of the wind and the water. "Either you abandon what you have worked toward your entire adult life in order to build a life with me at Fairfield, or I abandon Fairfield and every dream I have there to build a life with you elsewhere."

"Neither of us would be fully happy in either of those scenarios. I have been trying to sort out a solution, and I finally realized that it made no sense to mull this over without making certain you knew the reality of the situation as well as the desperation I feel to find an answer. I don't ever want you to think that I have given up or don't care enough to try."

They'd nearly completed their circuit of the island. Their horses were in view once more. Would she simply retake her saddle and ride away? Would she say there was no answer and they'd do best to simply move on?

No. He refused to believe that.

"How soon do you anticipate having these additional funds?"

"At the end of the fair," he said. "And I don't know how long the property I have my eye on will be available. If I hesitate, it might be gone for good."

She nodded. "Then, there is not much time for you to move forward."

"Not much at all."

"I haven't much either." She met his eye as they slowed their forward progression. "Fully expecting to be married and settling at Fairfield, there is a stallion for sale that I offered on so I can begin my horse-breeding endeavors in earnest. The seller won't hold the animal much longer, but the bank will not extend credit to an unmarried lady."

There were even more difficulties than he'd realized.

Penelope looked up at him once more. "Where will the money you are soon to receive be coming from? I can't imagine your family is now so pleased with you that they are tossing funds in your direction."

She deserved to know the entirety of it, so there was little point skirting the question.

"There is a fight being held the day after the fair," he said.

"And you mean to wager on the outcome? That seems very risky."

He shook his head. "I'm not a betting man."

"How can you possibly earn money from it?" Before he could answer, understanding dawned on her face. "You are not to be one of the spectators but one of the pugilists."

"I felt that you ought to know that as well, ought to know everything so you could decide if I were still to your liking."

"But it is my understanding that gentlemen don't participate in fights for purses or prize money."

"*Don't* and *aren't supposed to* are two very different things." He would do best to make his explanation quickly so she could begin whatever pleading or objection or disapproval she meant to invoke. "I've been fighting for years under the pseudonym the Cornish Duke. It's how I've earned most of the money I am putting toward my eventual land. I'm not the best pugilist in the kingdom, but I am quite good. I've won far more often than I have lost."

"Who are you fighting this time?" It wasn't a question asked in approval or disapproval. All Niles could make out was curiosity and concern.

"Sam Martin. He is known as the Bath Butcher."

"Because he originally worked as a butcher?"

He was relatively certain Martin's moniker had begun as a nod to a former profession, but it certainly wasn't the reason for it any longer. "It is, at least now, a reference to his abilities in the pugilists' ring."

"You could get hurt."

"Neither competitor usually ends a bout without at least some degree of injury."

She stood beside Midnight, watching Niles. "Could you get *more* than hurt?"

"It is rare, but people have died or been permanently impaired." He held himself at the ready for a barrage of denouncements.

"Winning this prize would allow you to buy the land you need to live your dream?"

"The losing purse will put me far closer," he said. "The winning purse, which is very unlikely to be mine, would see me able to purchase that land immediately *and* have more financial freedom than my current income allows."

"Then, Niles, I will say to you what a wise person once said to me."

"What's that?"

"You need to hit something. I will add that you need to hit some*one,* and you need to do so as expertly as possible."

"Because you don't want me to get hurt?"

"Of course I don't want to see you hurt, but it's more than that. I want to see you claim your dream, to have everything you've fought for."

"Even if those dreams are what keep us apart?"

"You asked yesterday if I believe in miracles. I meant it when I told you that I do. Somehow, this will work out for the best. Somehow, there will be a way around our current obstacles."

He wanted to believe it as well, but life had not always been miraculous. Seldom had been, in fact.

"And if there isn't?" he asked.

She used one of the benches between the gazebo columns to climb into her saddle once more. "If miracles choose to elude us, then I will cheer for you from Fairfield and from London when I am there. I will read of all you are accomplishing, and I will be so deeply happy for you." Emotion cracked through her words. Though she was at a bit of a distance, he thought he saw a shimmer of tears.

She looked as though she meant to say more but thought better of it. She simply nudged Midnight into motion and rode away.

Chapter Twenty-Nine

PENELOPE AND THE OTHER LADIES took up a game of Quarante de Roi the next afternoon. It was the first she'd seen of anyone since her ride with Niles. She'd taken her meals on a tray and had undertaken her morning ride when she'd known he wouldn't be undertaking his. Her mind had been too heavy for company. She had joined the ladies in the hope that their companionship would ease some of her heartache.

"It is a good thing the Gents scampered off like they did," Julia said as she mulled over the cards in her hand. "Lucas enjoys playing with Philip, but the poor little boy desperately needed a nap."

"He is a very attentive father, *oui*?" Nicolette said, eyeing her cards as well.

"Very," Julia answered. "And I take such comfort in knowing that our boys will never have reason to doubt that their father loves them."

"And," Violet added, "they will never have reason to doubt that their father loves their mother deeply."

Julia grew very still. In a quiet voice, she said, "I think Lucas's father is dying. His parents put on brave faces while he was home, but I saw those masks slip a few times after he left. I suspect they are trying to save him the pain of anticipating such a devastating loss. I know my Lucas; he would want to be told. But I don't want to be the one to tell him, to see the pain it will cause."

Penelope sat diagonal to Julia and was in a position to set her hand atop her friend's in a show of support.

"I do not think the mournful event is imminent," Julia continued, sounding a little steadier. "But I think it best that after our time here is concluded, we return to Nottinghamshire rather than traveling north to Brier Hill." She looked to Penelope. "That is our home in Cumberland."

Penelope nodded her understanding. "I hope I am not speaking out of turn, but I have seen a resoluteness in Lucas that makes me think, despite the grief he would feel at this news, he would not only hold up under the weight of it but would also be grateful to know what he is facing."

Julia nodded, as did the other ladies.

"It is such a difficult thing," Julia said, "to have to do something you know is the right thing but that brings pain to someone you love so dearly."

Penelope set her cards down; no one was paying the game much heed as it was. "What's to be done when doing that right thing is bringing both of you pain? What do you do when there's no reassurance that enduring the pain now will lead to anything but further pain?"

All the ladies abandoned their hands as well.

"We wondered what might have happened," Violet said. "When you did not join us for supper and Niles took to such utter silence all evening, we could only assume whatever occurred was significant."

Penelope confessed to them the situation in which she found herself: in love, helpless, and hopeless. She told them about Fairfield and Niles's parliamentary ambitions and all that came attached to that. He hadn't indicated that he wished the ladies to know of his plans to fight the Bath Butcher, so she left out that bit, simply saying that he anticipated having money enough for his Essex estate very soon.

"So, either I relinquish Fairfield, Niles forsakes his plans for Parliament, or we both give up any hope we have of being together." Her next breath shook a little. "Can fate truly be so cruel as to offer us only those three options?"

"My Henri and I found ourselves similarly without any hope for a happy future together," Nicolette said. "We were both willing to relinquish those things not related to love which were a crucial part of our happiness in the hope that our life together would soften some of the sting of losing what was otherwise crucial."

Penelope shook her head. "I don't wish for him to feel any sting, however softened. I don't want the life we could have together to be built on a foundation of loss and regret."

Nicolette leaned her arms on the table, holding Penelope's gaze. "In the end, *mon amie*, another option presented itself. After we had determined what path we could be content with for our journey, however imperfect, however long it meant waiting for our 'happy ending,' as the saying goes, only then did fate see fit to offer us something else, something better."

"You're suggesting I move forward with my plans for Fairfield, and he move forward with his plans for Parliament, and we trust that somehow, someday there will be an answer."

"I'm suggesting you don't give up hope," Nicolette said.

"Please don't give up." Violet squeezed her hand. "You and Niles are so remarkably good for each other. I've not ever seen him so alive, so entirely himself. And you smile more in his presence than at any other time. That you love each other is obvious. And that, Penelope, is worth fighting for."

"Why must everything be a fight?" Penelope released a sigh. "Is it too much to ask that *something* come easily?"

"If you sort out a way to arrange that," Julia said with a smile, "do share it with the rest of us."

Feeling a little better, Penelope found herself able to smile in return. "I swear to you I will."

"Kester and I spoke about your need to find a companion so you can set up house at Fairfield," Violet said. "He has insisted that if it would help you and if you would like to facilitate that sooner rather than later, we could travel to London from here rather than make our way to Livingsley Hall."

"That is very generous of you," Penelope said. "I do not wish to be a burden of any kind though."

Violet shook her head. "He has a sister in London, and we always enjoy visiting her family. It would be no burden to spend time in Town."

Liam's stinging accusations had undermined so much of the faith Penelope had in herself. These dear, new friends were helping her find her footing again. And Niles, her darling Niles, had seen fit to love her when she had begun to doubt anyone would.

"In the meantime"—Nicolette looked at them all—"there is a fair in only a few days' time. From what Henri has told me of English country fairs, we should find ample distraction from our worries."

"Indeed." Julia looked a bit less burdened.

Penelope hoped she did as well. "I've never been to an English fair."

"Neither have I," Nicolette said.

"They are delightful," Julia said. "And I can only imagine the scrapes our darling Gents will get themselves into over the course of it."

Little did any of them realize the enormity of the "scrape" Niles was actively planning to undertake. Penelope was trying very hard not to worry about him, but his opponent being known as the Bath Butcher did not help matters at all.

"I suggest we make a pact here and now," Violet said, "that we will make certain we all have a delightful time at the fair. I suspect we all need a bit of levity."

"Yes, let's," Julia said. "We will ensure each one of us enjoys herself, and we'll give the Gents a bit of competition for who is able to make the most of the day."

Chapter Thirty

"The important thing today is that you enjoy yourself," Aldric said to Niles as the Gents alighted from the two carriages in which they had ridden to the site of the Hamblestead fair. The ladies had ridden in a third.

"Enjoy yourself?" Lucas shook his head in disbelief. "That doesn't sound like a strategy our beloved and terrifying General would champion."

"I'm not actually terrifying," Aldric said.

Digby tipped his hat as he stepped past the General. "Beg to differ, my friend."

Aldric was undeterred. "The strategy *is* a good one, Niles. Allowing yourself to be at ease today and pass a pleasant interval will give your mind rest. So much of what you are facing tomorrow will be mentally taxing. Being keen of mind will go a long way toward surviving the bout."

"Surviving *is* one of my goals," Niles acknowledged. "But could I not have prepared for survival in my own clothing at least?"

Wilson had ridden up with the coachman, having received leave, like all the other servants, to enjoy themselves at the fair. He, however, had wanted to be present when Niles alighted to offer whatever help might be needed in putting his clothing to rights. Wilson had, after all, overseen the creation of Niles's current ensemble.

"You'll draw attention by fiddling with your clothes," Wilson warned in the very moment Niles hooked a finger around the cravat tied snugly around his throat. "And that would undermine the entire thing."

The young man wasn't wrong. Niles simply wasn't accustomed to wearing colors that weren't at least a little muted. Digby and Wilson had both insisted the borrowed frock coat and waistcoat wouldn't garner him extra notice, which he was keen to avoid. The ensemble would instead make him in many ways more invisible. He would be seen as simply another of the Quality and a gentleman far too fashionable for something as low-class as taking part in a boxing match.

"Keeping the hat a bit low will help make you less recognizable tomorrow," Wilson added.

Niles had never known a valet with Wilson's ease of manner around his employer's friends and associates. He couldn't help wondering if that would change over time, if the young man would settle into his role and take a more traditional approach. He hoped not, as he very much liked Wilson. But he also realized that Wilson would struggle to find his place in Lucas's household and among the other servants he would come to know in London if he were seen as not knowing his place. So many people had so very many expectations. It made being oneself a tricky thing to manage.

Apparently satisfied that Niles wouldn't make a complete mull of his efforts, Wilson wandered off into the fair.

The ladies' carriage arrived a moment later. As unsure as Niles was about his current appearance, knowing Penelope would emerge and spot him dressed as he was made him far more nervous. He'd hardly seen her the past few days. He'd spent a lot of hours in the outbuilding, practicing and building his endurance. But he'd also been avoiding her a little. They'd ended their conversation on the island on a note of hopelessness, acknowledging the worrying likelihood that life would tear them apart in the end. He didn't want that to happen and couldn't bring himself to face her without some small glimmer of hope to offer.

Now he not only had to face the possibility of seeing disappointment in her eyes over all that had happened, but he also knew there was a high likelihood that she would see how comparatively garish his current clothing was and think he looked ridiculous.

The women handed little Philip out of the carriage and into Lucas's waiting arms. Then they handed tiny baby Layton to Kes, who stood nearby as well. Lastly, Julia, Violet, and Nicolette emerged, their respective husbands greeting each of them.

"Part of enjoying yourself today, Puppy," Aldric said from directly beside him, "is allowing yourself the pleasure of Penelope's company. You've denied yourself that joy for several days now, and I don't think it has done either of you any good."

"Would it not be cruel to let our hopes soar today, knowing they'll fall to the ground tomorrow?"

"Win tomorrow and the purse would be enough for you to possibly aim for land near Fairfield," Aldric said.

"I can't beat the Bath Butcher." Niles knew that well enough. "I mean to make every effort to best him, but I am far too realistic to *expect* it to happen."

"I never thought my father would allow me the use of any of his estates, but he did. Miracles happen every day, Niles."

Penelope stepped from the carriage at that exact moment. She was, as always, breathtakingly beautiful. And her eyes, as was also usual to her, took in the entirety of her surroundings in a single, excited sweep. Heavens, but she would be delightful to pass through life with, eager to try and see new things but not needing him to be a person of renown or importance; she would be content and pleased with precisely who he was.

He crossed to the carriage and offered her his hand. She hesitated for just a moment before a broad smile lit her face.

"I didn't recognize you at first," she said, "and couldn't see your face very well."

"That was the hope." Niles helped her to the ground, then offered his arm. He lowered his voice. "It is rather important that tomorrow I not be easily recognized as the same gentleman who is wandering about today."

"That is wise," she answered equally quietly.

"I feel a little ridiculous," he said.

She squeezed his arm. "You needn't. 'Tisn't your usual appearance you're sporting today, but you're still quite handsome."

Lucas passed them, bouncing Philip in his arms.

Julia was directly behind, holding the baby. "We're off to see Punch and Judy," she explained.

"What would you like to see?" Niles asked Penelope.

"Are we to spend some time together?"

"All day, if you're willing."

She turned the tiniest bit toward him as they walked in the direction of the fair booths. "I have missed you so much these past days. I know that you've needed to prepare for tomorrow, but everyone is leaving in only a couple of days' time, and I'll need to leave when Kes and Violet do. I've worried I'd not have time with you before we are forced to part."

"I wish I had funds enough for purchasing an estate near Fairfield," he said. "Or alternately, had dreamed these years of an equine career rather than a political one."

She shook her head. "Our dreams aren't identical, but, Niles, they are so very well matched to the both of us. You understand and enjoy horses, which makes my dreams suited to your participation. And I enjoy learning things and hearing people's thoughts and points of view, which makes your dreams suited to my participation. We could be so very perfect together."

"Then, let's not abandon hope," he said. "It might take me years to have money enough for an estate near yours, but I am willing to keep saving and keep earning where I can."

"More fights?" she asked quietly.

"Those are getting riskier," he admitted. "Not merely because I don't dare get caught, but I'm also growing more out of practice, and that will eventually catch up to me."

They'd reached the heart of the fair and its rows and rows of stalls. He bent his head closer to hers so she would be able to hear him over the din of voices.

"I'll find something to supplement my income, and I'll not stop doing all I can until I have enough."

"As will I," she said. "Once I am able to hire the stable staff I need, I can begin with the horses I have. In time, there will be profit that I can save. Between the two of us, we'll have enough before we know it."

The questionable wisdom of the day would have dictated that Niles object to the idea of his would-be wife bearing any of the financial burden of allowing them to be together. But far from bruising his pride, her sincere and earnest offer buoyed him. He wasn't alone in this struggle. And he wasn't fighting for something that mattered only to him.

There was such strength in that knowledge.

"Fairings for you?" a woman at the stall they'd only just reached called out to them.

That stopped Niles in his tracks. "*Cornish* fairings?"

The woman nodded. "My mum's from Cornwall. Taught me how to make them."

Niles looked to Penelope. "Have you ever had a Cornish fairing?"

"I've not the first idea what it is."

"A variety of ginger biscuit," he said. "The very best variety."

"I love ginger biscuits," Penelope said.

He paid the biscuit seller and gave Penelope the purchased ginger treat. As they walked along, she broke off a piece and held it out to him.

"It's your biscuit, my dear. I'll not steal it from you," he said.

She laughed a bit. "I'm offering; therefore, it is not stealing. *And* I am keeping most of it, which pleases me to no end. I will enjoy it thoroughly."

He accepted the offered bit of biscuit. "One of the most ridiculous rows I ever had with Stanley Cummings—Julia's late brother, he was one of the Gents—was over a biscuit. A *tin* of biscuits, if I am being entirely honest. We knew at the time it was ridiculous, but we were both being stubborn."

"I am grateful you have learned to stop being stubborn about biscuits."

On they wandered, past stalls and crowds. It was an easy thing being in her company. Even dressed a little uncomfortably and with the worry of the next day's fight heavy on his mind, he felt entirely at ease. She lifted his burdens simply by being with him. He hoped he did the same for her.

They reached the open area where horses were corralled in the hope of being sold. He'd always enjoyed that section of any fair. It was no surprise that Penelope immediately stopped to study the animals. Offerings at country fairs like this were often sparse and focused on work horses. He didn't doubt Penelope would appreciate a horse no matter its pedigree or purpose, but Fairfield's focus would be riding horses or impressive matched teams to pull grand carriages. She was unlikely to find something here that would suit her needs.

"Niles." She spoke his name in an amazed whisper. "Look at that horse by the wagon."

He followed her gaze to a stunning white horse.

"I can't tell from this distance and angle if it is a mare, a stallion, or a gelding." Her focus hadn't shifted in the least. "Do you suppose it is pure white or a gray that has gone white?"

"We'd need to get a closer look."

But she shook her head. "That would afford its handlers a closer look at you and a reason to remember you. 'Twould be dangerous for tomorrow."

"And unfortunately," he said, "they probably won't discuss anything with you if you attempt an inquiry yourself."

"That is truer than it ought to be."

A quick glance around revealed they were in luck. Aldric and Digby were happening past.

Niles waved them over. "Penny would very much like to know more about the white horse at the back, but neither of us is in a position to lead the charge in asking questions."

Digby caught on quickly. "Because she is a lady, and you are a . . . duke."

Aldric was nodding along, clearly having realized the impediment at the same time Digby had.

"We'll lead the discussion," Aldric said. "You two remain nearby and keep your ears perked."

It was the perfect plan.

"My good man," Digby called out to the horse trader nearest the animal they were interested in. He waved him over.

"'Ow may I 'elp you?" The man watched them with awe and hope.

"What can you tell us of that white animal?" Digby asked the question casually, with the air of dandification that had prevented so many people over the years from taking his true measure.

"Spirited stallion," the man said.

"A stallion," Penelope whispered. That seemed to be the answer she'd been hoping for.

"But he ain't so full of the fire that he's difficult. He don't like doing the farm work I'd hoped he'd do, and it's a right struggle keeping him patient enough to see to it."

Under her breath, Penelope said, "That is *not* a farm horse."

Aldric eyed them without seeming to.

"I'd like to know where the horse came from," Penelope whispered quickly, "and if it is truly white."

To the horse trader, Aldric said, "I do not hail from this area. Are white horses common here?"

"This'n came from Lincolnshire," the man answered. "And though I've seen gray horses about, he's a different sort. Skin underneath's pink, if you can believe it."

"I'll believe it if I can see it," Digby said.

The man dipped his head and rushed toward his horse. Digby and Aldric both looked at Penelope expectantly.

"Pink skin tells us it is a true white horse," she said. "The man said it's a stallion. *And* from Lincolnshire, so there is the possibility it could be descended from Alcock's Arabian."

"You wouldn't be able to prove that," Niles warned.

"I know, but I have a true-white broodmare. We could breed white horses. I don't know of any other horse-breeding estate with that focus. When a true-white horse happens to be born, the interest is immediate. And when that horse becomes available for purchase, the asking price is incredibly high. To breed true-white horses with lines like this stallion has . . . . That'd be the making of Fairfield."

Niles took her hand while they were being paid such little heed. He was having to be careful not to draw notice.

"I don't want to get excited too quickly," she said. "I'm certain I can't afford him. But heavens, Niles, if I could . . . Being unmarried, I have no hope of the banks lending me money for the other stallion I was hoping to purchase. Having only one stud will slow down the building of my business. But to have this one, this *remarkable* one, would change everything. Fairfield could turn a tremendous profit in only a couple of years."

"Perhaps this is the beginning of that miracle we're hoping for," he said.

She released a tight breath. "It would require a miracle."

The man was returning, leading the horse by a rein. Niles squeezed Penelope's hand quickly before letting go.

"Age, overall health, more about its temperament," Penelope said quickly. "Let's make certain it definitely has not been gelded. Then a price."

Digby and Aldric continued asking the questions, managing to do so without seeming overly eager and without drawing undue attention to Niles. All the while, Penelope studied the stallion. So did Niles. It was exquisite. The pink of his nose, now near enough to be clearly seen, confirmed that he was truly white. And his eyes were blue.

This was a unique horse.

Penelope stroked its nose and rubbed its neck. And while the animal didn't seem to entirely trust her, it didn't snap or nip or object.

"True white. Beautiful lines. It hasn't been gelded." The slight shake in her whisper, Niles felt certain, arose from the enormity of this discovery. "Oh, Niles, I am getting my hopes up."

"So am I."

The horse trader quoted an asking price. Penelope froze. Niles didn't think he'd ever seen her so still. He'd been to Tattersalls and been present for equine purchases often enough to have had something of a guess as to what the trader would ask. He'd assumed the price would be high. Had Penelope as well?

Digby indicated they'd need to discuss it a moment. The four of them took a few steps away and spoke quietly.

"The price he's asking is far, far lower than it could be." Penelope shook her head. "And while I want to agree to it before he realizes his error, I'd also feel criminal accepting it."

"I know the man's family," Digby said. "I guarantee you he believes he is ruthlessly cheating you."

"What if we asked him to deliver the animal to Pledwick Manor for an additional fee? Then I could pay a little more and feel a little better without wounding his pride by insisting he doesn't know the value of what he has."

"Wise," Aldric said.

"Does this mean you can afford the stallion?" Niles asked. "Without having to petition any banks for a loan?"

She turned to him, shaking a little. With a look of absolute amazement, she nodded. "A horse like this shouldn't be at a tiny fair in an isolated corner of the kingdom. *I* never expected to be at a tiny fair in an isolated corner of the kingdom. My mind simply refuses to make any sense of this."

"Logical or not," Aldric said, "this opportunity is both real and, I suspect, fleeting. If you are going to seize it, you had best do so quickly."

"I haven't that much money on hand," Penelope said. "I would need to write to my solicitors to release funds, which would take at least a week."

Digby waved that off. "I can pay the man, and you and I can settle accounts once your funds reach you."

"I would appreciate that." Penelope still seemed to be holding her breath, as if afraid to let herself believe the truth of her unforeseen good fortune. "I would also need to keep the animal in the Pledwick stables until I can arrange for its transport to Surrey. That would be another inconvenience to you."

Digby smiled. "I will consider it repayment for you and Niles getting my little silver filly to feel at ease. The stable staff are all singing your praises."

Penelope looked at Niles once more. "It will still be years before Fairfield is profitable enough to help us find a solution to our separation. But this would make it possible."

How he wanted to pull her into his arms, to kiss her and hold her and tell her how well worth the wait a life together would be. Decorum required he do none of those things. So he contented himself with a smile of encouragement.

"I've always wanted to be part of a miracle," Digby said. "And purchasing horses is rather fun." With a flourish, he strode back to where the horse trader waited. Aldric joined him there.

The nervousness that had clung to Penelope gave way to excitement at last. Her eyes danced and shone. "Our fortunes are turning, Niles."

"And it's about time," Niles added. "Now we just need to plead for one more miracle tomorrow."

"I'd beg you to be careful, but I suspect that would make the undertaking *more* dangerous, as you'd be likely to hesitate and overthink."

"I intend to fight as hard and as skillfully as I can," he said. "And if fate is as kind tomorrow as she has chosen to be today, I'll not only not get mauled in the process, but I might also even win."

"That will be my request, then: not that you be careful but that you don't get mauled."

He chuckled. "I will do my best."

Her gaze remained on the white horse. It was truly a beautiful animal.

"What do you mean to do the rest of today?" she asked.

"Walk about with your arm through mine. Perhaps have another fairing. Wander about, and enjoy the company."

"That would be *my* company?"

He smiled. "If I'm lucky."

She set her hand in his. "Niles Greenberry, from this moment forward, I am choosing to believe that we are going to be very, very lucky."

Chapter Thirty-One

DIGBY HAD SECURED A ROOM in the Green Badger for the next day, where Niles could prepare for the fight in privacy, as much as he could with all the Gents there as well.

"I cannot promise this is the oddest thing you will do as a gentleman's gentleman," Digby said to Wilson, "but it definitely will not be commonplace."

"Do valets not usually cut their employer's hair?"

"Trim it, perhaps," Digby said. "But very seldom will you find yourself cutting it all off."

"I suspect Marston hadn't anticipated, when taking the position as my valet ten years ago," Niles said, "that he would repeatedly help me prepare for bouts in the boxing ring."

Another snip of the shears sent a tumble of hair to the floor. Niles wasn't vain about his hair, neither was he particularly attached to it, but the only time he ever cut it off entirely was in preparation for a fight.

Two hours remained until the battle was scheduled to begin, and it was starting to feel very, very real.

One more snip and Digby declared his hair "sorted."

Niles reached up and ran his fingers through what remained of it: about two inches of hair all around. It wasn't fashionable, but it was the safest way to go into a fight. "Thank you, Wilson," he said.

"Don't get yourself killed in this fight, and I will consider myself well thanked."

Niles rose from his chair, brushing the straggling bits of cut hair off his head. "Have you grown so attached to me, Wilson?"

"No, sir." Wilson's very direct manner of addressing them all was an endless source of hilarity. "But you're important to Lord Jonquil, and it's now my life's mission to look after the people he cares about."

"Look what we have for you." Kes set a twine-wrapped parcel on the dressing table.

Niles looked at them all, nervous and curious all at once.

"It's nothing bad," Aldric said. "Open it."

That was good enough for Niles. He untied the twine and peeled back the paper. Inside was a pair of yellow pantaloons and a black sash, precisely like those he'd always worn when fighting as the Cornish Duke.

"You didn't come to Yorkshire intending to fight," Henri explained, "so we felt certain you don't have your yellows with you."

"I don't." Niles had assumed he'd be fighting in the worn-out riding breeches he'd selected for the purpose. "How did you know where to find them?" He'd not given any instructions. Perhaps his valet had assisted.

"We had them made," Aldric explained. "Marston provided your measurements."

Niles held the yellow pantaloons out in front of himself.

"The Cornish Duke rises again," Lucas said with a grin.

"Let us hope His Grace isn't rising simply to fall on his face." Niles took the black sash from the bundle, hardly believing he was doing this again. "So much more is riding on it now than in the past."

"That's why you're going to go out there and give the Bath Butcher the hardest fight of his career." Aldric held his gaze, firm and unwavering. "Just stepping into the ring earns you £100. That gives you options, Puppy."

He'd been telling himself that all morning. That £100 wouldn't eliminate all the obstacles between himself and Penelope. And it wouldn't fix things immediately. But he could purchase the estate he'd been saving for and start his time in Parliament. He would save his income from that estate. Penelope would save as much of Fairfield's profits as she could. In a few years, they'd have enough for him to sell his estate and purchase something closer to Fairfield. They would finally be together, building the life they dreamed of.

But *winning* the fight would change the calculations. Property near her would be almost within his means. Months, perhaps a year, and they would have enough.

He'd decided to believe in miracles, and believing meant doing his utmost to bring about another one.

As the time for the fight drew near, Niles changed into the yellow pantaloons his friends had procured for him. Wilson and Digby helped him tie the black sash around his waist, carefully tucking the ends under so there would be nothing for his opponent to grab hold of.

The Cornish Duke always fought with yellow dots painted on his face—ten on each cheek, forming inverted triangles. It was a nod to the banner of the actual Duke of Cornwall but without copying it exactly. Stanley had been the first to suggest the affectation, not merely because it was appropriate for Niles's moniker, but also because it made him more difficult to recognize outside the ring. It had worked brilliantly.

Stanley had painted the yellow dots on Niles's face for his very first foray as the Cornish Duke. It had become tradition in the years since, whenever the Gents had helped Niles prepare for a fight, for them to take turns painting the yellow dots. It was a reminder that though Niles had lost Stanley, had lost his most ardent and unwavering source of support and encouragement, he wasn't alone. He had the best friends a fellow could ask for. It gave him confidence and reassurance.

Marston had created the yellow paint Niles needed for that day's fight, something he'd been doing for a decade. The Gents, in turn, painted the dots on Niles's face.

"How are you feeling?" Henri asked as they undertook the ritual.

"Determined," Niles said. "I know the odds are not in my favor, but the odds were decidedly against a pure white stallion being at the Hamblestead fair."

"Your Penny got her miracle," Lucas acknowledged as he finished painting the last of the yellow dots.

Niles stood. He rolled his neck, shook the tension from his arms, and squared his shoulders. "Now I'm going to go fight for mine."

The Gents offered final words of encouragement before slipping out of the inn. Niles would remain behind for a time in order to arrive separate from them so his identity would be harder to ascertain. Even in the silence left behind, their support remained with him, buoying him as he faced what was likely both the most important fight of his career and the last.

"I believe in miracles," he said. "I believe in Penny. I believe in *us*." He bounced a little with pent-up tension and energy, the way he always did before a fight. This time, though, he felt more focused. And he felt more confident, despite being inarguably outmatched.

Pugilists were meant to arrive at the ring with a second, not entirely unlike duelists on the field of honor. The Cornish Duke was known not to do so. The oddity had been attributed to a quirk of the already unusual boxer. Truth was, Niles couldn't risk his identity being known to any more people, and none of the Gents could fill that role.

He made the long walk entirely on his own from a side door at the inn, across a wide field, toward the din of the crowd. It was a lonely journey he knew well. He had kept his courage up during previous walks to the ring by reminding himself he was getting that much closer to claiming his dreams of owning an estate and serving in Parliament. During this solo trek, Penelope filled his mind. Winning this purse would mean they could be together sooner, with less waiting or struggling ahead of them. It was an opportunity fate wouldn't offer again.

We're going to build a life together. That's what I'm fighting for. For us.

The gathered crowd, quite possibly the largest he'd ever fought in front of, pulsated in a great mass around the fighting ring.

Niles knew his part.

He held his chin at a proud angle and walked with confident, almost arrogant steps toward his destination. As he approached, someone in the crowd called out, "The Cornish Duke!" His yellow pantaloons and yellow dots painted on his face made him easily identifiable.

This was the point in every contest when his nerves ebbed and the exhilaration of the fight began to invigorate him. He knew he was good at boxing, and that was a great feeling for one who was far more accustomed to applauding others for being adept at their various undertakings. And the possibility of adding to his coffers was exciting as well.

Martin was easy to spot, and not merely because he, too, was stripped from the waist up. Though only two or three inches taller than Niles, the Bath Butcher was far more solidly built, with thick, powerful muscles testifying to his profession.

He is not undefeated nor undefeatable.

The crowd roared as Niles stepped into the ring at the same moment Martin did. Niles took a fortifying breath but didn't allow his uncertainty to show. Confidence, even if it had to be somewhat feigned, was an important strategy.

But Martin looked every bit as confident as Niles was taking pains to appear. More than that, the man looked fiercely determined. The Butcher had lost his last two fights, highly publicized affairs that had led to questions about his future in the sport. The man would be fighting with every bit of strength and ability he possessed, intent not to lose again.

But this wasn't a matter of reputation for Niles; he was fighting for a future with Penelope.

The cheers and jeers that sounded all around him faded into indistinguishable cacophony as the fight began. Niles had learned early on not to pay any heed to whose side the crowd seemed to be on. Spectators were notoriously fickle.

Niles and Martin circled each other, each sizing up the other. The Bath Butcher was a hesitant fighter, taking his time and pulling back after each swing or jab. He also had a shorter reach than first impressions would lead a person to expect. Niles knew all that.

He also suspected his opponent was well aware that the Cornish Duke didn't deal blows as powerful as others of their profession and had been felled in the past by less devastating blows than others could endure.

Speed was Niles's greatest asset in this fight. Brute strength was Martin's.

The first four rounds were uneventful. Martin landed a few grazing blows. Niles managed a few of his own. He might have dealt more damage if the Butcher hadn't insisted on hovering just out of reach.

By the fifth round, Niles knew he had to take the fight to his opponent. Getting within striking range was a risk, but the fight would go on for ages otherwise. Niles's quickness would prevent at least some of Martin's blows from landing.

Niles stepped closer and feinted to the left. Martin took the bait and swung hard, but Niles sidestepped. Martin stumbled, and Niles landed a crushing blow.

Cheers erupted. Niles ignored them. He needed to remain focused.

The same tactic worked once more. Martin absorbed the punch but moved a little slower afterward. It would take a lot of well-landed blows to bring down the Butcher. Three more slowed him but didn't topple him.

Then the Bath Butcher's fist found Niles's face. Pain sent him stumbling backward.

Niles did his best to shake off the blow. He managed to duck another swing. But not the next one.

The Bath Butcher grew more spirited. Seeing it, Niles took a bolder approach as well.

They were both still on their feet when the sixth round began. Niles could see his opponent was flagging. He hoped he was hiding his own pain and exhaustion better than Martin was.

A life with Penelope. Niles's fist found Martin's jaw, sending him reeling backward. But the man made a surprisingly fast recovery, lunging forward in the very next instant. He landed a blow to Niles's midsection.

The air rushed from Niles's lungs. He staggered but stayed on his feet.

Fighting for a miracle.

Niles set his feet once more.

A future of our own.

He raised his fists to fighting position.

A life with Penelope.

Niles met the Butcher's fearsome glare with one of his own.

And swung.

Chapter Thirty-Two

PENELOPE COULDN'T KEEP STILL. ALL morning, she'd paced from one window to the next, one room to the next, watching the front drive, all the while knowing Niles wouldn't be returning for hours. But he *would* return. She refused to believe otherwise. People died in pugilist fights, but he wouldn't. People were horrifically injured, but he wouldn't be. He wouldn't.

"Boxing matches are a bit frowned on," Violet said, finding her at yet another window, "but they aren't technically illegal. And the local magistrate helped plan this one, so the Gents won't find themselves in a dangerous situation there."

The ladies had been told the Gents were attending the bout, but Niles's participation hadn't been revealed. And it wasn't Penelope's place to tell them.

"I have heard these pugilist events can turn to mob rule at times," Penelope said. "I will feel better when he—*they*—have returned. Safe."

Violet gave her arm a squeeze. "You don't need to pretend with any of us that Niles isn't special to you. We all know, and we all wholeheartedly approve."

"I wish my brother did."

"He came to England ready to sign the marriage agreement with Niles. He must have approved of him then."

"Yes, but he was not very approving when he left here."

"Of *Niles*?"

Penelope shook her head. "Of *me*," she acknowledged. "Of my hopes for resecuring the match with Niles, which Liam thought impossible, and of my determination to keep Fairfield, which he thought an arrogant and foolhardy dream."

"You realize, of course, that if he had a *brother* showing such determination to secure a good match and save his estate, he would be unspeakably proud."

That was undeniably true. "Were I a man, I would be applauded."

Violet gave her an encouraging look. "And even if your brother does not choose to be proud of you, perhaps *especially* if he doesn't, you should be proud of yourself. You've managed what very few could, and that gives you ample reason to believe you can weather the storms ahead as well."

Penelope hadn't really thought of that. So many of her plans had proven ill-conceived and had needed to be abandoned. It could be difficult to remember how much she *had* accomplished.

"I did purchase a horse yesterday," she said.

Excitement pulled Violet's eyes wide. "I saw it in the stables this morning. Penelope, that might be the most gorgeous horse I have ever seen."

That elusive feeling of pride swelled in Penelope's heart. "Finding the stallion at the Hamblestead fair was a remarkable spot of luck. But recognizing the enormity of what I found and having the means to take advantage of it was the result of a lot of years of very hard work." When had she ever acknowledged all the effort she had invested in the future she was reaching for? "And still, being here to attend the fair rather than on my way back to Ireland was the result of holding fast to what I know to be right."

"And that, my dear friend, is inarguably commendable."

"Have I thanked you and Kes enough for all you've done to help me?" Penelope hoped they knew how grateful she truly was.

Violet squeezed her hand. "You have thanked us, and we are happy to be in a position to help. You are one of us now, Penelope. And we would move mountains for each other."

"Julia warned me that once a person is made part of this group, she is part of it forever."

"Objections?" Violet asked.

"None."

After a quick hug, Violet left Penelope to continue her vigil. And it was not many minutes later that a carriage arrived, a Pledwick Manor coachman up top.

Thank the heavens.

She rushed to the entryway, reaching it in time to see the Gents flood in. Niles was not with them.

Aldric was nearest, and she pulled him aside. "Where is he?" she asked in a worried whisper.

"Wilson is bringing him in through a side door. We're attempting to keep today's events a secret from the staff."

That made sense, and the logical nature of the arrangement eased her concerns.

"To his room?" she asked.

Aldric nodded.

It was all the direction she needed. Penelope did her best to move with an aura of ease and nonchalance, not wishing to draw attention, all the while her heart begging her to speed her steps. Aldric would not have been so casual if Niles were horribly injured. And they would have remained in the village, taking a room at the inn so the local doctor could see to him.

She told herself all those things as she made her way up the stairs and down the corridor, but she didn't feel entirely reassured.

The door to his bedchamber was closed. She knocked, holding her breath as she waited.

After what felt like an eternity, the door opened, and Wilson eyed her from the other side.

"Is he here?" she asked, unable to keep the tone of pleading from her voice.

The young man smiled back at her. "I told him you'd rush to his side." He pulled the door open the rest of the way and motioned her in, then closed the door behind her.

Niles was sitting on the bed, looking the other way. She couldn't tell from this distance or vantage point how bad off he might be. Niles's valet stepped into view. Penelope froze. The staff weren't meant to know what Niles had been up to. Feeling a bit frantic, she looked at Wilson.

"Marston knows," Wilson said.

The valet smiled and dipped his head. "A good valet knows how to keep his employer's secrets, and I assure you, I have kept this one for years."

Feeling better on that score but not entirely relieved, she continued her walk to the bed, where Niles sat. She walked around to the far side, the direction in which he was looking. That he was upright seemed to her a good sign.

He turned his head a little more as she approached. What was it he didn't want her to see? His hands rested on his lap. His knuckles were split and bruised. Penelope sat on the edge of his bed. She very carefully slipped her hand beneath one of his, holding it without touching the wounds.

"Niles?" She spoke softly but made certain she didn't sound pitying or horrified. She knew him well enough to realize without being told that he was attempting to spare her while also worrying that he'd cause her grief.

"I'm a sight, Penny." Niles likely didn't realize how relieved she was simply to hear him speak. The words were a bit muffled, yes, but they were sensible and the sentence complete. She'd worried that his mind might be addled by a few too many powerful blows.

"You promised me you wouldn't get mutilated," she said. "I need you to prove to me that you didn't."

He kept his face turned away. "I believe the word I used was *mauled*."

"It amounts to the same in the end."

He didn't look at her.

"I know boxing matches aren't gentle affairs, and I don't expect you to look as though you've been for an invigorating ride through the countryside. I simply need to know the state of you, to be reassured that you are relatively whole."

Still, he hesitated.

"Niles, please. You're worrying me."

"I was trying to *avoid* worrying you." He turned toward her at last.

She made a quick accounting: a blackened and swollen eye, a gash on one cheek, a bruised nose, a split lip. And even at all that, she breathed a sigh of relief, one he seemed to misinterpret.

"I warned you I looked ghastly."

She touched his uncut cheek, gently because his whole face must have hurt. "You look far better than I had imagined. Better than I had feared."

"Your imagination must be incredibly vivid. Or morbid."

"Let's just call it *morvid*."

It was good to see him smile, however tiny the expression. He took hold of her hand, the one touching his face, and lowered it, clasped in his, to his heart.

"I have debated all day," she said, "whether I was more frustrated that ladies aren't permitted to attend pugilistic contests and are, therefore, left to fear the worst or more grateful because it meant not seeing you get hurt."

"Have you reached a conclusion?"

She scooted closer. "If I'd had to watch someone punching you, I'd have been hard-pressed not to march into the box or ring or whatever it is called and start throwing a few punches myself."

"We'd need to work on your technique first."

He was lucid and witty, speaking with the difficulty one would expect from a person whose face had taken a beating but without the misery that would come if his jaw were broken or he'd lost a great many teeth. And while his eye was swollen, it was not swollen shut.

Her perusal of his face led to a sudden realization that she had missed an alteration in him so significant that she began to doubt her powers of observation. "What happened to your hair?" It was cut quite short.

"Hair that is long enough to grab hold of is a significant liability in boxing."

That was surprising. "Is holding one's opponent by the hair permitted?"

"There are very few things that are not."

It sounded as brutal as she'd heard it was. Still, he had emerged relatively whole.

She looked at Marston, who was gathering strips of linen and what appeared to be jars of liniment. "His injuries are all ones he will recover from? I needn't be worried that something horrible is soon to come of this?"

"He'll be a touch miserable for a few days," the valet said. "But he'll entirely recover."

Penelope's heart at last eased. She wasn't going to lose him, and he wouldn't suffer endlessly for that day's bout.

With her most pressing concern addressed, she needed to know the outcome of the fight. The winning purse was enormous, significant enough that he would be very close to having money enough to purchase an estate near Fairfield. It would cut years off the amount of time they needed to wait to begin their lives together.

She turned back to her beloved Niles. "Did you win the fight?"

He hesitated for the length of a breath. "I didn't." He sounded genuinely ashamed. "The Bath Butcher is legendary. Not the very best boxer in the kingdom but a better one than I am. I did warn you of that. I fought very hard, Penny. I really did."

She lifted one of his battered hands to her lips and gently kissed a comparatively unscathed bit of it.

"I don't want you to be disappointed in me," he said quietly.

"I never could be, Niles Greenberry. You fought, quite literally, for the chance for us to build a life together. You did it knowing the odds were not in your favor. That is something I could never be anything but enormously proud of. You are remarkable. Don't you ever doubt or forget that."

"Seems a gentleman ought to keep a lady around who says things like that to him," Wilson said.

"You're not meant to speak out of turn, Wilson," Marston was quick to say. His eyes darted to Niles. "Even if what you are saying is entirely true."

Niles smiled at Penelope. "And she let me steal some of her Cornish fairings yesterday. How could I resist keeping her?"

"I purchased a few more fairings from the stall before leaving the fair last evening."

"I will now be sorely tempted to steal them from you."

It was good to hear him jesting. He was in obvious pain, and losing his match must have weighed heavy on him, but he wasn't drowning in his struggles.

"I might be willing to allow you to have some fairings, no stealing necessary. You would be paying a forfeit for them, of course."

"A steep forfeit?" Niles probably would have smiled at her if the two men weren't fussing with his face so much.

"I would think of something worth the exchange."

"In other words, I wouldn't be stealing but rather paying for the privilege of claiming my fairing crumbs."

"We need to get plasters on his cuts and bruises," Marston said, taking up position at the side of the bed. "The sooner we do it, the better they'll heal."

"I can help with the plasters or anything else that is needed," Penelope offered.

But Marston shook his head. "Some of the wounds that need tending are not accessible if he's to stay decently clothed."

She wouldn't insist that his dignity and privacy be violated, no matter how desperately she wanted to stay there with him.

"Do you both vow to take exceptionally good care of him? He means the world to me."

"Of course, Miss Seymour," Marston replied.

"We will," was Wilson's promise.

Penelope lightly kissed Niles's less-injured cheek. "Rest, my dear."

"You'll come look in on me again?"

"I'd like to see anyone try to stop me. I was taught how to deliver a powerful punch, after all."

Confident that her darling Niles was well looked after, Penelope slipped from the room.

She softly closed the door, then took in a quick breath. Her heart was racing with a promising possibility that had quite suddenly occurred to her. If this unexpected idea proved a good one, it could change everything.

Chapter Thirty-Three

Niles felt as if he'd been run over by a mail coach. He'd sneaked a glimpse of himself in a mirror and knew he looked like it as well. But he'd come away from a bout with the Bath Butcher with no broken bones, able to stand and walk, and with his wits intact. That was reason to be proud of himself.

That hard-earned pride, though, didn't entirely erase his disappointment. He'd known victory was unlikely, yet he'd harbored some hopes of securing the winner's purse. He could have been that much closer to beginning his life with Penelope.

There would be other fights he could take up, but he wasn't sure he dared. It wasn't merely that he was older now than the majority of his opponents would be, neither was he afraid of taking another beating. He'd drawn more attention during this match than he had in the past. Were his identity to be discovered, it would put an end to a great many things: his political aspirations, his acceptance in Society, his future family's standing. He wouldn't do that to Penelope.

This had been his chance at a windfall, and he'd come up short.

A quick knock sounded at the door in the rhythm Stanley and Lucas had always used. The Gents had come to look in on him, no doubt.

Wilson had remained in the room while Niles's own valet saw to duties that took him to other areas of the house. The young man opened the door but not far enough for anyone to enter.

"Is he decent enough for us to intrude?" Lucas's voice asked from the other side.

"It doesn't matter if he is or isn't," Wilson declared. "No one will be intruding on my watch." The young man was fearsome, that much was certain.

"Are you attempting to improve my manners, Wilson?" Lucas asked with a laugh.

"I'm attempting to look after your Puppy," Wilson answered. "If you receive a lesson in manners as a result, so be it."

A rumble of laughter echoed in. Lucas had not, it seemed, arrived alone.

"They can come in, Wilson," Niles said. "They'll do so regardless."

Wilson looked back at him. "If they cause a ruckus, I'll toss them out. I've been using your boxing building, and I'm not terrible at fisticuffs."

"We consider ourselves warned," Lucas said as he stepped inside.

As Niles had predicted, the rest of the Gents were with Lucas. But Niles had not guessed that Penelope would step inside as well. He wasn't disappointed, only surprised.

"Lud, Puppy," Lucas said, eyeing him up and down. "You look like something purgatory itself tossed out."

"Quite." Digby summoned one of his expressions of theatrical dandification. "The purple arising around your eye does nothing for your complexion."

Niles met Penelope's eye. "See what I have to put up with, Penny?"

She climbed onto the bed, where he sat propped up on pillows, with a blanket pulled up to his chest, which was wrapped in bandaging to ease some of the pain in his ribs. She settled in, seated directly beside him. To the Gents, she said, "I am fully aware of the scandalous nature of my current location, but as nothing untoward is actually occurring and he does, in fact, look like something tossed out of purgatory, I will trust the lot of you to keep your mouths firmly shut on the matter."

"Else what?" Kes asked.

"I'll tell Our Julia, Lily, and Le Capitaine that you are causing problems and let them exact whatever punishment they deem appropriate."

That threat hit its mark, and she very swiftly had vows of silence from all of them.

Everyone found places to sit or lean as Penelope reached to hold Niles's bandaged hand.

"How are you feeling?" Henri asked. "Truly?"

"Like I just fought ten rounds against the Bath Butcher."

"Accurate," Kes said with a nod.

"I don't think anything is broken though," Niles said. "And there's nothing that hurts that won't heal."

Penelope tucked herself against him, not saying as much but clearly showing that she was grateful he wasn't worse off than he was.

"Would you like to hear something that'll make you feel remarkably better?" Lucas asked.

"Coming from you lot, I'm not sure."

They grinned, all knowing perfectly well that they'd been known to be more than a little ridiculous at times.

"You want to hear this," Aldric said.

"I always listen to the General." Niles was beyond intrigued.

"Firstly," Digby said, "we have settled upon the perfect nickname for Penelope."

"Have you?" He turned to look at her, but she only shrugged.

"I have not yet heard this."

Lucas looked ready to burst. "Mag," he declared. "We've tested it out amongst ourselves and will not be swayed from adopting it."

"I might believe it is perfect if I had any inkling why you've chosen it," Niles said.

"It's a simple thing," Lucas answered. "She's our Puppy's Penny, but she's tiny, more like a quarter penny. But we couldn't call her Farthing, now could we?"

Digby looked horrified at the very idea. "Certainly not."

"We chose the next best thing," Henri said.

Ah. To his sweet Penny, Niles explained, "*Mag* is a cant term for a farthing."

She smiled broadly, looking at the Gents with every indication of delight. "I accept."

"Our second announcement," Digby said, "is that Mag has had a stroke of absolute brilliance, something frankly, we're all a little embarrassed to not have realized sooner."

"What is this brilliant idea, Penny—I intend to keep calling you Penny rather than Mag, assuming you've no objections?"

"None." She looked exceedingly happy. "I was thinking of the fairings we had at the fair, and I realized we'd sorted the difficulty with biscuits in just the way we ought to with land."

"Martin must have hit me harder than I thought, because my mind can't make sense of that at all."

Penelope smiled ever more broadly. "I'm explaining it poorly but only because I'm so pleased that there is a third option, just like we decided to believe there would be."

Niles looked out at his friends, hoping someone would explain it plainly.

Aldric took up the task. "Fairfield is not subject to an entailment, which not only means that Mag's great-uncle was able to leave it to her but also that it does not have to remain intact. The owner of the property is free to do with it as she sees fit."

"And she asked us if it was possible for a piece of the estate to be portioned off and sold," Digby continued the explanation, "and, assuming it was possible, if the requirement to own land in order to serve in Parliament dictated how much land a person had to own."

"It doesn't," Niles said. Anticipation spread like a bubble in his chest, the way it did when one was on the cusp of something significant.

Penelope sat up a little straighter, looking more directly at him. "There is a corner of Fairfield, a small clearing amongst some trees. It isn't near the stables nor part of the lawns or the kitchen gardens or the area where the horses would be running. What if you owned that part? You would own land, but it would be part of *our* home, adjacent to where you lived. Then, when you find your place in Parliament, you would be living among the people you would serve without having to live away from . . . me."

"There might be some question whether or not it is actually mine." He didn't want the possibility to lodge itself in his mind before he knew if it was, in fact, both possible and advisable.

"That is why it is important that you actually purchase it," Aldric said. "If the deed to the land is in your name and there is record of a purchase, it would be undeniably yours."

"Are you certain?"

"Believe me, I have spent a great deal of time these past months studying what it takes to make a *permanent* claim on an estate." Aldric had been given the use of one of his father's many estates but not ownership of it. It made sense that he was keen on discovering the exact ramifications of that.

"And," Digby added, "you could erect a building on the land, perhaps make it look like a cottage or some such thing so it didn't draw attention, but inside, you could hang bags of hay and keep strips of fabric for wrapping up knuckles."

"My very own boxing building?"

The Gents all nodded. Niles looked at Penelope and saw eager agreement on her face as well. Could this work? Could it truly work?

"Land in that area of Surrey comes dear," he reminded her.

"We did talk about that," Penelope said. "Paying a fair price would be important should any questions arise about your ownership, so I worried that that might make this impossible. But the Gents don't think so."

"If one is buying an entire estate with a house and significant land, then the price would be quite steep," Aldric said. "But you would be purchasing a very small parcel, without any roads leading to it, without buildings or improvements. A fair price for that would be well within your ability to purchase."

He wanted to believe it. "Henri, you are Archbishop for a reason, and I'm counting on you to live up to that moniker by not lying to me. Is all this doable and fair?"

"I have spent years searching for a place to call home," Henri said, "and I know the price of land and the intricacies of what determines that price better than almost anyone. And I can say with certainty that this is, by all accounts, both a fair and ingenious idea."

Niles held tighter to Penelope's hand, no matter that it made his hand ache all the more. This was the miracle they needed.

"There is one difficulty though," she said. "Don't look so crestfallen," she quickly added, apparently seeing his countenance drop. "It isn't insurmountable, by any means. For me to retain ownership of Fairfield, my brother has to sign the marriage contract that he initially negotiated with your grandfather, but to make certain there is no question of legitimacy to the sale of the parcel, you would need to purchase it before the contracts are signed; yet, if we are to catch my brother before he leaves for Ireland, we have to go directly to Cornwall."

"Where are your trustees located?" Niles asked.

"London."

That was not precisely on the way to Cornwall. "What do we do?" he asked the room in general. "Penny and I cannot be in two places at once."

"We have a plan," Lucas said.

"Four words that strike fear into the bravest of hearts," Niles said under his breath.

Penelope leaned against him once more. "It is a good plan, I assure you."

"You and Mag write up letters of intent to buy and sell respectively, requesting that my brother-in-law act as your representative," Kes said. "I'll take the letters to him in London. He is a barrister and, thus, is in a position to meet with Mag's trustees on your behalf in a way that satisfies the law. We can see to that while you two make your way to Cornwall."

"Can your brother-in-law sign on my behalf?" Niles didn't think so.

"No, but he can have all the papers drawn up, have Mag's trustees sign them, and entrust them to me to deliver them to you in Cornwall for the final signature."

"And once you do, I can sign those papers and then the marriage agreement without adding a question mark to the land purchase?" Niles ventured.

Kes nodded.

"What happens if Penny's brother won't sign?" Niles asked.

That brought the first hints of uncertainty to their faces.

It was Digby who spoke. "Then, you two will have yet another decision to make."

"I am choosing to believe it will not come to that," Penelope said. "Life ought not be so cruel as to take away two people's best chances for happiness."

It is a travesty how many people have to fight so very hard simply to be granted the right to live the life they ought to have been permitted all along. Stanley would have urged him to move forward eagerly, clinging to the hope that he would be permitted that precious chance to live a life filled with joy and love. How could he do anything other than keep fighting for it?

"Sounds to me, Digby, like you are about to lose an entire gaggle of guests," Niles said.

"But as I will be abandoned for a good cause," Digby said, "I'll be happy to see you go."

Penelope stretched enough to place a kiss on Niles's cheek. It happened to be his painful one, and he involuntarily winced.

"I'm sorry, sweetheart," she said.

"That does raise another question that needs addressing," Lucas said.

"What question would that be?" Niles asked.

"What explanation we plan to give the rest of the ladies for the sorry, sorry sight of you."

Chapter Thirty-Four

THE SWAY OF THE TRAVELING coach was not soothing enough. Niles had been uneasy and nervous throughout the days-long journey from Yorkshire. Now, mere minutes from his parents' home in Cornwall, he was struggling to keep his anxiety at manageable levels. If not for the peace and comfort of Penelope leaning against him, asleep with his arm around her, he would have been hard-pressed to keep his composure.

Something Aldric said to Henri—the two of them were sitting on the opposite bench with Nicolette—pulled a laugh from him. Penelope startled awake. For a moment, she looked extremely confused.

"I told them they were going to wake you," Nicolette said, reaching over and squeezing Penelope's hand. "These misbehaving Gents owe you an apology."

Niles tucked Penelope closer. She sighed, the sound both one of lingering sleep and what he'd come to recognize as tranquility. Even in difficult moments, Penelope had a way of bringing peace.

"Are you Gents causing trouble again?" Sleep hung heavy in her words.

"Again?" Henri objected. "We have never caused trouble in our lives."

"Puppy, your Archbishop is lying," Penelope said.

"How shall we punish him, Penny?"

Niles was less startled by the gorgeousness of her smile than he had been when they'd first met, but the sight of it still set his heart fluttering.

"Leave him to Le Capitaine," she said. "She'll sort him."

"Yes, she will." Aldric chuckled.

"Laugh all you want," Niles said. "The raisins have predicted you are the next Gent to fall."

"I make a point of never listening to raisins."

"Your true difficulty," Henri replied, "is that the raisins make a point of never listening to us. Some lady will soon claim your heart, and you will have to acknowledge how wrong you were to doubt."

Aldric shook his head. "There is no lady on earth the raisins would doom to that fate."

"But there are plenty your father would," Henri said.

"The duke has his heir, and his heir has an heir. I assure you, neither could possibly care less about my marital status."

"But the rest of us care a great deal," Nicolette said.

Aldric didn't allow that thread to be followed any further. "*Niles and Mag's* marital status is the one we're supposed to be focusing on."

Both Aldric and Digby had painful relationships with their fathers. Henri's connection to his father had also been difficult. It made Niles all the more eager to repair his relationship with his parents. He didn't always appreciate them as much as he ought to.

"How long until we reach your parents' home?" Penelope asked.

He swallowed down a sudden lump of nervousness. "A matter of minutes."

Minutes. He released a tense breath. Minutes away from a reckoning.

Penelope sat up straighter, her posture taking on a bit of tension as well. "I hope Liam hasn't already left for Ireland. What if we've missed him? What if he won't sign the marriage agreements? What if your parents and grandparents don't welcome you back?"

"Take heart, darling," Niles said. "We can endure the coming storm." He was reassuring himself as much as her.

"At least you look a little less like you've just lived through one," Penelope said.

His eye was still a bit dark from the bruising, and the scab on his face was plainly visible. Digby had provided him with a wig that was not highly powdered, which looked a lot like his hair had before cutting it. His appearance would not pass close scrutiny, but he looked enough like himself to be able to offer an explanation other than "I participated in a prizefight under a pseudonym and got pummeled."

"Is your family going to be very angry with you?" Penelope asked.

"I suspect they will be, but they'll behave with company about."

"Is that why we're here?" Aldric asked. "To be a buffer between you and the anger of the entire Greenberry clan, all three or four thousand of them?"

"I thought we made that very clear." Niles made a show of being confused. "Most of you will die, but your deaths will be heroic."

"I will be certain to write a very moving poem honoring that sacrifice," Henri said.

"What makes you think you are going to be one of the survivors?" Aldric shook his head. "I intend to rush in shouting, 'Target the Frenchman!'"

"You will do no such thing," Nicolette said fiercely.

The Gents and their ladies were godsends. From the moment Stanley had greeted him in that Cambridge courtyard so many years earlier, Niles's life had been changed for the better. He had been helped through heartbreak and misery; he'd been uplifted by their laughter and friendship. And he thanked the heavens again for them in this moment.

"I don't want your family to be unkind to you, Niles," Penelope said.

He pressed a kiss to the top of her head. "They won't be unkind. Upset and disappointed, yes, but I've not known them to be truly cruel."

"Requiring you to marry where you didn't wish to is not precisely a kindness."

"Perhaps not," he said, "but it is such a common unkindness that it doesn't overly matter to most people."

"Your unhappiness matters to *me*." She spoke every bit as vehemently as Nicolette had a moment earlier.

"A mutual sentiment, my Penny."

"Now I almost hope they do target the Frenchman," Henri grumbled before pretending to be sick to his stomach.

"First lies and now insults?" Penelope shook her head. "I begin to think your moniker was given ironically."

Through the carriage window, Niles spied a stately Cornish elm, one he knew well. He grew very still. "This is my parents' estate." His stomach tightened and twisted painfully. *My parents' estate.* He couldn't even bring himself to call it home, no matter that it had been his home all his life and was still where he returned every time he completed a journey. "I can't remember ever feeling so unsure of my welcome here."

Penelope leaned against him once more.

"Take courage, you two," Aldric said. "Remember, you've come bearing good news."

That was true. But would it be enough to overcome what he'd done and the hurt he'd caused his family?

Penelope lightly touched his cheek. "Aldric is entirely correct. While the timing was not what your family wanted, the outcome is precisely what they all wished for."

"Perhaps rather than begging for forgiveness," he said, "we should saunter in, bold as brass buttons, and declare that we've come to make all their wishes come true."

The carriage came to a stop. Beyond the windows was his childhood home.

They were met by the expected bevy of servants. The coach door was opened and the step put in place. Everyone inside the carriage alighted in silence. They were ushered as far as the entryway but were then told to wait while the butler took word of their arrival to Niles's parents.

"Being made to wait does not seem like a good sign, does it?" Niles rolled his neck, working very hard not to simply start pacing.

"It could easily be the fact that you have arrived with so many guests," Aldric suggested.

"Let's tell ourselves that." But Niles felt certain the others were as doubtful about the explanation as he was.

The butler returned. "This way, please."

Niles desperately wanted to hold Penelope's hand as they made the trek to the drawing room, but knew he would do best to keep strictly to the expectations of propriety. They needed to give his parents no further reason to think poorly of him.

He stepped over the threshold. How was it a room could be so pleasantly familiar and so uncomfortably uninviting at the same time?

"Lord Aldric Benick," the butler began his introduction as soon as he stepped inside the drawing room. "Mr. and Mrs. Fortier. Miss Seymour. Mr. Niles Greenberry."

His parents stood inside, watching their arrival. Unfortunately, Niles could describe them the same way he'd described the room. Achingly familiar. Heartbreakingly uninviting.

Still, he knew what civility required of him in that moment. "Father, Mother, I believe you know everyone in the group other than Mrs. Fortier"—he indicated Nicolette—"who now resides in Suffolk but is originally from France. Mrs. Fortier, this is my father and mother, Mr. and Mrs. Greenberry."

"*C'est un plaisir de vous rencontrer,*" Nicolette said with a curtsy.

"*Le plaisir est pour nous,*" Father returned with a bow.

Mother was never one to neglect her social obligations, but she did not offer a greeting or welcome of her own. In fact, she was not paying Nicolette the least attention. Mother's unwavering gaze was on Niles.

His heart dropped. He'd caused his mother pain. That was not something he could ever feel good about.

She moved toward him. Niles held his breath. He would endure whatever castigation she delivered. And somehow, he would find a way to mend all this.

"Niles." Mother spoke his name quietly, barely louder than a whisper. But he didn't hear any anger in her tone. She wrapped her arms around him as she'd done so often over the course of his life.

He embraced her in return. "I am sorry for all the difficulties I have caused you these past weeks, Mother."

"You told me often enough that you dreaded the very idea of an arranged marriage," she said, holding him tight. "I am your mother; I ought to have listened."

This was not the reception he'd anticipated. He didn't quite know what to do.

"And I ought not to have placed you in the position I did," he said. "I admit I panicked a little."

She stepped back. "You set off a bit of a panic here as well. The family is divided on this matter: some insist that you were entirely in the wrong, while others have begun to declare that they will follow your lead should your grandparents arrange a marriage for them."

That was not at all what he had intended. He glanced very briefly at his father, who was offering greetings to the new arrivals. "Where does Father fall on the matter?"

"At the moment, I believe he feels conflicted."

"That is far better than livid, which is what I had anticipated."

She patted his arm. "Make no mistake, he is not best pleased with you. But we've also spent a lot of time since your defection discussing what we might have done differently, and he has begun to realize, as I have, that as your parents, we should have given more importance to your happiness and less to the demands of tradition."

"Thank you." His growing amazement rendered the words a little breathless. He'd expected denouncement but was receiving compassion and embrace instead.

"You look as though you had an accident," Mother said. "You're bruised, and there's been a cut on your face."

He gave a reassuring smile. "I grew a little too enthusiastic during a game of sport."

"You do have a tendency to do that." Mother leaned in a bit, lowering her voice. "You and Miss Seymour do not seem to be at odds."

"We aren't," he said. "Quite the opposite, in fact."

Mother turned wide eyes on him. "That is unexpected."

"It certainly was."

She shook her head. "That will make this evening very interesting."

"How so?"

"We are to have supper at your grandparents' house, and neither of them has reached the place of equanimity that I have on the matter."

This welcome reception, then, was not an escape from the reckoning he'd anticipated but merely a delay.

"Niles." Father's greeting was not nearly as tender as Mother's had been. He didn't pull Niles into a hug, nor say his name in the same soft way. But there was no obvious animosity in his eyes. If anything, he looked as uncomfortable as Niles felt. "It is good to have you home again."

"I am sorry my original letter went astray. It was not my intention to cause the distress that I did." But that wasn't entirely forthright, and he thought it best not to add to his deceptions. "I knew staying away would cause difficulty, of course, but I hadn't meant to leave you guessing what happened to me."

"Mr. Seymour wrote to us after finding you in Yorkshire. He explained that you said you had been unwell."

That you said you had been unwell. Not that Niles *had* been unwell. That he *had said* he had been. There was significance to Mr. Seymour's explanation but even more to Father's recounting of it.

"Lord Aldric's letter was far more eye-opening," Mother said.

"Lord Aldric wrote to you?" Niles hadn't been informed of that.

Mother squeezed his arm. "He said you were more yourself than when he had first arrived at Pledwick Manor, which set my mind at ease. He also said we were fortunate to have a son like you, and that far too many people don't treat you as they ought."

"I believe," Father said, "his admonition was that too many people don't *listen* to you as they ought. It was not difficult to understand what he was telling us."

"I didn't ask him to write to you."

Father reached out and set a hand on Niles's shoulder. "I know you didn't. But I'm glad he did. It forced me to look at things a little differently."

"But Grandfather doesn't see things any differently?" Nervousness trickled over him once more.

His parents exchanged uncomfortable glances.

"Mother said our time at Ipsworth tonight will be interesting."

Father raised an eyebrow. "*Very* interesting."

Chapter Thirty-Five

NILES PULLED ALDRIC ASIDE AS they all gathered in the entryway, awaiting the carriages. He'd not yet had a chance to speak with the others, as they'd all been ushered to various bedchambers shortly after arriving in order to dress for dinner at Ipsworth.

"My parents told me you wrote to them from Yorkshire."

Aldric looked a little unsure how Niles felt about that discovery.

"Thank you," Niles quickly added. "My father said your letter is the reason he began thinking differently about my situation and the family's demands. *Thank you.*"

"Stanley would have marched here directly and diplomatically given your family a piece of his mind." A corner of Aldric's mouth pulled in a hint of a smirk. "I am not easily suited to the role of diplomat."

"No, you're not." Niles smiled a little himself.

"I thought a letter might allow me to say what they needed to hear without raising their hackles. And unfortunately, I thought they would be more likely to listen to me than to you."

Niles couldn't argue with that. "The Gents have always heard me in ways no one else ever does."

"Mag does." Aldric motioned to Penelope with his head.

She was chatting amicably with Mother, at ease even in this difficult situation. "My Penny is remarkable."

"Keep that in mind when we reach Ipsworth. If my evaluation of your parents' few hints is correct, your grandfather is excessively put out with you. Remember how remarkably fortunate you are to have found your Penny and that building your life together is worth whatever discomfort you have to endure tonight."

"I will," Niles said.

That declaration was put to the test within moments of arriving in his grandparents' drawing room.

Introductions were quickly undertaken. Grandmother was the perfect hostess, warmly welcoming everyone. Grandfather was equally gracious, except when his eyes would happen upon Niles. He didn't glare, but he did narrow his eyes and tense his jaw.

Nicolette, employing the grace of manner so often associated with the French, smoothed the way. "What a delight it is to be here, Mr. and Mrs. Greenberry. I have never before seen Cornwall, and your grandson was certain your family would kindly allow me to impose a little in order to have a glimpse of this beautiful area of England."

Grandmother motioned for Nicolette and Mother to sit with her, speaking, as they walked to the settee, of the sites nearby that she felt the newly arrived Frenchwoman would find particularly delightful. Henri followed in their wake, staying near his wife.

"Mr. Greenberry," Aldric greeted with a bow. "Always a pleasure to see you."

"The pleasure is mine, Lord Aldric." Grandfather's gaze quickly shifted to Penelope. "Miss Seymour, welcome back. Your brother did not tell us you were returning."

"He did not know."

"He does intend to join us for the evening meal," Grandfather said, "but he returned later than he'd expected from his excursions and is still dressing."

"Liam is here, then?" Penelope pressed.

Grandfather nodded. "He is."

That, Niles would wager, was both a relief and a source of unease for Penelope. It was for him as well.

Without any preamble, Grandfather addressed Niles. "Might I have a few words with you before we eat?" He looked briefly at Father. "Privately."

"Of course." Best get this over with.

He followed Grandfather into the empty sitting room across the entry hall.

They'd not gone more than three steps inside when Grandfather spoke. "Do you have any idea of the havoc you have wreaked in this family, Niles? The humiliation? The worry over your health that you did not relieve but left Mr. Seymour to do? Your mother was certain you were near death's door."

"Why is it Mr. and Miss Seymour were the only ones to make the journey to Yorkshire if my family was so convinced I was taking my last breath?"

Grandfather took his own breath. "I exaggerate, I confess, but the chaos you have sown is no exaggeration. A rift has begun in this family, a divide between those who see the value in the age-old tradition of finding suitable spouses for the Greenberrys and those who think you have the right of it and all your cousins should simply run away from home should your grandmother and I dare to work tirelessly at making good matches for all of you."

Too many people don't listen to you as they ought. Niles deserved to be heard, and he meant to try one last time. "I have told you ever since I was old enough to understand these things that I know myself and my heart well enough to be absolutely certain I could not be happily married to someone I did not already love." He spoke firmly but not confrontationally.

"Your grandmother and I were strangers when we married," Grandfather countered. "And we love each other deeply. Your parents weren't entirely unacquainted, but they found and built that love after they were married."

"And I cannot express how grateful I am that the four of you had such happy outcomes. But my heart does not work that way. I've always known it didn't. You were dooming me and the poor lady you chose to a life of frustration and misery. I couldn't, in good conscience, cause such acute lifelong suffering for either of us."

"If you found her so entirely not to your liking, I wonder that you brought her here with you." It wasn't confusion but doubt that filled Grandfather's words.

"I didn't say she wasn't to my liking," Niles countered. "I said that *an arranged marriage* wasn't. Though it has proven a good approach for others, it would have been anguish for me."

"And you felt the best way to tell me this was to hide in Yorkshire?"

"I have been telling you *for years*," Niles said. "But no one in this family would listen."

Footsteps sounded behind them. They both turned. Penelope crossed to Niles but watched Grandfather. "If I had known that the letters exchanged between you and my brother hadn't so much as been shown to Niles through the entire negotiation, I would never have agreed to it. Arranged marriages are difficult enough without leaving one half of the would-be couple entirely in the dark. He ought to have had a voice in so enormous a decision."

"Is that why you went to Yorkshire?" Grandfather asked her. "To give him a voice?"

"I went to meet him, to find out who he was, to discover if there was a chance of moving forward."

"And what did you discover?"

"That you have a remarkable grandson, Mr. Greenberry. Any lady would count herself fortunate to know him."

To Niles, Grandfather asked, "And what did *you* discover?"

"That you chose well. She and I have similar interests. We get on well. Every time I'm with her, I like her even more. I love her."

"Sounds to me like you could have skipped the theatrics of the past weeks and gone ahead with the match," Grandfather grumbled.

"No, sir," Penelope said. "The choosing is important. Crucial. If you have any doubts on that score, simply contemplate the lengths he has gone to in order to have that choice."

For the first time since Niles's arrival, Grandfather looked a little less sure of himself, even a little humbled.

"Miss Seymour and I were able to come to know each other in Yorkshire," Niles said. "Which is more or less what I'd been asking for all these years: a chance to know someone before *deciding* whether we could happily build a life together."

"And what am I to do with the rest of this family?" Grandfather asked. "There is dissension in the ranks, Niles. The tranquility we have known is under threat."

"I can tell you this: I haven't experienced the least tranquility on this matter for twenty years. I know I am not the only Greenberry who has felt that way. What you have seen as familial tranquility has, in truth, been silent misery. I would hope this family would want to be *actually* happy rather than simply pretending to be."

Penelope took Niles's hand, squeezing it reassuringly. She had come to know him well enough to, it seemed, sense that speaking so bluntly to his grandfather was not an easy thing.

"I really have worked exceptionally hard to make good matches for my children and grandchildren," Grandfather said. "I have given that far greater consideration than most heads of family do."

"Perhaps," Niles said, "instead of abandoning your efforts altogether to appease those who object, you might consider allowing them the opportunity to meet their potential spouses before anything is decided upon, to make your grandchildren's ability to have a choice a crucial part of the process."

"I will give it some thought." It was an enormous concession, truth be told. Niles couldn't manage a response.

Aldric spoke from the doorway. "Pardon the interruption, but I think Miss Seymour would appreciate knowing that her brother has joined everyone in the drawing room."

Penelope took a tense breath. Her shoulders squared. "If you will excuse me." She turned and, chin at a determined angle, walked out of the room.

Chapter Thirty-Six

PENELOPE HAD KNOWN SHE WOULD be uneasy when the time came to face Liam again. But she hadn't expected to be shaking.

The drawing room was still and quiet when she entered. Liam stood facing the door. Both Mrs. Greenberrys watched him. Nicolette and Henri didn't seem to know who to watch.

"What are you doing here?" Liam asked.

'Twasn't the most loving of greetings. "I'd hoped to see you before you continued on to Ireland."

That obviously surprised him. "Did you miss me that much?"

"I have missed you, and I was deeply disappointed not to have been given the chance to say goodbye in Yorkshire." She chose not to point out in that moment that *he* had prevented that farewell.

"You knew what inn I was at," he said. "Would it have been so difficult to have followed me there?"

"I sent a letter to the inn I *guessed* you had stopped at," she corrected. "And the response you sent back indicated you were not overly keen to see me, not merely at that inn but ever again."

Liam's eyes darted about the room. "I would never be so dismissive of my own sister. I cannot imagine why you are maligning me this way."

Everyone was watching them now, listening intently as Liam tossed her into the figurative muck. She had held out some hope that his anger had cooled and that this reunion would not be entirely awful. Being wrong about that was heartbreaking. And while she would like to keep the peace with her brother, she was standing in a room with hopefully her future in-laws, whom she needed to not think of her as a heartless liar.

"I have your letter still, Liam," she said. "I would be willing to read it aloud so we can all determine if I have truly so wholly misinterpreted your words."

Liam's expression froze. A tiny bit of color crept over his face. He took a nostril-flaring breath, releasing it slowly. To the senior-most Mr. Greenberry, Liam said, "I do not wish to delay the meal any longer than it has been. Please, begin without us while I have a private conversation with my sister." And in a rare showing of public poor manners, Liam didn't wait for a response nor for his host to indicate if the plan was to his liking. He simply took hold of Penelope's arm and began leading her out of the room.

Niles stepped into their path. He met Penelope's eyes, his unspoken question obvious.

"I'll be fine," she reassured him.

Liam led her around Niles and out of the drawing room. They made their way from the entryway, down a corridor, and to a door leading out onto a terrace.

When he finally released her arm, he said, "I am beginning to suspect that I will never stop being humiliated by you, Penelope."

"What have I done this time?"

"I have spent the past two days smoothing things over with the Greenberrys, salvaging their opinion of us by explaining that you and Mr. Niles Greenberry simply didn't suit and that it was in everyone's best interest to forgo the planned match. I made so many excuses for you, for him, for us, and just when I feel I have made progress, you arrive making sheep eyes at their son and grandson and undo it all." He spoke in a tense, quick clip. "In their eyes, I will now either be an idiot or a liar."

"We will simply explain that Niles and I made our decision after you left and that when you arrived here a few days ago, there was no reason for you to think anything had changed between him and me."

"Which will only convince them that I am irresponsible and neglectful. Is that really so much better?"

Penelope pushed down her growing frustration. She knew she had caused her brother difficulties, but he seemed determined to think the worst of her and lay at her feet the blame for everything. She could argue with him, point out the many ways in which he was being horribly unfair. Everything she did met with his disapproval. Everything she did was wrong in his eyes. But she didn't want to be at odds with him. If there was a way to make this right, and she wasn't sure there was, she wanted to try. "What do you need from me?" she asked, leaning against the low wall of the terrace, wrapping her arms around herself as a shield against the chilled air. "What can I do?"

"I don't know," he muttered.

The both of them feeling sorry for themselves wouldn't help anything. "There must be something," she insisted. "We cannot leave things this way."

"Most of Dublin society views it as a tragic thing that the older of the Seymour siblings was not male, as you are considered far more competent than I." He began pacing, something she didn't think she'd seen him do before.

"I have never heard anyone express that sentiment," she said.

"Not to you, no." His words were clipped and tense. "They view me as a laughingstock. I had hoped that view wouldn't spread to England."

"I truly don't think it has," she said. "I don't even honestly think that opinion is held in Dublin."

"I have shielded you from a lot of it, Penelope."

Was that true? She'd not noticed even a hint of what he insisted was a widespread view of their family. Surely if his worries were founded, it could not have been kept from her entirely.

He continued on. "You no longer have to interact with Dublin society if you don't wish to, but at least until Mother feels she'd like to venture to London, Dublin is the entirety of my social circle. And they think I'm a dunderhead."

"You will return this time having seen your sister married into a respected English family. Surely that will be to your credit."

But he shook his head. "They will say, 'Miss Seymour got herself married into a respected English family.' I will receive no credit for it."

She chose not to press her suspicion that he was imagining more in other people's evaluations than was actually there. How he felt this would impact him was the crux of the current matter.

"Liam, I cannot be blamed for what other people might say or think. It is unfair to hold their opinions against me."

He stopped walking and turned to face her. "You truly wish to marry Mr. Niles Greenberry?"

"I do." She bounced a little to keep warm.

"And I suspect you actually followed me here, not because you missed your brother but because you need me to sign the marriage agreement?" He eyed her the way a barrister might upon catching a criminal lying in court.

"I *have* missed you," she insisted. "And had your letter not dismissed me so entirely that I knew that feeling was not mutual, my missing you might have been reason enough for me to follow you here. But yes, I also need you to sign the marriage agreement." Her teeth were chattering a little. "If you will not do so as a kindness to your sister, I hope you will at least do so as proof that you are the competent head of your family the world ought to see you as."

"You intend to subject me to extortion?"

Frustration pushed a sigh from her. "I do not intend to lower myself to extortion."

"Neither do I," he said. "But I do have a requirement."

At that, her uneasiness turned to unabated anxiousness. "What requirement?" The question was almost indiscernible, cold shaking her from deep within.

But footsteps on the terrace stopped whatever response he might have made. They both turned to look.

Niles was walking toward them, holding her red wool cloak.

Liam looked none too pleased. "I believe I told you this was meant to be a private conversation, Mr. Greenberry."

"It has apparently escaped your notice, Mr. Seymour, that your sister is chilled to her core." Niles set the cloak on Penelope's shoulders. "Your demands for a private conversation cannot be allowed to supersede her right to not develop an inflammation of the lungs."

"I didn't—" Liam had the decency to look a little ashamed. "I didn't realize. I should have. I'm sorry."

Niles fastened the frog closure near her neck.

Penelope pulled the voluminous length of the cloak around her, sighing at the relief it provided from the cold air.

Niles moved to stand beside her. He set an arm around her, another buffer from the chill. "Now, Mr. Seymour, please continue your discussion about the not-extortion condition under which you will sign the marriage contract."

"This is a private conversation," Liam insisted.

"As the outcome of it impacts me as well, I believe I ought to be included."

Liam's expression grew ever more determined. "My condition is simple, really." He looked directly at Penelope. "You marry in Dublin. I will be seen to be part of your good fortune, and you will be seen treating me like the competent head of the Seymour family. I don't mean groveling but a show of respect and confidence in me and enough deference that I won't be laughed at."

"I have always respected you, Liam. And I do have confidence in you. That you insist on believing otherwise is frustrating."

"Society is driven by perceptions," he said. "I need the people who have influence on my future to believe I am worthy of having one."

"Showing to all the world that I love you and believe in you is no burden at all," she said.

"Prove it." Liam's expression grew more unyielding. "The *only* reason you were not going to be married in Ireland was because the Greenberrys asked that the ceremony take place here. I am asserting some authority in that matter now. Agree to marry in Dublin and show society there that I am worthy of respect, and I will sign the marriage agreement."

That was asking more than he probably realized. All of Niles's family was in Cornwall, generations of them. They had been married in the local church for centuries. Most of his family would likely not go to Dublin. And the Gents would not necessarily be able to make the journey either.

"You'll not budge on this?" she asked.

"I cannot. Too much depends upon it."

To have the future that was now within reach, Niles had to endure more pain. She didn't want to inflict that on him, but what else could be done? "Niles and I will need to talk about this."

Liam met her eye with a gleam of triumph in his gaze. "Discuss it between the two of you. I will return inside."

She watched him walk through the terrace doors. "Do you think I ought to warn him that I now know how to punch like a pugilist?"

"He deserves one just now, I'd say." Niles pulled her fully into his arms. "Give him a moment to get farther away, then we'll go inside as well. Even with your cloak on, you are cold."

Despite her heavy mind and heart, she could smile at that. "Thank you for coming to my rescue."

"An incomplete rescue, I'm afraid. He is still holding our future hostage with his demands of you."

"Of both of us."

They walked together, his arm still around her, through the terrace door. The pace was slow, giving them time to talk before they crossed paths with anyone. The rest of the group would have already begun their meal. Liam had insisted.

"I've spent so much time the past weeks castigating myself for being such a selfish and unfeeling sister. But I am beginning to fear that Liam's grievances against me are broader and of longer standing than I realize. I am not certain they can be overcome."

"You are not selfish or unfeeling," Niles said. "That your brother has convinced you otherwise is inexcusable."

"I have begun to feel relief at knowing I'll be living in England and he will be in Ireland." She leaned her head against Niles. "Which adds weight to his accusations regarding my selfishness."

"Wanting a respite from unkindness is not selfish." Niles kissed the top of her head.

"Will you promise me, Niles, that you'll always do that?"

"Do what?"

"Kiss my head like that. I never fail to feel better when you do."

His arm slipped from her shoulders to her waist. "For you, my Penny, I would do anything at all."

She stopped and turned to face him. They stood at the end of the corridor, far enough inside to escape the chill but not near enough to the drawing room or dining room to be overheard. "Does that 'anything at all' include getting married in Dublin?" Liam ought not to be demanding this of them, but since he had, there was no avoiding the decision they had to make. "I realize it would mean you wouldn't be married in the chapel where your family always has been, and very few of your family members would be in attendance. And with the state of Lucas's father's health, he and Julia most certainly wouldn't be there. And Henri and Nicolette's income does not allow for such journeys, especially after having very recently made several. Aldric has a new estate to see to. Digby has not been granted much peace at his estate and must long for a bit of it. Kes and Violet must long to be back home as well. It is possible not one of the Gents would be there, and they are so important to you." Emotion cracked through the words.

He brushed his hand along her cheek. "Penelope Seymour, do you not know that *you* are important to me?" He smiled softly. "Fate has given us this miraculous chance for us both to pursue the dreams we have but to do so together. I would marry you on a mountaintop or in the depths of the sea or at the farthest reaches of the earth, with only the two of us there if need be."

"Dublin seems a less complicated option than any of those," Penelope said. "And unlike underwater or mountaintop weddings, those solemnized in a chapel of the Church of Ireland are recognized and binding in England. That makes Dublin the less scandalous option as well."

"Far less."

She breathed more easily. "This isn't the insurmountable obstacle I thought it was?"

"We have overcome far more difficult impediments."

Penelope sighed; she couldn't help herself.

He tipped her head upward. Their eyes met. "We should tell your brother to begin planning a Dublin wedding. But we'll keep our decision to ourselves for a few minutes."

"Why?"

Niles brushed his hand along her hair, tucking a tuft of it behind her ear. "Because Liam deserves to stew for a while." He leaned closer. "And because I intend to take my time kissing you."

"Yes, please," she whispered.

He lowered his mouth to hers, his lips caressing hers unhurriedly. Penelope's cape fell back as she hooked her arms around his neck, holding him close, reveling in the feel of his arms wrapped around her.

"We're getting married, Penny," he said, his breath tickling her lips.

"Yes, we are."

He lifted her from the ground and spun her about. Though she hadn't giggled a day in her life, she did so then. And that giggle turned to a laugh of absolute joy as she spun with him. They were going to be together. Always.

Chapter Thirty-Seven

Dublin, one month later

NILES HAD NEVER BEFORE WONDERED what the horses at Tattersalls must feel like, being out on exhibit and inspected by everyone who happened past, but he was currently skipping over wondering about it and jumping straight to knowing. He had now been on exhibition and subjected to inspection for a fortnight in Dublin.

Liam Seymour had wasted no opportunity to prove to local society that he had managed a good match for his sister. Niles's many important connections were rattled off to anyone who would listen. The Greenberrys' standing in Cornwall was, perhaps, a little *over*emphasized. While it was deeply uncomfortable for one who preferred being unnoticed and overlooked, Niles was far more put out at the treatment Penelope was subjected to.

In every public interaction, his fiery and fearsome Penny deferred to her brother. She gave Liam credit for the match, for the connections their family had gained, for essentially every success anyone referenced or even hinted at. And through it all, Liam preened and smugly accepted the acclaim heaped on him.

"We need never return to Dublin if we'd rather not," Penelope had said when Niles had expressed his concerns to her. "I can endure this for the next few days."

"You shouldn't have to," he had insisted.

And in true Penelope Seymour style, she had smiled confidently and said simply, "I know."

Niles's soon-to-be mother-in-law proved to be precisely the person Penelope had described in Yorkshire: elegant, commanding, and utterly exhausting. While Penelope wasn't cowed by her mother, Mrs. Seymour noticeably dampened her daughter's spirits.

"I am beginning to understand even better your attachment to Fairfield," Niles had said after one particularly exasperating meal at the family home.

"It wasn't entirely about escape," Penelope had said, "but I will confess *this*"—she'd spread her arms out, indicated the entirety of their home and all who lived in it—"has certainly played a role."

Niles suspected, watching her the night before the wedding, that Penelope was as weary as she was excited. He was attempting to formulate an argument that would convince her family to allow her to remain home for the night, where she could be herself and not be required to scrape and bow to her brother and mother.

As if to prove no one strategized as naturally and effortlessly as the General, Aldric arrived at the Seymours' Dublin home just in time to be the excuse they needed. As Niles claimed the closer connection to Aldric, he ought to have been the one to undertake the introductions, but Liam jumped so quickly at the opportunity that there was no chance.

"Mother," Liam said, "this is Lord Aldric Benick, younger son of the Duke of Hartley. Lord Aldric, this is my mother, Mrs. Seymour."

"It is an honor to make your acquaintance, Mrs. Seymour." Aldric offered a bow that deferred to the lady of the house while still acknowledging his far higher standing. He always managed that and did so without offering the least offense. He was a marvel in many ways. "And a pleasure to see you again, Mr. Seymour." Then he turned to Penelope, and his very formal expression turned far more familial, the sort of brotherly affection Liam ought to have displayed every time he was with his sister. "Miss Seymour. Tomorrow is the happy day, I believe."

Penelope hooked her arm through Niles's. "It is. And all the happier now, knowing you will be here with us."

"We can have Mr. Greenberry moved to another guest chamber," Mrs. Seymour insisted. "The one he is in now is the finest we have. You would be happiest in that room."

"Mother." Penelope sounded appropriately horrified.

"I have obtained lodgings elsewhere, Mrs. Seymour," Aldric said. "No need to displace the groom."

As regal and self-assured as ever, Mrs. Seymour said, "We are to attend a soiree this evening at the home of a very well-respected family, Lord Aldric. They would be most honored if you were to grace them with your attendance as well."

One glance at Penelope and Niles must have told the weeks-long story. Without needing to be asked to save them from more misery, Aldric said, "I look forward to spending the evening here in your lovely home with my good friends." He indicated Niles and Penelope with the smallest movement of his head.

Aldric managed to evade all attempts to change his mind and, within the hour, Mrs. Seymour and Liam were both gone, and there was peace in the house at last.

"Thank you for this," Niles said. "I suspect Penny was at the end of her endurance."

From his seat across from them, Aldric said, "The Gents would do absolutely anything for Mag."

Penelope curled into Niles, and he set his arm around her. "We didn't think any of the Gents would be able to come to Ireland for the wedding."

"The others wanted to be here," Aldric said. "They truly did."

Borrowing a page from Penelope's book, Niles answered, "I know."

"And I haven't the words to express how much Stanley would have wanted to be here." Aldric allowed a small nostalgic smile. "This is what he always wanted for you, Puppy."

Penelope wrapped her arms around Niles.

"He was the most remarkable person I've ever known," Niles said. "He changed my life."

"Mine as well," Aldric said quietly.

"If he were—" Niles swallowed. "If he were here, I would ask him to stand up with me tomorrow. Would you be willing to do so in his place?"

A rare show of emotion entered his eyes. "It would be my very real honor."

January 1788

Fairfield was beautiful in the winter. Niles looked forward to seeing it in all the other seasons. But more than that, he looked ahead with eagerness to spending those seasons with Penelope. They'd been married a month, and he found himself amazed at how much his love for her grew every single day.

"Everyone has a dream," Stanley had often said, "but only the truly fortunate ones get to live theirs."

I'm living mine, Stanley. And I think you'd be happy for me.

He and Penelope had ridden out to his land at the far end of Fairfield. They'd settled on the name Penfield, "pen" being the Cornish prefix referring to a place located at the far end of something or somewhere. It also, in Niles's mind, was a reference to Penelope's name.

"This is going to be a lovely spot," his darling wife said, looking over the clearing where, come spring, construction would begin on his personal boxing salon. She smiled at him. "I'm beginning to fear you will be so pleased here that you will never return to the house."

"You'll simply have to join me here," he said.

She held her hand out to him. "I'll join you wherever you'd like to go, my darling."

"London, perhaps?"

She nodded. "I'd follow you to London."

"To the next Gents house party?"

"Gladly."

"And if Henri makes good on his many years of threatening to swim back to France and the Gents are forced to retrieve him?"

"I know how to swim," she answered.

She was an utter delight, and he was the most fortunate man in the world.

Niles pulled her into his arms. She melted against him. "I love you, you know," he said.

"I do," she said. "And I love you."

He'd imagined all his life loving someone and being loved in return, but even those long-held hopes paled in comparison to what he'd found with Penelope. They'd needed a miracle, and fate had provided one.

He was not merely fortunate but doubly so: he was living his dreams *with her.*

Niles bent toward her and captured her lips in a slow and tender kiss. His darling, wonderful Penny. He had waited so long to find her and could not wait to spend the remainder of their lives together.

About the Author

Sᴀʀᴀʜ M. Eᴅᴇɴ ɪs ᴀ *USA Today* best-selling author of more than seventy witty and charming historical romances, which have sold over one million copies worldwide. Some of these include 2020's Foreword Reviews INDIE Awards gold winner for romance, *Forget Me Not*, 2019's Foreword Reviews INDIE Awards gold winner for romance, *The Lady and the Highwayman*, and 2020 Holt Medallion finalist, *Healing Hearts*. She is a three-time Best of State gold-medal winner for fiction and a three-time Whitney Award winner.

Combining her obsession with history and her affinity for tender love stories, Sarah loves crafting deep characters and heartfelt romances set against rich historical backdrops. She holds a bachelor's degree in research and happily spends hours perusing the reference shelves of her local library.

Sarah is represented by Pam Pho at Steven Literary Agency.

www.SarahMEden.com
Facebook: facebook.com/SarahMEden
Instagram: @sarah_m_eden